FULL CIRCLE

Full Circle
First edition: November 2023
Vered Neta

Layout & formatting: Arjen Broeze, Kingfisher Design

ISBN Paperback: 978-1-61947-082-8
ISBN Ebook: 978-1-61947-083-5

© 2023 Vered Neta. All rights reserved. No part of this publication may be reproduced, stored in a retrieval system, or transmitted, in any form or by any means, electronic, mechanical, photocopying, recording, or otherwise, without the prior permission in writing from the proprietor(s).

VERED NETA

FULL CIRCLE

From the Depths of Uncertainty,
Purpose Arises

Dedication

*Dad, this book is dedicated to you for filling my life
with the remarkable stories of history
and making me realise just how important it is.*

Thanks for being my history hero!

Acknowledgments

No author exists in isolation, and the creation of this book is a testament to the collective support and contributions of many remarkable individuals to whom I owe immense gratitude.

Foremost, my sincere thanks extend to Lucy V. Hay—my mentor, coach, and cherished friend. Her unwavering encouragement, insightful feedback, and invaluable guidance played a pivotal role in shaping the narrative you now hold. Lucy, your belief in me has been a constant source of inspiration throughout this journey.

Special appreciation goes to Lucy Linger of the Bang2Write community, whose perceptive feedback on the initial script prompted a transformative shift in the narrative, opening new dimensions to Ana's story.

I am indebted to Michelle Goode, my editor, whose meticulous work ensured that my voice, as a non-native English speaker, resonated authentically throughout the story.

Heartfelt thanks also go to Arjen Broeze from Kingfisher Design, whose technical expertise proved invaluable in navigating the intricacies of modern book publishing.

To the vibrant Bang2Write community, including Fiona Leitch, Jon Meyers, and countless others—your writing advice, constructive feedback on early drafts, and unwavering weekly encouragement transformed my solitary writing journey into a shared adventure. Each of you created a safe space for me to share my work, and for that, I am deeply grateful.

Lastly, profound love and appreciation are reserved for my beloved husband and confidant, Yehonathan (Nisandeh) Neta. Your unwavering support, belief in my abilities, and constant reminders that I can achieve anything have been the driving force behind this endeavour. Thank you for being the wind beneath my wings.

Chapter One

BOSTON – NOVEMBER 1989

'Are you OK? Shall I call an ambulance?'

Ana had no idea why the woman, a stranger, was asking her these questions until she realised she was sitting on the pavement. She got up, embarrassed and dizzy.

What the hell happened?

'I'm fine. No need to call for an ambulance,' she reassured the woman, 'I'm a doctor.'

Ana walked away towards the bus station. Once there, she sat down and tried to recall what had just happened. The last thing Ana remembered was stepping out of the store. A huge group of people had been standing in front of the electrical appliance shop. She remembered thinking how strange it was and felt compelled to see what they were watching. In the window display, the latest models of televisions were lined up next to one another. All were tuned into CNN, showing events happening somewhere in the world. Ana rarely had any interest in politics or news. She was about to turn and walk to the bus station when her eye caught the images.

Her beloved Prague.

Don't look back! Ana could hear her mother's voice calling after her. But she couldn't stop staring at the scenes unfolding on the screens. Thousands of people marched with signs, calling out for freedom. They faced lines of policemen; some on horses and some with guns or batons. She couldn't believe she was watching it on a screen and not immersed in her own memories. Memories she had worked hard to forget for the past two decades.

That's when her knees collapsed, and she'd blacked out.

How did I end up here?

***

It was Ana's day off. On any typical day, she would allow herself to sleep in and take her time, but today, she had errands to do. She never liked leaving the holiday shopping to the last moment, so she decided to get it over with.

By the time she woke, Dan had done the groceries and prepared an excellent brunch. She always felt pampered by him when he made such gestures. In their first few years of marriage, she'd felt spoiled, or worse, like she was taking advantage of Dan's good nature. When she'd asked him about it, his first response sounded like he was joking.

'Can't a man cook for his wife without being considered a "sissy"?' Ana had smiled but wasn't reassured by it. When she kept asking him about it, he finally told her his motives.

'I grew up in a family where food was the way to show affection. Food was more than just nutrition: it was a way to celebrate, share and show how much you care for and love your family. Why is it so wrong if I'm the one who does it and not you?'

Ana had finally relaxed, recognising it was Dan's way of telling her he still loved her after all those years together. In time, she'd started to look forward to it and appreciated her good fortune of finding such a man.

But today, Ana didn't have time to linger. She checked the bus timetable and, seeing she would be just in time to catch it, she set off downtown.

The streets were already decorated for Thanksgiving and Christmas.

It feels like they start the celebrations earlier and earlier each year.

Today, Ana wanted to get Yael, her daughter, something for Chanukah, the festival of light. This year, it took place at the same time as Christmas. Both she and Dan had made a point of celebrating both Chanukah and Christmas so Yael would not feel different from her friends.

Ana recalled seeing a unique artistic Chanukah in a special shop during the summer months. It was made from clay, and each candle holder was shaped like a different fairy, while the backdrop had a colourful Tree of Life symbol. She knew Yael would appreciate it, given her artistic talents. Ana hoped it would still be there.

When she reached the shop, Ana was relieved to discover the Chanukah was still on display. Ana stood outside, taking a second look. Was it as beautiful as she had remembered it in her mind? Yes, it was even more unique and impressive. Ana was happy to discover it was on sale. She paid and asked the shop owner to gift wrap it. She would never have time to do it herself; even if she did, it would never look as good as they did in the store. Ana had learned long ago that it was best to leave certain things to the professionals. She was happy that it didn't take too long.

Stepping outside, she saw the crowd.

***

Serves you right for following a crowd, her inner critic mocked her on the bus back home. *You should know better by now!*

Arriving back home, Ana realised how late it was. She could hear Yael was home, filling the space with her constant chattering. Her daughter always talked about people, places and events Ana couldn't keep track of. She was grateful Dan was his usual attentive self as their only child told yet another involved and long-winded story.

Once dinner was over, Yael went up to her room under the pretence she was doing homework. Both Dan and Ana knew she was more likely chatting with her friends on the phone, but they let it go. They both joked that kids needed to believe they were fooling their parents. Once they became parents themselves, most kids would discover how their parents knew all about their supposed transgressions. It was one of those well-kept secrets parents had; you only discovered it when you entered the club.

Dan switched on the TV. He was zapping between the endless channels when he landed on CNN. It was a Breaking News segment that caught Ana's attention.

'It's Prague again,' she muttered and stopped Dan from turning over. 'What's going on? I saw clips of it today on the street. People were glued to the TV shop's window as if a revolution was taking place.'

Dan raised the volume. The same images came up: protesters filling the streets of Prague; the notorious riot police trying to beat back the demonstrators, hoping to tamp down the demand for freedom. But it looked like the people seemed to have grown immune to the brutality of the regime. The show of force only motivated them to resist even more. Students were joined by citizens of all ages. The reporters said that more than half a million people were filling Prague's streets and taking over Wenceslas Square.

Ana watched the scenes with a stoic look; she still couldn't believe her eyes. She sensed it was real but couldn't bring herself to accept it. She was startled as one of the reporters said, 'Change is in the air.' She was about to get up from the sofa when Yael strolled into the room.

'They're calling it the Velvet Revolution,' she announced without taking her eyes off the screen.

'Yes, they are,' Dan said. 'Where did you hear about it?'

'They've been showing us these images for the last two weeks at school, ever since the Berlin Wall collapsed. They're saying it's history in the making.'

'Why do they call it the Velvet Revolution?' Ana felt out of touch with the conversation between her husband and daughter.

'Don't you know?' Yael asked her with an astonished tone.

'You know me; I don't have time for news or TV.'

Yael stared at her mother as if seeing her for the first time.

'You're not interested in news or politics? But it defines our lives and dictates how we live.'

'No, it doesn't. You are the only person that defines your destiny. You are the only one that would create or destroy your life, nothing else. And don't let anyone tell you anything different.' Ana cringed as she heard a firmer tone in her voice than she'd intended. *I sound like my mum.*

'Why are you so against it?' Yael asked.

Dan was about to answer, but Ana silenced him with a look.

'Nothing new. They think "change is in the air," but they have no clue. I've been in that movie, and it didn't end well.'

'You never talk about your home country. Why is that?'

'I believe there is no point in looking back.'

'But I want to know about your past,' Yael pleaded, 'I want to know *you*.'

Ana looked at Dan. He shrugged his shoulders, then nodded.

'Maybe it's time?' he said. 'You don't want her to be as clueless about you as you were about your mother… Would you?' Dan couldn't have said a more powerful sentence to convince Ana.

'Well, I guess,' Ana sighed, looking at her eager daughter, 'it's time you heard how I arrived in the United States. But first, you need to understand who I was.'

Chapter Two

PRAGUE – JUNE 1966

Ana was standing on the stairs of her high school with her classmates for the traditional graduation photo. Their school was a typical old, grey building; ugly but functional. The party wouldn't spend much money on buildings with the sole function of educating young people. Everyone and everything was supposed to be uniform: a conformity factory. There was no room for individuality. People were supposed to follow the party's doctrine no matter what.

The school faced one of the oldest churches in Prague. It was a constant reminder of what old Prague used to be: the centre of culture, art, and beauty. For six years, Ana would take her breaks on those steps and take in the splendour of that building. The church had since been shut down when the Communist Party took control of the country. Even so, nothing could ruin the magnificence of that church. The sun would play on its stunning stained glass; the ornamental baroque sculptures decorating the spiral of the tower. Ana loved running her fingers on the wooden doors of the church just to feel the carving of the old stories in them. It strengthened her when she was doubting herself or when things looked bleak. The sight of the church was the one point of beauty in her day.

Standing on the first row of the stairs, Ana could see Pavel and Helen, her parents, in the crowd. Pavel towered over everyone else and was easy to spot. But Ana could *just* see her tiny doll-like mother standing next to him. As usual, Pavel was holding

Helen's hand as if making sure he would not lose her in the crowd. Ana couldn't remember a time when her parents were not lovingly touching each other. Sometimes, she believed they came into the world united by an invisible link. Now, when she looked at them, they were both shining with pride. She'd graduated with honours, and her speech at the ceremony was already hailed as one of the best and original speeches the school had heard for many years.

Ana knew her future was promising. Unlike many other youngsters, she knew what she wanted to do and had it all planned out. Her final interview at Charles University would take place the following week. Thinking about that interview made Ana nervous. She was a problem-solver: exams and tests were easy for her.

In contrast, she found interviews more daunting. She had no idea what they'd ask her or what they expected to hear. What answers should she give that would guarantee her a place in the prestigious medical school she had her heart set on? She didn't know anyone who had ever managed such a feat. Most people she knew didn't go to university, as it was considered too intellectual for the party. If they did go, they studied subjects the party called 'useful', such as engineering. Those degrees would guarantee them a job when they graduated. Medicine took at least six years to study and then another three as an intern without any promise of a secured career. But that wouldn't hold Ana back.

If only I knew what to say to convince them to accept me. Her thoughts were cut off by a nudge from her friend Ludmila.

'Smile! They're going to take our photo. You should look happy!'

'What's the big deal?' Ana replied. 'It's not as if I finished anything important.'

'What do you mean not important? At last, we're adults. Hell, no more studying for me. I'm out of here.'

'I love studying and can't think of anything better than spending my time learning,' Ana whispered back, trying to hold a smile on her face for the camera.

Later, when Ana walked to collect her books from her locker, she bumped into Ludmila again. Her friend was, as usual, surrounded by boys trying to impress her, but Ludmila had eyes only for Ana.

'Gregor here invited me to a party to celebrate the end of our miserable life as students. Want to join us?'

'I can't. I have to prepare for my entrance interview to Charles University.'

'Come on, the best thing about graduation is we're free to do whatever we want! Why would you want to put yourself into another institution that dictates your life for you?'

Ana rolled her eyes. She was tired of apologising for her love of learning. Ludmila had been her friend for a long time and should know this by now. She flashed Ludmila a grin, hoping her friend would take a good-natured ribbing.

'Get real, you're not free. You'll have to find work and do what your boss tells you to… while he does what the party tells him to… then all of them follow what Moscow tells them to do. No one experiences complete freedom, if you ask me!' Ana realised that, even with good intentions, it came out condescendingly.

'Suit yourself,' Ludmila said, turning her back on Ana and walking away.

It wasn't the way Ana wanted to end the day, but there was no way of taking back her words.

That night, Helen made a special dinner. It wasn't lavish; food was scarce. The Svebodas could never afford the black market's vouchers for Tuzek shops. Pavel's salary as a factory worker was not enough for anything more than staples. Helen insisted that bringing home products not on the ration list would attract too much attention and were not worth risking everything for.

'Walls have ears and doors have eyes' was her motto. Helen was constantly under the impression that someone was following or watching them. Ana had grown tired of her mother's overly cautious nature. But even Ana had to admit her mother was a genius at stretching their meagre resources. No matter how lacklustre the ingredients, Helen's ingenuity and resourcefulness transformed the most basic foods into something festive. She had an eye and a talent for making something out of nothing.

Tonight was no different. The table was set stunningly, highlighting the beauty of the dinner plates and the silverware. Helen had picked flowers from their back garden. She had made napkin hooks from old branches and collected pebbles from the river to decorate the table. Though she'd never had the experience, Ana felt as if they were dining at an expensive restaurant. She'd seen such places in movies or read about them in books. Helen had made an effort to make a three-course meal starting with potato soup, then grilled fish with some cabbage, and her signature dessert – bublanina - a light sponge cake with cherries, apricots and pears. While Helen was busy organising the food on the plates, Ana glared at the blue tattoo number on her left wrist. No matter how many times she'd seen that number, she still wondered what it really meant. *And what does it mean for me?* she'd wonder.

Ana never could understand or connect to her mum. Her dad, on the other hand, was her hero. Looking at Pavel across the table, he reminded her of Paul Newman with his blue eyes and big smile. For her, Pavel was like a Nordic God. He wasn't a man of many words, but when he talked, every word sounded like old wisdom being revealed.

Pavel watched Helen serving the food with admiration in his eyes that never ceased to surprise Ana. None of her friends' parents ever showed as much affection to each other as her parents did. Sometimes, she was embarrassed by it, but she found it adorable these days. She hoped, one day, someone would look at her with as much love as her father had for her mother.

'Are you nervous for your interview next week?' he asked.

'I don't know if I am nervous, but I feel unprepared.'

'What do you need to prepare for? They only want to get to know you. You don't have to have a dress rehearsal for being yourself.'

'That's just it, I don't know what type of person they want or are looking for. What if what I say comes across as foolish? What if I appear unfit to attend the University?'

'Never doubt yourself as a person. You can doubt what you think or believe, but never doubt the person you are. At the end of the day, you are an amazing young woman. If you show them who you are, they will recognise how fortunate they would be to have you as their student.'

Ana felt overwhelmed by her father's strong conviction. She wished she could feel as confident as he did about her chances of getting into medical school.

'I hope you're right and that all they're looking for is to get to know me as a person and not what I know or don't know.' Ana could see her father had more to say, but she appreciated that he allowed her to reach her own conclusions. 'I guess all I can do is be as authentic as possible.'

'That's the best way to go. That way, you can relax and maybe even enjoy the interview.'

'That's taking it a bit too far,' Ana countered with a smile.

Ana cleared the table, washed the dishes, and cleaned the kitchen. Helen protested, saying it was her night and she should not be doing it. But Ana liked doing chores. The simple act of washing, drying, and clearing the kitchen was her meditation, allowing her to get out of her own head.

Returning to the living room, Ana saw her mum sitting in her usual armchair with a book. Her dad sat at the cleared dining table reading his daily 'Rude Pravo'.

'Mum, why don't you play something for us? You haven't played for a long time, and I miss it. Let's have some music to celebrate the end of this wonderful evening.'

'It's too late; the neighbours will complain,' Helen replied.

'Not if you play something they will enjoy too,' Pavel said in an encouraging tone. 'Just choose a piece everyone in the building would love to hear.'

Helen hesitated but stood up and opened the piano lid. Within the first few notes, she transformed the room into the best concert hall in the world.

Bach's sonatas were never more moving than when Helen played them.

***

The following week, Ana walked into the main entrance of Charles University. She tried focusing on her breathing to stop her thoughts from going at ninety miles an hour and spinning out of control.

Remembering how she used to relax before important exams at school by touching the church doors, she now repeated the ritual by touching the walls of the ancient Charles University. She told herself it was a building that had seen many great minds entering since the 14th century. The ancient stones gave her strength. She sent silent prayers to all the famous people who had studied there at one time or another; that they'd support her in the interview so she could join them.

Sitting outside the interview room, Ana kept repeating in her mind what her dad had said: *Just be authentic and you'll be fine.*

When the door finally opened, she entered a room that emanated centuries of learning and knowledge. Painted glass windows decorated the room with the richness of past centuries. In contrast, the furniture was proof of Czechoslovakia being under the Communist regime. Nothing fancy or artistic was allowed.

Ana sat down on a simple chair facing a dais from which four men looked down at her. In her mind, Ana kept repeating her newfound mantra: *I deserve to be here. They'll be lucky to have me.*

The first few questions were easy and allowed her to loosen

up; she even enjoyed the conversation. She could express her ideas and thoughts, which she had plenty of. Just as Ana thought it was over and felt she'd nailed it, the question she feared the most came.

'Why medicine? Why do you want to become a doctor?'

A sinking feeling overcame Ana. She never could articulate her reasons for wanting to become a doctor. How could she express that it was what she'd always known she was supposed to do with her life? How could she explain it without sounding naive, or worse, spiritual and strange? Ana paused for a minute, then decided to do what Pavel had recommended.

'I can't think of a better way to live my life than by easing the pain of others and helping them to regain their health to live a happier life,' she said. 'I think it's the reason for me to be alive. I know this might not sound scientific or rational, but for me, it's my purpose in life to aid people, to support them… And if needed, to save them from harm.'

There was silence.

After a while, when she had the courage to raise her head, Ana saw all the men smiling and nodding.

Thank God. Ana could finally allow herself to release a breath of relief.

She was *in*.

Chapter Three

PRAGUE - 1968

The wind was blowing straight into Ana's face. Her eyes were watering from the pitch cold wind, and any time she opened her mouth to breathe, it felt as if her brain was freezing.

It was January, and the winter was colder than any they had had in many years; at least, that's what the papers were saying. Ana didn't need anyone to tell her how cold it was.

Walking to the hospital, someone pushed a flyer into her hand. She carelessly skimmed through it, but it was all about some political rally that would take place the next day. Ana didn't have any interest in getting political.

Between studying, work and helping at home, I don't have time for anything else.

She was looking for a trash can to throw the flyer into when she noticed a crowd gathering at the entrance of one of the university's buildings. It irritated her. It was her shortcut to the hospital, and they were in her way! Worse, she was freezing cold.

Damn, now I will either freeze going the long way or get crushed going through that crowd... I hate crowds! Ana braced herself and started to move through the throng of people when she heard someone call her name.

'Ana, I didn't expect to see you here in this demonstration!' She turned around and found herself looking at Pjoter, or rather at his chest. He was so tall she nearly had to crane her neck to look into his eyes.

'I'm not. I'm only passing through. I have a hospital shift, for which I'll probably be late now. What is it all about anyway?'

'Dubček. He's talking about his new ideas for change. He is challenging the status quo! You should stay for a while and listen to him.'

Ana glanced at her watch and realised she could spare five minutes. She could also do with the warmth of the bodies surrounding her before returning to the cold. 'Fine, but only for a few minutes. I don't want to be late.'

'You won't be able to hear him from down there. I'll take you on my shoulders so you can see and hear better.' Without warning, Pjoter grabbed Ana. In one swift movement, he raised her onto his shoulders. She was now sitting high like a child on a parent's shoulders.

In other circumstances, she would feel embarrassed, but she could see other girls sitting on top of their friends' shoulders as well. The place seemed more like a music festival than a political rally. After her initial surprise, Ana paid attention to what Dubček was talking about. He was undoubtedly a passionate speaker, but Ana had never been interested in politics.

After a while, she became bored. She was more concerned she might be late for her shift in the hospital. She leaned down and whispered to Pjoter.

'It's getting late. I must get to the hospital for my shift. Could you put me down?'

'No problem!' Pjoter hauled her down from his shoulders. 'I hope it inspired you. Look at this crowd. We just might have some hope!'

Ana didn't want to offend him by saying she saw no real change coming. Instead, she smiled and gave him a little wave.

'See you tomorrow at class.'

Turning away, she ploughed through the crowd to the other side. She was so busy moving through people that she wasn't aware that someone was watching her keenly after Pjoter had raised her on his shoulders.

***

A few days later, Ana was heading home, trying to enjoy her beloved city. She had always been in awe of the beauty of Prague, even on days as cold as these.

The cobbled streets, the euphonic chiming bells of Prague churches. There was a reason Prague was named the 'City of a Hundred Spires'. Usually, she couldn't stop smiling when she walked through her city of dreams, looking up frequently to drink in the stunning architecture. Most of all, she loved walking across Charles Bridge, her heart overflowing with happiness at the sight of the castle complex on the hill above Mala Strana, the far end of the bridge and the archway between the two towers that would lead her home. But the narrow streets of Prague seemed to be doing everything they could to slow her down that day.

Ana was contemplating dodging the cold by slipping into the Lion's Head pub around the corner. She needed to get warm enough to feel her face and fingers again before continuing her journey home.

As she got closer, she noticed it was full of students, all cheering and talking loudly. She knew she would be bound to bump into one of her classmates and get stuck there longer than she wanted. She took a deep breath, rubbing her hands together as fast as possible. After a few moments, she could feel the tips of her fingers again, so she dipped her head against the bitter, cold wind and continued walking as fast as the slippery street would allow her to return home.

Once in the protected courtyard, Ana could breathe easier without risking brain freeze.

Entering her home was like stepping into a sauna. Ana could feel her body thaw almost as soon as she crossed the threshold. Her parents were in the living room, sitting close to the radio.

That was an unfamiliar sight.

Most evenings, her father would prefer reading the paper, while her mum would keep herself busy either mending clothes, hemming, or knitting during winter. On rare occasions, she would play the piano to her father's delight.

'What's going on?' Ana asked while taking off some of her many layers of clothes. 'Anything left to eat? I'm starving.'

'Sit down,' her mum replied, getting up from the sofa and walking towards the kitchen. 'Take a break from your studies. Honestly, between your studies and work, you'll drive yourself to exhaustion. I have your dinner warm in the oven. I'll get it for you.'

Ana did as she was told and sat down. 'What is going on?'

Her dad was still glued to the radio. 'It seems as if the whole city is on fire,' Ana continued. 'Everywhere I went, people were huddled around radios, listening and cheering as if something big was happening.'

'You really don't know?' her father responded with a

surprised look on his face. 'Where have you been living the last few months?'

'You know me; my focus is only on my studies. I try to avoid anything else like the plague.'

Pavel observed his daughter, shaking his head. 'The world just passes you by?'

'No. I need to stay focused on what is important for me.' Ana felt annoyed by the implications of what her father was suggesting.

'But you're a part of this world. You can't close yourself off to what is taking place around you. It's not healthy and not right.'

'So, what would you like me to do, get involved in politics? Waste my time discussing things I have no control over?' Ana never liked arguing with her father, whom she admired so much.

'I didn't ask you to get involved. I only meant that you should pay attention. Listen to the people around you, watch for signs of what is taking place. If you don't, you'll end up missing the important things in life!'

'Well, for me, graduating is the most important thing in life right now.' Ana was not willing to admit that her dad might have a point. But she had no clue how she could combine her busy study life with anything else. She couldn't afford to lag behind on her revision and coursework. 'So, what is going on?'

'Why don't we both listen to the news?' he suggested. 'Dubček is going to make an announcement on the radio in a few minutes. There has been a lot of speculation on what he will say.'

'Whatever he says, it will not change anything,' Helen said

as she entered the room with Ana's dinner. 'People can talk as much as they want. But in the end, Moscow gets what Moscow wants. Don't you forget that.'

Despite herself, Ana didn't like the sound of what her mum was saying at all. It sounded as if Helen was trying to keep the status quo even when there was a chance for change. Ana used to call her mum - at least in her mind - a defeated soul and a pessimist. She didn't like to discover that she and Helen shared common beliefs.

'I heard Dubček talk at a rally outside the university the other day. I have to say I wasn't impressed. However, I did notice how the other students were inspired by him. Maybe I wasn't impressed because I didn't know enough about what he was talking about?' she mused.

'Better stay clear from any political actions. It will not end well, trust me,' Helen responded before she could continue.

Ana wished she could have contradicted her mother, but the station ident was playing on the radio signalling that the news was about to start.

'It's an historic day,' the reporter began. 'Today Dubček announced his plans to build an advanced socialist society on sound economic foundations. He is committed to creating socialism that corresponds to the historical democratic traditions of Czechoslovakia, in accordance with the experience of other communist parties. His plan includes increasing freedom of press, freedom of speech and freedom of movement.'

Ana could hear cheers and shouts coming from the other apartments on her floor.

'It's about time,' her father muttered.

The only person who seemed cautious was her mother. 'Moscow's not gonna be happy with this,' she said.

But even that did not spoil her dad's mood. 'We're Czech, we've always been free.'

Helen laughed a short, cynical laugh. 'I don't think Brezhnev will agree with you.'

Pride burst through Ana as her dad stood up.

'I didn't fight the Nazis to live under the fear of another dictator,' he said. 'We're born free. We should have the right to live that way.'

'Freedom is an elusive idea; staying alive is far more important.'

'You don't get it,' he said, 'there is change in the air, I can feel it. We can't miss this opportunity by being on the defensive from the start.' It seemed to Ana that her mother had more to say but chose not to. Helen picked up her knitting and ignored both of them.

Typical of her, she thought to herself, but before she could say anything there were rapid, strong knocks on the door.

Helen's knitting needles stopped clacking and she exchanged fearful looks with Pavel, who was standing up to walk to the door.

'I told you walls have ears,' Helen whispered, partly to herself and partly to Pavel.

Chapter Four

Ana was working in the hospital going over some blood tests. She loved her job in the lab. Not only was she learning more there than in her studies, but she was also getting paid for it. But what she loved most were the quiet hours in the lab, alone with her own thoughts.

She was at the reception counter when a young man stepped in. From the moment he crossed the threshold it was clear he did not belong. He wore no lab coat, plus he didn't exude the quiet, studious air the other lab technicians had. He was certainly not in the right place.

'Can I help you?'

He turned around and for a second, Ana stopped breathing. He resembled an old drawing depicting a poet or a dreamer. He was a head taller than her. *Well, that isn't hard,* she thought, *I am more the size of a fairy than of a human.*

But what really caught Ana's attention was that he was staring at her with his deep blue eyes. His expression was intense. There was something familiar about him.

'You're Ana... Ana Sveboda, isn't it?'

The sound of his voice unlocked something in her. '... Jan?'

'God, you're all grown up.'

'Well, that's what happens when time passes,' Ana chuckled. 'It *is* you, Jan, isn't it?' She double-checked; she didn't want to make a fool of herself. He nodded.

Without a second's thought, Ana came round the reception

desk and hugged him. He folded her into his embrace, almost enveloping her in his big arms.

'How did you find me here?'

'I saw you the other day at the rally. So, I enquired where I would be able to find you.'

'Well, that's one good thing that came out of that rally, I guess.' Ana smiled, 'When did you return to Prague?'

'About a year ago, I came back to study.'

'Are you in Charles University?'

'Yes.'

'Me too!' she said, 'How come I didn't see you before?'

Jan laughed. 'It's a big university, you know.'

'I'm studying medicine, like I always wanted.'

'I remember. I study history and philosophy, which means I'm on the other side of the city than most of your courses.' Jan grinned. 'But forget studying. Have you joined the Student Union? I saw you with Pjoter. Hasn't he convinced you to join?'

'Who? Ah no, he's just someone who studies with me. I bumped into him that day when I was trying to get here as fast as possible.'

One of the tests beeped, signalling that it was finished. Ana had to go and get the results.

'Hold on. I just have to get that, wait here.' She wasn't going to let this opportunity of reconnecting with him slip away. Jan smiled at her, and with a thud of her heart, Ana realised how attractive he was.

How come I never noticed he's so good looking? Maybe because you were only ten years old the last time you saw him!

When she came back Jan was still talking, but she was too

busy hushing the voices in her head. When she could finally focus, she was surprised to hear him say, 'I rather make history than study it.'

'What do you mean?'

'We're living in exciting times. You have to take part in it, otherwise you're not truly living.'

It sounded like her dad's words a few nights before.

'Mama will kill me. She says it's not safe. Besides, I really want to be a doctor.'

'Who says you can't? You can do both. In times like this, we have a social responsibility to be part of what is going on. We can't leave it in the hands of the old generation.'

As Ana listened to Jan, she noticed his whole face lit up when he was talking. There was fire in his voice and eyes. It was impossible not to get caught up with his enthusiasm, and Ana was no different to anyone else.

She realised she wanted to spend more time with Jan, just like in the old days, when they were inseparable.

But how could I do that? Where would I have time for him in my busy schedule? Then it all became clear - to spend time with him, she'd need to join the Student Union. Her dad would approve.

The challenge would be to get her mother on board.

'Why don't you come for dinner on Friday? I'm sure papa would love talking to you.' Ana knew that if her dad could get excited by what Jan is talking about, it would be easier to convince her mum to allow her to join the Student Union.

'Great, thank you.'

'We're still in the same place,' Ana said, 'but now I'm afraid you have to leave. I have loads of work waiting for me and you're not supposed to be here.'

She moved back to stand behind the reception counter and waved to Jan as he left the lab. She couldn't help noticing that she had a big smile on her face.

Jan was back in her life.

Chapter Five

BOSTON - 1989

'Ohh… Who's Jan? Was he your first boyfriend?'

Yael couldn't hold herself back when she heard Ana getting excited about a boy. She'd always wondered what her mum had been like as a young girl. Tonight, she had learned more about her than she had during her whole life.

'Jan is a separate story. It's getting late, it's way after your bedtime. How about we continue tomorrow once I come back from work?'

Though Yael wanted to hear more, she realised her mum had a point. She was tired and wanted to have her whole attention on her mum's story.

'You promise? You'll continue telling me your story tomorrow?'

'I promise,' Ana replied.

***

'Honey, I'm home,' Ana called when she entered her house.

It was hers and Dan's private joke. Unlike so many men and women of their generation in the nineteen eighties, Ana would go to work while Dan worked from home. No matter what time she returned, he would welcome her back, smiling, and asking about her day.

Not tonight, however. Ana listened out for her family, hanging her coat in the hall.

'That's so not fair! All my friends will be there!' Yael's petulant voice filtered through from the next room.

Ana hung back, picking up her post from the hall table. Part of her didn't want to get involved in whatever her daughter's tantrum was about.

Yael had been such a delightful little girl when she was younger; Ana had adored taking her to the park, plaiting her hair, and baking with her in the kitchen. Yet, since Yael had become a teenager, that little girl was gone and a belligerent stranger was in her place: brittle and demanding, always wanting what she couldn't have.

'I didn't say you can't go!' Dan shouted, 'I *only* said either me or your mum would have to be there.'

That's unusual, Ana thought. Dan was an easy-going person. He rarely raised his voice. That must mean Yael was kicking off about something. Sighing, Ana abandoned her post and entered the family living room.

'What's going on?' she demanded.

Both Yael and Dan whirled around in Ana's direction. Dan looked wan and long-suffering, like he'd been arguing with their only child for some time. In contrast, Yael was red-faced, her limbs in jagged shapes; the epitome of a stereotypically angry teenager.

'Dad won't let me go to Rachel's party this weekend!' Tears tracked down Yael's face. 'He says that if there are no adults present, then I can't go. He doesn't trust me!'

Before Dan could start shouting again, Ana shot him a look that said, *'I got this.'*

'Don't be ridiculous, darling,' Ana declared, 'We both trust you completely. It's just that we also remember what it's like to be young. Things might get out of control very quickly. It's good to have a grown up around to keep things calm.'

Dan looked relieved that Ana had taken control of the conversation. He was an expert in communication, but when it came to his own daughter, he floundered.

'Why is this party so important for you, anyway?' Ana asked.

Yael's mouth dropped open. 'Are you serious?'

Ana massaged her temples. 'I mean; you see these kids at school every day? God knows you're on the phone with them for hours, which is something we need to discuss by the way… But why is this specific party so important for you?'

Yael's lip curled in a sneer. 'You'll never understand. I'm not like you. I don't want to only study and be a bookworm like you were at my age!'

Her daughter's contempt was like a knife to Ana's heart.

'If this is what you took from what I shared with you last night, then we have nothing to discuss. Go up to your room. You just proved you're not mature enough to make decisions.'

'I knew it! I'm going to be the only girl in school who doesn't have a social life!' Yael stormed out of the living room, slamming the door behind her so her parents would understand how upset she was.

As Yael left the room, Dan and Ana stared at each other and declared at the same time: 'Teenagers!'

Chuckling to himself, Dan gave Ana a hug. 'Were you really like what she said?'

Ana shrugged. 'I wasn't allowed to go out at all, let alone go out to a party on my own. She should be grateful we even considered it.'

'What do you mean?' Dan asked, knowing that anything that had to do with Ana's past had to be handled with kid gloves.

The question took Ana by surprise, and she allowed the memories that were beginning to flood her consciousness.

'You know, maybe it's something Yael has to hear, and then she will understand me better that way.'

'Good idea. I'll come up with you. In the end, we do need to show a united front,' Dan remarked with a smile on his face.

When they entered Yael's room, Yael's face was red and there were remains of tears on her face. When she saw them, she instantly tried to recover and pretend she was only angry. Ana sat down on the bed next to her, while Dan leaned on the door in a relaxed way.

'I'm sorry,' she said quietly. 'I should have responded differently. I don't like it when we fight, and I certainly wouldn't want it to come between us.'

Ana put an arm out and Yael snuggled up against her.

'Remember you wanted me to carry on with my story? How about we continue it now?'

That seemed to relax Yael, and she leaned back in bed waiting to listen.

Chapter Six

PRAGUE - 1962

Ana stepped into her building's courtyard with a heavy step.

There was a lot going on in her mind. She was excited for the invitation she'd got today at school, but she also knew she would have to phrase her request in such a way that Helen would agree to it. No way would her mother allow her to go out at night without supervision or protection. Ana would have to find a way, or an argument, to convince Helen to allow her.

Ana was so absorbed in her thoughts she nearly bumped into Mrs. Hudek. The old crone - along with Mrs. Fischer and Kadlek - were their building's infamous trio. They were so nosy, everyone called them 'The Three Witches' behind their backs. They always seemed to be sitting at the centre of the courtyard, gossiping and shoving their noses into other people's business. Nothing escaped their attention.

'Watch out!' Mrs. Hudek called before Ana crashed onto her. 'Earth calling Ana! Get your head back from the clouds. One of these days you'll get into trouble.'

'Sorry,' Ana muttered to avoid an argument.

Why the hell are you sitting in the middle of the courtyard and creating an obstacle in this small space? was what she'd really wanted to say, but she knew better. If she did, it would open the gates of hell and her parents would never hear the end of it. *Honestly,* she thought, *some days I think the witches are part of the Communist Party, controlling young people.*

She made her way into the narrow passageway on her own side of the building. It smelled of cooked food and sweat. Today, she could smell boiled cabbage. It made her realise how hungry she was. After a whole day in school and then her after school job at the local pharmacy, Ana realised she could do with some sustenance. Food was never on her mind when she was busy doing things she loved.

As Ana entered her parents' small apartment it felt like a haven. Somehow, no matter how difficult the world was out there, when she crossed the threshold to her home she was always wrapped in a cocoon of safety. It was great to come back to a place where her mere presence received all the attention, and her needs were met before she even expressed them. But Ana recognised this came at a cost.

Mum can't keep me here forever. Despite herself, Ana felt irritated by her mum's obsession of keeping Ana safe and at home. *Thank God the party does not allow home-schooling, otherwise I would be kept here forever!*

The smell of fresh bread wafted from their kitchen. She could hear her father whistling as he helped Helen prepare dinner. Helen barely allowed anyone to help her, but Pavel always liked being next to his wife and giving a hand when she allowed it.

'I'm home,' Ana called. She knew her parents would have heard her entering the apartment, but they liked it when she announced it. Pavel came out of the kitchen with a big smile on his face.

'There's some hot water left; you better take a quick shower before someone else in the building finishes it. We'll wait with dinner for you.'

'That would be great.' She dropped her bag and made her way to the bathroom.

'Tell us about your day?' Pavel asked her after they'd finished eating.

Ana took a deep breath and decided to handle the situation as if taking a Band-Aid off: quick and fast.

'I had an exciting day. Ludmila invited me to go to a small party at her place this weekend. It's okay, right?' Now it was out there, and she knew she had to shut up and wait. But waiting was not something Ana was good at. She counted the seconds in her head, calculating what would be an appropriate time of silence before saying anything else. She didn't have to wait too long.

'No. You know the rules. You can't leave the house after dark.' As ever, her mother shot Ana's request down in flames. Maybe it was the fact she'd anticipated such a response, or maybe it was because she had already been scolded by Mrs. Hudek earlier. Whatever the case, her mother's well-meaning protection pushed all of Ana's buttons at once.

'Are you going to lock me in this house forever? I'm not a baby anymore!'

Helen was surprised by Ana's uncharacteristic outburst. She pursed her lips. 'Well, you're certainly behaving like one now.'

Ana realised that making a scene would not help her case. She calmed herself, taking deep breaths through her nose and exhaling via her mouth. She had to hold on to her feelings. It was the only way to bring Helen around.

'Okay, fine. What would it take for you to trust me enough and let me have more freedom?'

'I would never take your freedom from you. I love you too much,' Helen replied. Ana could hear in her voice how stunned her mother was by what she'd said.

'Well, you're doing it right now. I want to go to a party and you're not allowing me. I've been so lonely since Jan left. Now I have a chance to go out and meet new friends and you don't allow me to do it! What kind of love is that? If you keep doing it, you might lose me forever!'

Helen looked like a deer caught in headlights. Her face became white, and her lips trembled. She was trying to say something, but no words came out. For a few seconds, her whole body was frozen. Then the shaking began, as if she was a terrified animal.

'Helen, oh my,' Pavel said. He rounded on Ana. 'Look what you've done to your mother!' Pavel jumped up and went around the table, taking his wife by the shoulders. He helped her out of her seat and hugged her, before taking her to their bedroom.

Ana was left alone in the living room. It wasn't the first time she'd seen her mother like this, but she had no idea what she'd said that had brought on this reaction. She didn't regret asking about the party. It was normal for teenagers to want to go out. Why was she never allowed to do anything? *That's mum for you. Playing weak and feeble to get what she wants. As always, she has to be the centre of attention.*

It took some time before her dad was back in the living room.

'She's relaxing now.'

'Great,' Ana said, sarcasm dripping from her voice, 'now we'll never get to the end of this discussion!'

Pavel's face changed instantly. 'You had no right to say those words!'

Fear and confusion surged through Ana. She rarely saw her father so angry. His icy tone froze Ana's own anger in a second.

'Have you no shame?' he continued. 'Your mother lost everyone she loved – *everyone!* - in the war. If there is anything or anyone that makes her life worth living, it's you. Now you threaten to leave by indicating she would lose you – for what? - a party?' Pavel had to stop to breathe before he could carry on.

Ana was so stunned she wasn't even able to reply. Her father's face contorted with fury at her lack of response; he thought she was belligerent and uncaring.

'You say you're a grown up? No, you're not! A grown up is someone who is able to see beyond their own needs and wants and sees the other person's point of view. You're just a child pretending to be a grown up.'

With that, her father left the living room and walked into the kitchen.

Ana was left on the sofa, her mind reeling. She knew that no matter how much she could try to deny what he said, he was right. She *was* behaving like a child. The words she said to her mother were mean and insensitive.

She watched as Pavel came out of the kitchen. In his hand he had a warm drink of milk. It wasn't the first time her dad had given her a peek into her mum's inner world. It reminded Ana of the first time she saw him do it.

***

Ana had been eight years old. It was night-time. She'd woken up but wasn't quite sure what had pulled her out of her dreams.

She was lying in bed listening to the sounds of the apartment when she heard her mother crying and shouting words in a language Ana couldn't understand. She got out of bed and tiptoed to her parents' bedroom along the corridor.

Their door was ajar. The bedside lamp was on; its yellowish light gave the whole scene a dreamy look. Her dad was sitting on the bed next to her mum, hugging and rocking her, whispering into her ear.

Ana couldn't hear everything he was saying, but one sentence sounded above the others: 'It's OK, I'm here. It's OK, I'm here.'

After a while, Helen calmed down and fell back into the bed like a rag doll. Pavel handed her a glass of warm milk and said, 'Drink this, it will help you fall asleep again.'

'I don't want to sleep,' her mum said, 'I'm afraid.'

'Nothing to be afraid of. I'll be here, nothing will happen to you on my watch.'

Helen finished drinking and closed her eyes. Ana could see her father keeping watch, even after Helen fell asleep. That was Ana's cue to tiptoe back to her room.

She tried doing it as quietly as she could, but there was a creak as she stepped on a wobbly floorboard. Ana froze and turned to see Pavel smiling at her from the bedroom doorway. She knew she was in the clear.

'Can't sleep?'

'What's wrong with mama?'

'It's the war,' he replied. That didn't make any sense to her.

'But the war is over. Why does mama have nightmares about something that is not happening now?'

The next sentence her dad said would stay with her for the rest of her life.

'Some people have to free their mind before the war inside ends.'

Ana hadn't fully understood it at the time, but years later it would make all the sense in the world.

Chapter Seven

BOSTON - 1989

Ana had finished telling her story. It took her a while to return to the present moment. Yael and Dan gave her time to linger among old memories.

'So, grandma was a Holocaust survivor?'

'Yes. she was. And I guess I had no option. But it doesn't have to be like that with you.'

'What do you mean?' Yael asked.

'I can't compare my situation with my mum to you and me. My mum had no other option with what she'd had to go through. But I do. I'm the grown up here, not you. It's my responsibility to find a solution for this conflict.'

'Your mum is right,' Dan added. 'As parents it's our job to find a way to understand our kids, not the other way round. We know it's also not like you to behave that way.'

'What's really going on?' Yael was still hesitating.

Ana could sense Yael was debating whether to trust them or not. She hoped that by now Yael would know that the best way to deal with things is telling the truth.

She relaxed once Yael took a deep breath and mumbled as fast as she could, 'There's this guy that Rachel knows, from another school. I like him and he'll be at the party.'

Once Yael's words were out, both Ana and Dan understood. If Yael would have had the courage to look at her parents, she would see a glimpse of a smile on Ana's face, looking at Dan who was grinning. They both understood it was all about first love.

Ana peeked at Dan with a question mark in her eyes and he nodded.

'I'll tell you what we'll do,' she said, 'You can go to the party, but we'll pick you up from Rachel's place at eleven sharp. No arguments or delays.'

Ana had barely finished her sentence when Yael grabbed her and hugged her. She jumped out of bed to give Dan a kiss.

'I have to call Rachel and tell her. I phoned before to tell her I can't come. I want to make sure she doesn't change any plans. Thank you so much. I love you!'

Ana and Dan were about to leave the room when Yael said, 'You still didn't tell me who Jan is. I still want to hear the full story.'

'How about we continue it this weekend?'

'Sounds like a plan.'

Chapter Eight

BOSTON - 1989

November was 'clear out month' for Ana. Each year she was surprised to find how much she managed to collect during the previous twelve months. No matter how much she tried to get rid of stuff, there was always more to be thrown away.

'I swear, it's like all our stuff is multiplying like rabbits,' she joked with Dan as they surveyed the huge amount of junk that needed clearing.

As she went through her drawers, Ana found an envelope full of old photos hiding under a pile of papers. Intrigued, she picked them up and started sorting through them. Ana was not someone who lingered on the past, so she was confused about why she had them.

'These look old …Whose photos are these?' Yael asked, appearing through the door and snatching the pictures out of Ana's hands before she could say anything. 'Hey, that's you!' Yael laughed. 'Who are the other girls? You're so young in these photos; when were they taken?'

'It's impolite to look through my photos without asking permission,' Ana said, snatching the photos back from Yael. Ana could see her daughter was startled and confused by her fierce reaction; her eyes were glassy with tears.

'I only wanted to get to know you better. Is that so wrong?' Yael left the room.

Ana sighed. The last thing she wanted was for Yael to resent her. She always hoped she would have a better relationship with her daughter than she'd had with her mother.

If only I could take those words back.

'You wouldn't believe what I found this morning in my drawer.' Ana told Dan when they were driving to a second-hand shop to drop the boxes off.

'What? Don't keep me guessing. You know I'm not good at it.'

'I found an envelope with old photos from the old country. I had no idea I had them. I was trying to recall how I got them when Yael grabbed them from my hand and wanted to know who the people in those photos were.'

'What did you tell her?'

'I told her it was rude to snatch it without asking for permission.'

'So, you didn't use it as an opportunity to continue your story?'

'No.'

'You know she wants to be closer to you. You did promise her to tell her the full story.'

'I don't think I'm ready. Not yet,' Ana muttered, more to herself than to Dan.

They kept driving in silence.

Once they arrived at the second-hand shop and unloaded the boxes, she felt better. It was good to let go of old stuff lying around without use. It felt as if the energy was cleansed, and space was opened for something new in its place.

'I'm sure you wouldn't want her to be alienated from you,

the way you were with your mother?' Dan remarked once they were back in the car.

'I'm scared she'd think I was selfish.'

'You have nothing to fear. You didn't do anything bad.'

Ana flashed Dan a look. He sighed, realising his faux pas.

'Okay, I'll continue the story tonight,' she said, 'but only what I feel comfortable with.'

That evening, after dinner, Ana went upstairs and brought down the envelope. Yael was on her way back to her room when Ana motioned for her to join them in the living room.

'You asked me about these photos, and I think I did a bad job answering,' Ana said.

'You think? You practically chopped off my head for asking.' Yael was still offended.

'I know, and I'm sorry. It's just not that easy for me to talk about that period. But I promised to tell you the story, so let me continue as much as I can.'

Ana's tone was as soft as she could manage, hoping it would put things right between her and Yael.

Yael shifted her weight from one leg to another, darting a look at Dan, then at Ana.

'OK,' she said. 'Let's hear it.'

Chapter Nine

PRAGUE - 1968

Ana was collecting her books at the end of a long study session. A glance at her watch told her she had a few hours before her hospital shift. She debated whether to spend that time in the library writing her next assignment or getting to the lab earlier and catching up on the work.

'Hi Ana, how about joining us for the celebration?' she heard Pjoter's voice above her. She always had a challenge looking at him; he was so tall.

But he's good-looking and smart. Ana was upset that her thoughts could imitate her mum's voice. *Now you sound like her!*

Ever since Jan had come to have dinner with them, her mum had been nagging her that it was OK to admit that she was in love with Jan. It infuriated her that all her mother could think of was a romantic relationship. To Ana, Jan was a friend. He was the one she could talk about anything with, share dreams with, and the one she trusted the most.

'Sorry, Pjoter. Have to finish my paper. I'm going to the library.'

'Then I'll walk with you.'

Pjoter and Ana started walking towards the library. Ana had no idea what to say, and the silence between them felt awkward.

'I heard you joined the Student Union?' she asked.

'Yes. I believe it's the right thing to do. It also gives me a bit of a break from only studying. Why don't you join?'

Ana was happy when they reached the library. How could

she explain that what stopped her from joining was her mother? She would sound so childish, which was the last thing she wanted Pjoter to think of her.

'I'll think about it. I can certainly use a break from my studies. But how do you do it with all the work they give us?'

'I just do the minimum I need to keep me in the program. I'm not aiming to be at the top of our class like you.'

Ana was surprised to hear someone admit to such a thing. She would expect it from someone in high school but not in university. *What's the point of choosing to study if you don't want to excel in it?* She felt she was missing something most other students took for granted.

Ana didn't have much time to contemplate it. She only had a short time to collect the books she wanted for the essay she had to hand in the following week. From experience, she knew it took a long time to find those books. She would have to do the work itself once she was back home.

It took Ana nearly an hour to find the books she wanted. The librarian was not very helpful, so she had to locate the books on the shelves herself. To her irritation, the ones she most wanted were already loaned out, so she had to find a substitute for them. She hoped the magazines she would cite would be enough for her paper.

Leaving the library, Ana noticed a big crowd walking down the street, but didn't give it much attention. Her mind was only on the work she had to complete in the lab.

Hours later, when Ana emerged from the lab, she could hear music down the street. She didn't pay much notice, but when a loud wave of cheers and shouts followed, she started wondering what was going on. It was January, and no one in his right mind would spend time outside more than necessary. All she wanted was to get home to warm up.

Turning around a corner, she found herself amid a crowd all moving together singing and shouting. On the one hand she was happy: the crowd protected her from the cold, but after a few minutes she realised she would be unable to get to where she was headed. She was surrounded on all sides, and it seemed like everyone was going to a specific place. If she wanted to get out of this crowd, she would have to force her way out.

There was no way she could stop. People were pushing her from all directions. She started to feel claustrophobic and had a hard time breathing. The combination of being surrounded by all these people and being so small was not helping. Fear started creeping in.

I have to break through.

She started moving against the tide but was pushed forward and nearly fell down. She was afraid the crowd would trample her, when out of nowhere a hand reached in and pulled her out.

'You really shouldn't be in the midst of this crowd. It's the second time I'm saving you from being stepped on.' Pjoter smiled at her.

'I didn't plan this. What's going on?'

'We're celebrating. Dubček was elected to head the Party and they say he will start a new era for Czechoslovakia.'

'Ah. So, this is what a political rally looks like. I guess it's not for me, after all.'

'It's not like this every time. We're only celebrating right now. Join me?'

'I really have to get back home.'

'Then I'll walk with you. We don't want you injured, do we?'

That night at home, Ana was sharing her day with her parents. She tried to avoid talking about the street incident. If she was honest with herself, she was still shaken by it, which was the last thing she wanted to admit to her mum.

'Funny thing, when I came home tonight there were lots of students celebrating Dubček's win on the street,' she said.

'I hope you were not one of them,' Helen cut her off.

'Why? And what if I was?'

'It's too dangerous. Moscow is not going to like Dubček's win. They will retaliate. You shouldn't take the risk of being connected to his ideas. It would be you who would pay the price, not those politicians. Think about your future and what you want.'

Ana watched her father as he buried his face in the papers, pretending he wasn't listening to Helen's words. It was a sign that he disagreed with her.

'What do you think, dad?' Ana asked, to give him an opportunity to express his thoughts.

'I think your mum has a point. However, I believe Dubček would be able to walk the line between bringing new ideas and not alienating Moscow. We just have to wait and see what he stands for.'

Typical. Dad will always find a way to be diplomatic enough to pacify mum, instead of saying what he really thinks. At that moment there was a knock on the door. Helen got up to open it.

Jan seemed as if he'd run the whole way to their place. His eyes were sparkling, and he had a big grin on his face. He was thrilled with something.

'Good evening, Helen. I was passing by, and I saw light in your window and thought to ask Ana something. Is she back already?'

'Come in. Would you like something to eat?'

'No. I'll just be a minute. Hi, Ana, hi, Pavel. I thought I saw you and Pjoter in the street celebration, but I couldn't reach you.'

Ana saw Helen's face darkening. Now she felt ashamed she'd hidden this fact from her parents.

'I was only caught up in it on my way back from the hospital. Pjoter saved me from nearly being trampled by the crowd. I had no intention of being there.' It was the only way she could explain her indiscretion.

'Doesn't matter. What I wanted to tell you is that tomorrow there is a rally where Dubček is going to announce his new direction. Why don't you join me?'

'No. She can't,' Helen interrupted. 'She has her future to think of and Dubček's direction is not part of it.'

If her mother hadn't said anything, Ana might have refused the invitation, but now she felt that if she agreed with her, she would seem like a school kid who needed approval from her mother. That was not how she wanted Jan to think of her.

'Well, I don't care what you say, I'm going with Jan to this rally. And if dad wants, he can join us, just to make you at ease.'

It was the first time Ana had stood up to Helen. She wasn't sure she liked it, but it felt like the right thing to do. She wasn't going to let Helen keep her small anymore.

When she looked at Jan, she saw that he was surprised by her determination. There was an awkward silence in the room.

'Ok then. I'll pick you up tomorrow at six.'

Jan left as fast as he could. Helen was staring daggers at him.

If looks could kill, Ana thought, *Jan would drop dead before he reached the entrance.*

'That boy isn't good for you,' Helen said. 'Mark my words, he'll be the end of you.'

Chapter Ten

When Jan left that night, Ana was exhilarated by the prospect of going to hear Dubček the next day. It was hard for her to fall asleep. She knew that defying her mother's wishes had shaken their family's unspoken agreements. But Ana felt it was time. She wasn't a child anymore, and she had a nagging urge to break some of those unspoken rules. Jan and the Student Union was just an excuse for her to do that.

Ana had no idea when she fell asleep. One moment she was fantasising about living her life without her mum's limitations, and the next minute Helen was waking her up.

'Are you still planning to go to that rally with Jan?' she asked.

'Obviously. Got to run,' Ana replied, grabbing her books and a piece of bread before rushing out the door. She didn't want to have a discussion with her mum on the topic, knowing very well she would try to prevent her from going.

The whole day, Ana was restless. She couldn't wait for the day to end so she could join Jan at the Student Union house.

Finally, her lessons were done. Ana grabbed her stuff and headed to the main building where she knew Jan would be waiting for her. Before she even noticed, Jan was walking towards her with a group of students.

'This is Ana. She's joining us today.' Jan introduced her to the group. Ana waved to Pjoter. He welcomed her with a wide smile.

The whole group started walking and conversation and banter were exchanged between the guys. Though they all welcomed her, Ana felt like an outsider, not knowing who or what they were talking about.

'You study medicine, don't you?' A girl, who looked like an Amazonian with bright red hair, approached Ana with a smile. 'I'm Tereza, it's great to have another woman in our group.'

Ana smiled back. Being a loner for most of her youth, Ana was never sure how to behave in the company of others.

'How did you know I study medicine?'

'You're always bringing samples to my lab to be checked. You always look so serious as if it's life and death. Never saw you smile or pause for a minute. You're either studying in the library or in the lab.'

Ana wasn't sure if it was a compliment or an insult. 'What do you study?'

'Depends on the year. I keep changing my studies, I can't find one topic that captures my heart enough to dedicate four or more years of my life to it.'

'So, what do you do in the lab?' Ana asked, shocked by her casual attitude.

'Oh, that's my work. I'm a lab technician. That much I was able to master.'

Ana was flabbergasted. The thought that someone would not finish what they started was like a foreign language to her. Her whole life she'd believed in completing what you start. Anyone who doesn't was without a doubt a frivolous person.

How can Jan associate himself with someone like her? There was no time to dwell on those thoughts as they'd arrived at Vinohradská St where the main radio station was located. A crowd was already gathered around the station. Ana could see the loudspeakers outside the building allowing the crowd to hear Dubček's speech.

Whether it was the heightened atmosphere or the anticipation or her mum's warning, Ana couldn't help experiencing excitement one moment and anxiety and fear the next. To add to it, she was once again surrounded by a wall of people. With her diminutive height, she felt like she was being locked in a cell created by bodies of people.

'I need to get to Jan. Help me push through,' Ana said to Tereza. Without any hesitation the Amazonian-like woman parted the throng of people and elbowed Ana towards Jan.

'Look, Vaclav Havel and Milan Kundera are here. I love their work, did you read them?' Jan didn't seem dazzled by their presence. 'What did you think about their writings?' Ana asked, hoping to get a hint about why Jan was not excited by their attendance.

'I like their writings, but I believe we should aim higher. They're still holding back. We can't have real free thought if there is censorship. Let's hope today's speech will change it.'

That was when the crowd in front of the radio station parted like the red sea before Moses. For a second, Ana got a glimpse of Dubček and other party members walking into the station.

Soon after, the whole street could hear Dubček's words announcing his new direction for Czechoslovakia.

'On this day, as we celebrate the twentieth anniversary of *Victorious February*, it is time for us to build an advanced socialist society on sound economic foundations that corresponds to the historical democratic tradition of Czechoslovakia.'

The crowd broke the silence with cheers so loud, it was impossible for Ana to hear the next few sentences. The mood on the street was electrifying, and no one was immune to the excitement and the hope for something new to come.

Ana experienced a rush of emotions she'd never felt before. She looked around and it seemed like she wasn't the only one. Old and young people all had that light in their eyes. Some were crying, some were whispering, and some were singing.

'Our aim is to build a society of socialism with a human face, and we start today with the abolition of censorship of the press and enhancing freedom of speech and movement.'

The sound on the street was as if a bomb had exploded. Hundreds of people shouting and crying out Dubček's name. Strangers were hugging each other. People broke into songs and the whole street turned into one big celebration.

Once the crowd started moving, there was no way for Ana to control her own movement. She was carried along with it and felt like a leaf floating with the stream. Even if she'd wanted to break free, she couldn't.

Feeling a panic attack brewing, Ana felt momentarily spooked, but then she felt Jan's hand in the palm of hers and knew she was safe. There was no way for them to communicate, so Jan squeezed her hand to let her know that he's there for her and she's shielded.

Jan and Ana moved along the streets of Prague until they reached the main square. Some students had guitars with them and broke into songs and dancing circles. The whole place felt like one big party.

'Hi guys, my boyfriend's apartment is close by, how about we continue this party at his place?' Tereza cried out to Ana, Jan and Pjoter.

Ana liked the idea of getting away from the crowds. Even though Jan was holding her hand, she still felt suffocated. She had no idea who Tereza's friend was, but anything that would take her away from this shoving and pushing was better.

'Lead the way,' she said, and started following Tereza.

At last, Tereza took a turn, and they were away from the mass of people that were still running down the main streets.

They were standing in front of what looked like a cafe, but Tereza signalled them to go down into the basement.

Ana was flabbergasted. She had never seen a room like it. The place was huge. You couldn't even guess how far it extended. There was no furniture anywhere, only mattresses covered with oriental-looking cloth and huge pillows that appeared to be serving as chairs. There was music playing, but nothing she had ever heard before. *No doubt it's American music.*

The room was lit with dimmed lights that twinkled like stars, which were enchanting but did not allow much visibility.

'Hi love, come meet my friends Ana, Jan, and Pjoter,' Tereza called into the room. Only then did Ana notice the room was full of sweet-smelling smoke.

From one of the mattresses a tall man stood up and strolled towards them. He was much older than any of them. He looked to be in his late thirties. He was tall, built like a brick, with hollow cheeks that gave him an intimidating look. But then he smiled and his whole appearance changed.

'Any friends of Tereza are my friends. Join me.' Tomas gave

a passionate kiss to Tereza while fondling her buttocks. Ana didn't know where to look. Tereza didn't seem to mind and only clung to him more.

'I just got some good stuff from my connections in France,' he continued. 'Would you like to try it?' He offered a weird-looking cigarette to Ana. Ana took it, but as she had never smoked before she had no idea what to do with it. She just held it in her hand and stared at it like it was a foreign object.

'It's going to be wasted on her,' Tereza said while grabbing it from Ana's hands. She took a long inhale from the cigarette.

That sweet smell that the room had was now even more present. Ana finally realised it came from the cigarette. She looked around and saw Jan and Pjoter sitting down on those mattresses. Tereza passed the cigarette to Pjoter, and he took a long inhale from it.

'Oh, that's really good, Tomas. Trust you to get your hands on such good stuff.' Pjoter's words were slurring, and he reclined even more on the mattress. He passed the cigarette to Jan.

Ana stared at Jan, curious to know what he would do. She was torn. On one hand she wanted to stay in this unfamiliar and intriguing place, but on the other hand there was a growing, nagging feeling that Helen would by now be sick from worrying about her. She knew she had to go back home.

'I'll walk Ana home,' Jan declared, having sensed her unease. Ana was relieved. It proved to her that Jan understood her situation. In a strange way, he could read her mind.

They walked back home, each absorbed in their own thoughts. Just before they reached her street, Ana stopped and turned to Jan.

'Was that cannabis that Tomas was smoking?'

'Yes.'

'Were you going to smoke it?'

'Why not? It's harmless. You of all people should know the benefits are higher than the propaganda they tell us against it.'

'Why me?'

'Because it has been used for centuries for medicinal use. Besides, there are countries, even communist countries, where smoking is a cultural element and is part of the society.'

Ana contemplated this. This whole evening, she'd felt like Alice falling down the rabbit hole, discovering a whole new world.

A world that challenged her on *everything* she was certain about.

She was lost for words.

'I know,' Jan said, 'Give it time.'

Ana was relieved. She didn't think she could feel any happier, but his next few words made the whole evening even better.

'I'll see you tomorrow.'

Jan turned around and walked away, leaving her staring at the entrance to the courtyard where *the three witches* were sitting, controlling their neighbourhood.

Some things never change, she thought.

Chapter Eleven

Having finished her shift at the lab, Ana was now waiting for Jan to come and pick her up. They planned on going to another Union meeting. To use her time more effectively, Ana decided to distribute some flyers she had still in her bag. She was hoping they would encourage people to join the rally the next day.

The last few weeks had changed her so much. She could hardly believe she was standing in the middle of the hospital handing out flyers. Most of her life, Ana had tried to be as invisible as possible while striving to achieve her dream of becoming a doctor. Now, her studies and her work took a back seat. She'd stop and talk to anyone who would be willing to listen to her. She'd discovered that she had a great talent for explaining the political situation in a way that got people excited about the future. For some reason, people related to her and were moved by what she had to say.

All at once, Ana noticed Helen entering the lab. She'd totally forgotten it was the time of the month when Helen came to pick up her medicine. Ana tried to shove the flyers into her bag but wasn't fast enough.

'What were you handing out to people, can I also get one?'

Ana didn't know how to get out of this situation. She knew Helen would not approve of what she was doing. She hesitated.

Helen grabbed her bag and took out some of the flyers. 'Are you insane?' she said. 'This is exactly what will get you in trouble,' Helen whispered vehemently. 'Do you really want to throw your life away for some political ideas?'

'I'm not going to throw my life away. I am doing what dad suggested… getting more out of life than just studying.'

'That's not what he meant. Get rid of them, now!' Helen was about to throw the flyers into the closest bin when Jan came running into the lab.

'What's going on here?' He looked at Ana, who was unable to respond.

'I knew it,' Helen said. 'It's you who influenced her to do this. Do you care for her so little that you'd let her throw away her dream for this?'

'You're insane if you think that distributing some flyers will ruin her chances. Why can't you trust that she knows what she's doing?'

'She doesn't know what she's doing. She's only doing it because you convinced her it's the right thing. I'm telling you,' Helen said to both of them, 'this won't last, and those who support this soap bubble of hope will pay the price for it.'

'Now who isn't trusting Ana? Who is treating her like a small child who doesn't know what she's doing? At least in the Union we all see and appreciate her talents and respect her for them.'

Ana was flattered by Jan's defence of her but wasn't sure she was happy with him attacking her mother in such a way.

'You have no clue what you're talking about,' Helen shrieked at Jan. 'You're too young to understand anything about how this world operates. Sure, now it seems as if there is new hope, but trust me this is going to disappear one day as quickly as it arrived. And then what? What will you do when all that you've loved and cherished is taken away from you?'

'You're too stuck in the past,' Jan shouted back. 'You're

too afraid that life can be much more than this dreary life of survival. You're basically a coward who not only won't dare to dream but will kill the dreams of the people around you.'

'That's enough!' Ana cried out. Jan was way out of line calling her mother a coward. She didn't like it that people who she loved were fighting and saying such mean things to each other. Ana could see the first signs of an attack coming over Helen.

I have to take her out of here. I have to take her home NOW.

'Mum, sit down here. I'll bring your medicine and I'll take you home.' She helped Helen to sit down on a bench next to the receptionist area in the lab. She took Helen's prescription and went to pick it.

When she returned, Jan wasn't there anymore. *Good. I can't deal with both of them at the same time.* She gave Helen one of the pills with a glass of water. Her mum didn't say anything. She had a faraway look and simply obeyed Ana's instructions like a small child. Ana helped Helen to get up, grabbed her bag and, holding her hand, took her back home.

Ana knew perfectly well that there would be no Union meeting for her tonight.

On their way back home, Helen's condition worsened. She started mumbling to herself and her body was shaking. It started with her hands, but as they kept going Ana had to hold Helen several times when her legs began giving up on her.

Ana was happy to reach home without her mum collapsing.

'Dad, I need your help,' she called as they entered their apartment. Before she could say anything, Pavel was next to her.

'I got her. Go warm up some milk with honey.'

Ana was relieved that she didn't need to explain anything. Her father was familiar with such attacks and knew all too well how to take care of Helen when they happened.

Ana went into the kitchen and prepared the drink she had seen her dad give her mum all those years ago. She had no idea why that specific drink was so powerful, but it seemed as if it always did the trick. Within less than fifteen minutes, Helen would relax and fall into a deep sleep only to be awakened the next day. Most of the time, she would have no recollection of what had taken place.

Ana never knew what triggered those attacks. It was part of the mystery surrounding her mother. It was as if there was an unspoken agreement that no one would speak about it afterwards. She hated that she had to pretend as if nothing had happened. But today, she knew she'd played a part in triggering that attack. Making the drink was her way of trying to apologise. She added some honey to it and walked to her parents' room.

Helen was in bed, still shaking with an absent look on her face. It was as if her body was a separate entity than her.

Helen was not there.

Pavel was holding her hands and whispering some comforting words. Ana couldn't clearly hear what he was saying. She handed the glass to him and stepped out of the room.

Ana couldn't relax. On the one hand she felt bad that her mother had got one of her attacks due to what she did. On the other hand, she was angry.

How long will I need to give up on what I want in life for fear of triggering her? She kept repeating the conversation that had taken place between Jan and her mum. *I could have said... I should have said... I would have...*

None of it helped her feel better. The only thing that did make her feel better was the realisation that Jan thought highly of her.

Ana was so preoccupied with her thoughts that she hadn't noticed Pavel enter the room.

'That was a strong one. What happened?' There was no accusation in his tone, only real concern for Helen.

'She came into the hospital to pick up her medicine and found me distributing flyers for the rally tomorrow.' Before she could explain that she wasn't the real issue; that what Jan had said was the cause, Pavel interrupted.

'How can you do this? You know what she thinks about these developments. Why would you do it?'

'So now I can't follow what I believe in, just because she's scared? Maybe Jan was right calling her a coward,' she exploded.

The silence that followed was booming.

Ana had never seen her dad react so strongly to anything. The room turned ice cold. Pavel stared at her, and she could hear the wheels in his head turning.

'He called her what? And you think he was right calling her that?'

Ana couldn't answer that question honestly. She had also been pissed off by Helen but calling her a coward was something she felt was not right somehow.

'You young people,' Pavel continued. 'You have no clue what courage means. You think walking down the street shouting some words and making signs or flyers is courage? It's a juvenile activity. I'm here to tell you that neither me or my friends, who fought with me against the Nazis, had a tenth of the courage of what your mum and her people had to have to survive. Never, *ever* call or think of her as a coward. She is the bravest human being I have ever met.'

'But that's just the point. She never tells me anything. I have to guess everything. I don't know who she is and she's not making it easy for me.'

'Well, I guess that is your problem, not hers. You are the most important thing in her life, and she would do anything to protect you and make sure you achieve your dreams.'

'I don't want or need her protection. I just want to live my life the way I think is right and she's not letting me do it.'

'Now you sound like a selfish, spoiled kid. How about you grow up a bit and start noticing how you affect the people around you?' With that, he left the room.

Ana was stunned by the fact that he'd called her childish and juvenile.

Am I really? For wanting to live my life on my own terms?

Chapter Twelve

Pavel's words kept on turning around in Ana's head for days after.

She did her best to keep her activities with the Student Union hidden from her parents. She felt guilty about it. She never used to hide things from them. But now, she had no idea how to share it with them without causing tension.

Gone were the days when Jan was welcomed in their house. That also was hard on her. Jan had become more and more important to her.

One afternoon, Ana came rushing into the house. She only had a short time between her hospital shift and the meeting at the Student Union. She agreed Jan could pick her up from home.

'I'll make you something to eat,' Helen said when she saw Ana rushing in. *That's a good sign. Maybe she's not angry at me anymore.* Helen disappeared into the kitchen and the smell of fried cheese came seeping into the living room.

'That smells so good, mum.'

When Helen emerged from the kitchen it seemed as if she would forgive Ana for anything. The second her mum set the dish on the table; she gobbled it down as if there was no tomorrow.

Later, a knock on the door signalled to both of them that their momentary truce was up. Ana jumped up to open the door, still munching on her last bites of dinner.

'Ready?' Jan asked.

Ana grabbed her coat and bag and left the apartment with Jan before Helen could say anything.

'Be safe,' Helen murmured after them, more to herself than to them.

Ana could see the *three witches* at the entrance. She motioned to Jan not to talk any political talk as they passed by them. She knew their daily gossip could stretch to the police, which would be dangerous for both her and her parents.

'Your boyfriend?' asked Mrs. Hudek with a smile.

'No. I recognize him. That's the same young boy that used to defend her when she was small. Still playing the knight in shining armour?' Mrs. Kadlek asked cynically.

Ana grabbed Jan's hand and pulled him away. Only when they were in the street and far enough from their ears, she released a sigh. 'Witches. Can't stand them, why can't they stop putting their noses in other people's lives?'

'Let it go. Let them think what they want, their day will come once we're free from the control of censorship and Moscow.'

'You're right. I just hate this feeling… Like everything I do is watched and can be reported to someone, and if we step out of line someone pays the price for it.'

'What you need is some good ol' fashioned fun. Let's find Tereza and her gang of misfits. I heard Tomas managed to get his hands on some records of the Beatles.'

Ana wasn't sure she liked the idea of spending the evening in the company of Tereza and her friends. She found Tereza both intriguing and scary. It wasn't her physical looks, which were breath-taking, but more her attitude to life and how she looked at Jan. Ana regarded Tereza as someone who doesn't take life seriously. That was something Ana could never understand.

Truth is, you're afraid Jan would be attracted to her. Ana tried hard to block the intrusive thoughts, thinking she again sounded like her mum. Ana would never be willing to admit her mum knew her better than herself. She wanted to prove that she *doesn't* know her that well. Being with Jan and his friends gave her that opportunity.

Prague was buzzing with new ideas, and as winter had dissolved into spring, hopes were rising, and new voices and ideas were spreading like forest fires.

Ana was so gripped by her thoughts that she barely registered when Jan opened the door to the university dorms. Before she could ask any questions, her attention went to the loud music being played. Being accustomed to mainly classical music, hearing rock 'n' roll with Czech words to them sounded like a weird combination. Through the hallways, students were dancing to the music and laughing.

At the entrance to the last room in the corridor, Ana observed that there was hardly any space between the three bunk beds, but that didn't stop more than ten people cramming into the room. On each of the top bunks were guys playing guitars. They played so well together; Ana was sure they must be a band. After a while, Ana recognized that, though the music was rock 'n' roll, the words were political and were making fun of the Soviets and their attempts to control the world.

It took her a while, but Ana finally felt like she could unwind and start enjoying herself. Just when she found a spot on the floor to sit and listen to the music, Jan held out a hand.

'Shall we dance?'

Nothing could make the evening better than his question. She had no idea what kind of dance she was supposed to dance, but it didn't seem to matter as long as she could be close to him. She soon found out there were no specific steps or rules for this type of dancing. *Another way of expressing our freedom. Maybe that's why Moscow is against rock 'n' roll so much and forbids it to be played.*

Ana was having fun, but then she noticed Tereza standing at the door.

'What are you staring at?' Jan asked. Ana hadn't realised she was staring.

'What is Tereza wearing? I've never seen any pants that cling to your body like what she's wearing.'

Jan burst out into laughter so loud that Ana could feel her face turning red by the minute. She grasped that she'd made a stupid mistake; something she was not used to doing.

'Hi Tereza,' Jan called over to her. 'Ana wants to know where you got those Levis?'

Tereza was busy talking to one of the guys who were playing the guitar and ignored his question. But when he repeated it in a louder voice, Ana wished the ground would swallow her up.

'I'll tell you later,' Tereza answered, and continued talking with the guy who played the guitar. It seemed as if she was trying to convince him to break his jam and introduce something new for the party.

It took only a few minutes before he agreed, and they all dragged a table into the corridor while Tereza and her friends brought an old record player out. It was clear that it had seen better days, but no one cared as long as it was playing.

To everyone's surprise, Tereza pulled out several records from her bag. All of them were groups and singers that were banned in Czechoslovakia. Tereza looked at the crowd with a twinkle in her eye and chose a record. The sounds of the Beatles filled up the whole dorm.

To Ana's surprise, everyone broke out, singing the lyrics. Various people not only were singing but dancing, and when the song reached the chorus, the whole dorm was singing 'Help'.

At first, Ana watched like it was a scientific experiment, but soon she found herself joining in with the others, wiggling her body to the rhythm of the music. *This can hardly be called dancing*, her rational voice was telling her.

After one of those dances, Ana was breathless and hot. She stepped outside into the cool air and took a deep breath in. She didn't realise how crowded the space had been.

Looking around, she noticed Tereza standing outside smoking a cigarette. Ana looked at Tereza's Levis and flowery, loose top with beads embroidered all over it. It looked so good on her. *How does she get this stuff?*

'I love your top,' she called out to Tereza. 'You always dress so colourful and fun. I constantly think of spring when I look at you,'

Tereza laughed. 'That's the best compliment I ever got. How about we go back to my place and have fun there with Tomas and his friends? Much livelier than here.'

Ana hesitated. It was getting really late, and she still had to finish her essays and other assignments. Lately, she'd been late on her deadlines.

'Come on, live a bit,' Tereza continued. 'You're always so serious, just like Jan. What's the point of fighting for freedom if you're always burdened by responsibilities? Why not live for the moment?'

Ana stared at Tereza. The concept of living for the moment was not something she'd ever heard of or understood. In her gut, though, she sensed Tereza had a point.

She wasn't aware that her inner conflict was showing through her facial expression. Only when Tereza started giggling did she return to reality.

'It's not a matter of life or death. Don't you ever stop thinking so much? You know, sometimes it's good to just have fun in life.' Tereza sat down on the stairs and patted the space next to her.

Ana hesitated; she was wearing her finest clothes. She had expected to spend the evening with Jan and had wanted to look good. However, standing up looked even more strange, so she sat down, but not before making sure she wasn't sitting on anything that might get her clothes dirty.

For a while, both Tereza and Ana were silent. It felt good not to have to say or do anything. It was a strange experience for Ana, whose whole life had been about constantly doing things. It dawned on her that she might have something to learn from Tereza's attitude towards life.

'How can you afford to buy these lovely clothes from the Tuzek shop?' The minute the words came out, Ana was horrified. In her book, you don't ask questions like this. But if Ana was horrified by her own question, she was even more flabbergasted by Tereza's answer.

'Oh, I pay in a different type of currency. I have sex with Tomas. He's one of their buyers. He has way more vouchers than he needs.'

Ana's jaw dropped. She had never heard anyone speak so casually about sex. Tereza grew suspicious.

'What? Don't tell me you haven't done it with Jan by now?'

Ana's face was now red as a tomato. She had no clue what to say to Tereza, but Tereza didn't need her to say anything.

'Well, I'll be damned, you're a virgin. I'm sorry, I didn't realise. I didn't mean to shock you. But I thought, what with all your talks about freedom, you also allowed yourself to be free from the old, conventional way society deals with sex.'

'For me,' Ana said, finally finding her voice, 'it's all about political freedom. Having the right to have more voices heard than just the party's voice. It's not about abolishing everything else.'

'What's the difference between freedom of thought and having the freedom to choose what to do with our bodies?' Tereza challenged her. 'What is the difference between my desire to have freedom with my body and your desire for freedom of the mind?'

'I never thought about it.' *There's truth in what she's saying,* Ana thought.

'Of course you haven't. You're following Jan everywhere and are influenced by him. But he's a man and has no clue how it feels having your actions and desires censored like women have experienced for ages.'

A new point of view had suddenly opened up to Ana. She got clarity on the fact that freedom means much more than what she'd thought during the last few months. She now saw Tereza in a different light; she wasn't a shallow person whose only interest was fun and parties. In truth, she had more dangerous ideas about freedom than what she and Jan had in mind. She grasped that Tereza's ideas are the ones Helen would call a *dangerous game*.

'You do realise that your notion of freedom could lead to the downfall of the traditional way of life?' Ana asked.

'Will that be so bad? Isn't that what you and Jan are all about? I know, I should be more careful who I share my views with, but I don't intend to stay here much longer. I'm going to find a way to get out of here.'

'Where to?'

'Austria, and from there the United States. That's where true freedom is,' Tereza said in a dreamy voice.

'You'd leave everything behind you and go to a place where you don't know anyone? Be among our enemies?'

'Who says they are our enemies? Isn't that just propaganda the party spreads? What if they want the same things as we do? Have you ever listened to them?'

'How can you listen to them? All international broadcasts are censored. That's part of what Jan demands to change.'

'Well, Tomas has a way. He's connected to pirate radio stations where you can tune to any channel you wish. If you want, you can come over one night and listen together with us.'

That would be the end of me, mum would never let me leave the house if she knew! Though the voice in her head was loud, something was stirring inside of Ana. It was as if a door had opened and, though she wasn't yet walking through it, she felt the attraction and the pull towards it.

'I don't think I could leave everything behind me and move to another country.'

'Hmmph,' was all Tereza replied, but kept her gaze on Ana for a long time.

When the silence was too much for Ana and she felt like getting up and ending this strange encounter, Tereza surprised Ana.

'So, what are we going to do with you and Jan?'

'There is no me and Jan, we're just friends.'

'Sure you are, but you're in love with him and he obviously adores you.'

'I'm not so sure about that.'

'If you want to know, just show up at his place, or better, make him invite you and see what happens when you don't talk politics.'

On that cue, Tereza stubbed her cigarette out, stood up and walked inside.

Ana could hear the party still going strong. She also noticed the famous Prague clock ringing *eleven bells*. She had no idea where the time had gone. The last few hours had felt to Ana as if she was on a different planet. Now, hearing the bells, she was thrust back to her ordinary life; a life she was no longer sure she wanted.

The last few weeks had felt like a roller coaster. It's not that she didn't like it, just that she felt like she was going off the rails and away from her pre-planned path.

She stood for a few seconds watching the city in front of her, then came to her senses and started walking back to her parents' place.

'Wait,' Jan shouted, trying to catch up with her. 'I'll walk you back home; don't want to give Helen or Pavel another reason to hate me.'

Ana stopped. 'I'm not a baby, I've been walking these streets on my own for years.'

'I know, but if your parents see I'm bringing you back home safely, maybe I'll get back in their good books.'

Ana was astonished that Jan was aware of the dynamics between her parents. They continued walking in silence.

'Did you like the party?' Jan finally asked her.

'Sure, though I'm confident we broke more than fifty regulations. But I did enjoy it.'

'I still sense there's something else. What is it?'

Ana took her time to think, despite already knowing the answer.

'I support President Dubček in what he's aiming to do. God knows we all deserve more freedom.'

At the same time, a voice at the back of her mind demanded to know, *What's more important, freedom or being alive and safe?* Despite sounding like her mother, Ana couldn't ignore that voice, especially now that she grasped the depth of the changes Dubček was suggesting.

After a few minutes she stopped, deciding to be brave enough to express her own thoughts on this issue.

'I know you expect me to say it's a good thing. And it is. I'm all for having more freedom. For not being told by the government what to think or how to lead our lives. But tonight, I experienced how far these ideas can go, and I can understand why Moscow would oppose it. We need to be smart in how we lead this movement.'

'Then why don't *you* lead the way?'

Ana stared at Jan blankly. 'What do you mean?'

'We need more people to join in and express their support for what Dubček is doing. The unions are the ones that hold the key. If you could speak to them and inspire them to join us, that would be a huge success.'

'How am I supposed to get to speak to the Union leaders?' Ana burst out laughing.

'Every revolution starts from the bottom,' Jan said with a serious tone. 'You don't need the leaders. You need the workers. Talk to your dad, I'm sure he'll be willing to help you.'

'I've never spoken in front of a group. What would I say? Why would they listen to me?'

'We can work on that together.'

The chance to work together with Jan on something was tempting enough for Ana to consider it. They kept walking, each caught up in their own thoughts. Just before entering her street, Ana stopped and turned to Jan.

'I think I will bring more value if I speak to the students and get them involved. Right now, it's only those that are part of the Union that are active, but there are many more students that are passive and do not care. If I get *them* participating and excited about it, it will make a bigger impact.'

'I think it's an excellent idea, but for now, let's get you back home safely and give those *witches* something to talk about.'

Jan put his arm around Ana's waist and walked her into the courtyard. *The three witches* were not there, but Ana could see a face in the window of the upper floor where Mrs. Fischer lived.

Chapter Thirteen

Ana raised her head from the paper she was reading. She stared at her parents, waiting for their verdict on her speech for the upcoming meeting.

After three weeks of hard work, she'd managed to organise a group of students who were willing to meet with her and listen to what she had to say about the political situation. There was silence in the room and Ana couldn't take it any longer.

'So, what do you think?' Her father stood up and walked towards the window where the radio was playing loud music. It had covered their conversation while Ana was reading her speech in case someone was listening to them.

'I'm proud of you,' he said when he turned around to look at her. His eyes shone, and Ana felt overjoyed that her father thought her speech was good.

'Do you think it would get them to join the Student Union and become active?' It was the main question she had on her mind. Anything other than positively encouraging students to register would be a failure to her.

Pavel looked at her and smiled gently. 'It's impossible to do it with only one speech. You're asking them to move from being passive and scared to willing to give up on safety for an ideal.'

'But you did it.'

Pavel sighed and walked back to sit next to Helen on the sofa. 'Those were different times. The Nazis invaded our country. Now we have the country. It's not perfect, but we have one. The risks you're asking those students to take are higher.'

Ana was disappointed by his answer, but she knew he had to say it for Helen's sake, knowing Helen's ideas about rocking the boat and taking risks.

'But I am proud of you,' he continued. 'You fight for what you believe in, and that's what is important. I can understand why it's important for you. I didn't fight against the Nazis to find myself living under a different type of dictatorship. But if you really want to get those students to join, you need to understand what the stakes are.'

'You promised me you'd be careful with all this involvement with the Student Union.' Helen's voice was quiet, but firm.

'No, mum. I didn't promise. You did. We need more people demanding changes. We can't have people sitting on the side lines. I'm trying to get them involved. How can I be careful when this is my aim?'

'I knew it. It's Jan who is dragging you into this mess. That's what I was afraid of. You have your future to think about. What will happen when this whole false hope collapses? Don't you get it? More demands will bring pressure from Moscow. You forget what Stalin did. People disappeared, never to be seen again.'

'If people are silenced and their activities are strictly controlled from above, it is like living in a concentration camp,' Ana answered back. She looked at her father, wanting to get some assurance from him.

'It's a fine line that you need to walk,' he said. 'Sometimes in life it's better to be wise than right. But I guess that comes with age. I can still remember my own passion when I was young and followed what I believed in.'

'You might be right,' Helen muttered between her teeth, 'but it would be a concentration camp where people are allowed to sing, and not die. I know what I'm talking about. I've been there, you haven't.'

'Those days are over, Helen. We moved on.'

Helen looked at Pavel and hesitated for a moment. 'People might move on, but some things never change. Freedom is a dangerous game.'

'Freedom is not a game, it's our birth right!' Ana exploded at Helen. It was one thing to accept that fighting for freedom could be risky, the way Pavel explained to her. But she wasn't willing to look at life the way Helen advocated, where being safe was the most important thing in life. There *had* to be more to life than just being safe.

'Try convincing others who think differently,' Helen continued in a calming tone. 'You're too young to understand the danger of it.'

Helen stood up and walked out of the room, making sure she had the last word.

Ana felt torn between her desire to impress Jan and her father, and the tales of cautiousness her mother kept pressing upon her.

Chapter Fourteen

Stunned by the standing ovation she'd got, Ana kept shaking hands with the students. They all wanted to thank her for the fantastic speech she gave. What made her thrilled more than anything was seeing the line of students waiting to register to the Union.

'It seems like you've done it again. You're becoming really good at these speeches. I can't recall when we had so many students joining the Union as we have today. A lot of it is due to your talks,' Jan said, giving her a hug.

'I'm still nervous before each time. I keep thinking, this is the time I'll screw it up, or people will leave before I say two sentences.'

'You have no clue how good you are. I can still remember the first speech you gave.'

'I could hardly string two sentences together. I was in my head constantly and words refused to come out of my mouth.' It made her chuckle when she realised how far she had come from the first time she'd made a speech.

'Let's get out of here and take you back home before Helen has a heart attack. I know she's not happy with your involvement and blames me. Let's not stretch it too much.'

When Ana stepped out into the street the air was fresh. She took a deep breath and could smell spring in the air. It wasn't the same bitter cold that sniped at your face and made your eyes tear up. It was a gentle cold that refreshed the spirit.

Ana felt energised as they walked towards her home through the silent streets. She could hear their footsteps on the cobblestones, which made her giddy. She didn't know whether it was the adrenaline, or walking with Jan, but she felt like a child.

She started skipping for joy, *just to change the rhythm of walking from serious to light-hearted*, she reasoned. *Or maybe I'm following Tereza's advice of not being serious all the time.* Noticing Jan was no longer walking beside her. She turned around and saw him looking at her.

'You really are remarkable; do you know that? You're so charismatic when you stand on that stage. You have a way of simplifying complicated ideas, so people get excited about them.'

Ana felt her face turning red and hot. She was embarrassed and pretended to search in her bag when she remembered something.

'That reminds me. Thanks for this book. Another brilliant one. Just to remind you, I wouldn't have been able to get where I am without your support.'

Jan took the book and went through it, noticing all the places she'd made notes in the book. 'I only showed you the door. You're the one that walked through it.'

Ana thought about it for a moment. 'Isn't that what friends are for - showing the way and supporting them in moving to the next level? You're the first person, other than my parents, that believed in me. You changed my life.'

Ana couldn't believe the words had come out of her mouth. Feeling nervous, she didn't dare look at Jan and kept staring into her bag. Jan was silent and, after what felt like an eternity, he put his hand on her shoulder.

'I really believe in you, Ana. More than that, I love being with you. I think you are the voice and the face for breaking barriers.'

There was nothing more to say. They kept walking towards Ana's place, and when they arrived at the courtyard Ana looked up and saw a light on. Her parents were still awake.

'Would you like to come up? Dad would love to see you.'

Jan hesitated, 'Isn't it too late?'

'It's never too late for dad for philosophical debates.'

'I really would love to come up. I like talking to your dad. I could never talk with my dad like I can with yours. But it's your mum that I'm afraid will dislike it.'

'You're right. Mum would ruin the celebration with her pessimistic outlook on life.'

'You know what? How about you come over tomorrow, to my place? We can work on your next talk and see how we can take things further.'

There was nothing Ana wanted more. *It's what Tereza suggested, and I didn't have to do anything for it.*

'I can't tomorrow,' she said with a sinking feeling of regret. 'I really must catch up on my studies.'

'You're right. Me too. How about we meet on the weekend?'

It was the perfect ending to a wonderful evening for Ana. She couldn't be more excited and skipped all the way up to her apartment.

Chapter Fifteen

Ana hardly slept that night. She was so excited about the prospect of finally going to Jan's place and it being just the two of them, alone.

She realised she had never truly been alone with him since their childhood adventures. On the other hand, she didn't know what she would do with him if they were on their own. Talking about politics was always a safe topic between them. She longed to kiss him and feel his lips on her.

But I'm not like Tereza. What if I freeze and don't know what to do? What if he rejects me? Then I'll lose him both as a friend and as a boyfriend. Those thoughts were swirling around her head for the whole week. However, she somehow managed to focus on her overdue essays.

Being top of the class for the last few years afforded Ana some slack, but she knew she had to do well, or she'd end up falling behind.

It had been a week since she'd last seen Jan. She had been looking forward, with trepidation, to the weekend, and had been unable to concentrate on her work.

The library, her favourite place, had always been the best place for her to focus. Yet, now it took her twice as long to go over the material. She kept being disturbed, either by people who came to tell her how great her speech was, or to ask when the next rally would be. All of a sudden, the library was not as peaceful a place to study as it used to be.

What was more disturbing, however, were her own thoughts, which kept switching between what she would do with Jan when they met, to her mother's fears for her. One moment she would hear Helen's warning about how Moscow would react to what takes place in Czechoslovakia, and the next she would have visions of what she would do with Jan if she followed Tereza's advice. None of those thoughts helped her to focus on her essay on the latest research about the measles vaccination.

Looking around, Ana noticed Jan sitting at a faraway table next to the big windows. She got up and approached him. His table was covered with daily newspapers. She noticed some were in Russian.

What the hell is he doing? 'This is a surprise,' she said, 'I've never seen you in this library before!'

Jan raised his head from the books and papers and stared at Ana with a blank expression on his face.

It's as if he doesn't recognise me, she thought. *What is going on with him? He looks like he hasn't slept or eaten for days.*

'Oh. Hi Ana, didn't notice you. I was too busy with this article I'm about to write.'

'An article? What's it about?'

'It's a call to all politicians to take off the gloves and demand more freedom and less censorship. I'm afraid Dubček is too scared of following through with his promises and will retreat.'

'Who are you going to publish it with? Don't you think it's too risky? I mean, they would arrest you for sure for this.'

'Someone has to voice it. And if they don't publish it, I'll print it myself and make flyers and post them all over the streets.'

Ana felt uneasy hearing Jan speak this way. There was fever

in his voice, and she became even more concerned about how thin and pale he looked.

'When was the last time you had a good meal?' she asked, hoping to change the topic.

'What day is it today? Who cares about food, anyway. I must finish this article now, so thanks for stopping by.'

His words confirmed Ana's fears. She was not willing to be dismissed by him, but she understood that confronting him head on would not be helpful.

'I'm about to finish here and go home for dinner, why don't you come with me? I'm sure dad would be happy to give you some feedback about the article and maybe more perspective to it.' His face lit up.

That worked.

'That's a great idea,' he said, 'and I can certainly use Helen's great cooking. I would love to come.'

Ana returned to her table, marked a few more sections on her essay and scribbled some bullet points for later, but her mind remained on Jan.

Something's wrong. She could feel it in her whole body but couldn't put her finger on what it was.

Ana recognised there was a difference between being passionate about a cause and being reckless. She sensed Jan was close to crossing that line. She had no clue how to stop him, but she was determined to do whatever it took to prevent it from taking place.

On their way home, Ana made trivial conversation with Jan and was happy to hear him momentarily back to his normal self. They both joked about the latest finds Tereza had managed to get from her friends at the Tuzek shop: t-shirts with Che Guevara on it, records by The Beatles and The Doors. She relaxed when the conversation went on to discuss who's better, The Beatles or Elvis. This felt normal to her.

'Do you want to hear what my article is about?' Jan said, bursting her bubble. She'd hoped he'd forget about it. What made her even more concerned was the fact he seemed to have lost the recollection that he'd already told her about it.

'Sure.' However, when Jan gave her the main points of his article, her fears were doubled. 'Jan, I think it's a bit too early to demand these changes you're talking about. Remember, Rome was not built in one day. Change is a risky thing, and we need to be smart about it.'

'You sound like Helen. I always thought she was a coward. All this time I thought you were on my side and believed in this cause.'

'Of course I believe in it. And yes, I want to see more steps taken towards freedom. But I am also a realistic person. I don't want you to take too many risks. We both know what the Communist Party is capable of. I don't want to see you on trial and sentenced to death the way Slansky was.'

'This is not you talking, these are Helen's fears. Remember what your dad said - the only way evil prevails is when good people do nothing. I can't sit and do nothing.'

Ana was shocked by the fierceness in Jan's tone, and yet again hurt that he'd accused Helen of being a coward. It's not as if she didn't see her mother as such, but in the end, she was *her mother*. Hearing Jan say it made her want to defend her. She didn't want to get into a big fight, though. She felt that if she did that, she would ruin her chances of having a date with him. She had to find a way out.

'You have a point there. But my dad also said that it's a tricky line to walk between being wise and right. How about when I come to your place tomorrow, we go over the article and make sure it's both wise *and* right?'

'That's a great idea. I need to go back home and get it finished. See you tomorrow.'

Before Ana could say anything, he turned around and disappeared, totally forgetting the reason he was there in the first place - to have dinner with her.

Not a good sign. But I'll see him tomorrow.

Chapter Sixteen

The next day Ana made sure she'd finished all her essays before heading to Jan's place. It took enough courage to go there without having to think about overdue assignments.

She'd never been in his place before. When she arrived, she was shocked to find herself in front of a rundown building. It wasn't that it was old; that was expected in this part of the city. It was the fact that it was dilapidated. From the fading colour of the walls, the cracks in the doors and the shabby look of the building, Ana could tell that no one had taken care of this building for years.

She climbed the crooked steps and knocked on the door. There was no answer. She knocked again. She could hear noises inside.

He didn't forget. There is someone there. It was several more minutes before the door half opened and Jan's face peeped through.

'Ana, what are you doing here?'

Damn. He did forget.

'We agreed to meet here today. I'll help you with your essay.'

'Right, right. Was it today? I totally lost track of time. Come in.' Jan moved aside and opened the door wider so Ana could enter the room. He immediately closed the door behind her.

If the outside of the house looked crumbling, Jan's apartment was in even worse condition. He had only one room that served as a sleeping place, dining room and kitchen all in one.

The place was filthy, with papers everywhere and leftover food that had probably been on the table for several days. It smelled horrific, and Ana could see bugs creeping all over it. She nearly gagged. The sink was also full of dirty dishes and pots.

This place was not what she had imagined for her first attempt at romance. There was nowhere to sit. It looked more like a hermit's cave than an apartment.

Jan looked even worse than when she'd seen him in the library. His black hair was greasy like it hadn't been washed for weeks. His once clean-shaven face was covered in stubble. But most of all, he had dark shadows under his eyes as if he also hadn't slept for weeks.

'Can I open the window? It's really stuffy in here,' Ana said while walking towards it. She felt some fresh air would help her breathe a bit easier. Jan just nodded and watched her. 'Can you help me?' she asked after a few futile attempts to open it. 'It seems stuck.'

'I don't think it was ever opened. Remind me, why are you here?' That's all it took for Ana to lose it.

'If you don't want my company, then why did you invite me? If you don't want my help, then why do you insist on telling me about your plans? You invited me. Don't you remember that?'

Jan looked stunned. It seemed as if Ana's ferocious outburst had moved him.

'I'm sorry. I have no idea what day it is. I've been working on this new article of mine for days and totally forgot we agreed to meet. If I had, I would have certainly cleaned this place up. I mean look at it, it's a pigsty. Now I'm embarrassed.'

This relaxed Ana. She could see he was genuinely regretting

he'd forgotten. Also, his distant look had gone, and he seemed back to his charming self. Ana didn't know what to do now. She knew she couldn't stay in this filthy place, but she still wanted to be with him.

'Look,' he said. 'Whatever it was we planned to do, this place is not in shape for it. I need to clean it up before anyone else steps foot in here. How about I make it up to you. Give me a few days. I'll meet you for a nice picnic in our usual place on the river?'

That was much more like what Ana had in mind as a setting for her romantic ideas towards Jan.

'OK,' she agreed. 'But promise me you'll not only clean this place, but also take care of yourself. Start with taking a shower.'

'Oh, I smell that bad?'

Ana nodded. *If he can joke about it, he's in better shape already.* 'I also have exams this week, but how about next Sunday?'

'You got it. And I promise this time I will not forget it.'

Ana hoped it was a genuine promise but couldn't do anything more. She walked out the door, doing her best not to touch anything.

On her way back home, Ana felt excited at the thought of a picnic with Jan. Yet, his volatile mood swings still disturbed her.

She had a nagging feeling that something was not right with Jan but couldn't express what it was.

Chapter Seventeen

It was Sunday, and Ana and her parents were having their lunch together.

Ana was quieter than usual. Both Pavel and Helen had noticed it but continued the conversation between them. When they were reaching the end of the meal and Ana still hadn't touched her plate, Helen leant over towards her.

'Is everything OK, Ana? You hardly touched your food, is something on your mind?'

Ana heard her name, but not what her mother had asked her. Her thoughts were still on what had taken place at Jan's that day. She had mixed feelings about it, switching from being concerned for him to angry at him for forgetting his invitation. She didn't know how to handle this surge of emotions. Ana looked at her parents sitting across from her, waiting for her to say something.

'I had a fight with Jan today.' She didn't know how to continue.

Am I going to tell them what really took place? She didn't know how much she could say without giving her mum proof that Jan was dangerous for her.

Looking at her mother, she was surprised to see her smiling. 'Why are you smiling?'

'I'm smiling because all lovers have fights, and it's how you recover from the fight that will tell you how strong the relationship is,' Helen said, looking more at Pavel than at Ana. Pavel was nodding in agreement.

'I don't think I'm in love with Jan. For sure he isn't in love with me. We're just friends. But I am worried for him.' This got their attention and their smiles disappeared.

'Why are you concerned for him?' Pavel asked.

'I saw him a few days ago in the library and he was talking about writing an article to the newspapers to demand bolder actions.'

'I knew it,' Helen said. 'I told you from the first moment he was back in Prague that he was a dangerous young man.'

'You see, that's the reason I didn't want to talk about it. I knew you would take it as proof he's dangerous. But I think he's a danger to himself. You should have seen him. He looked as if he hadn't eaten or slept for days.' Ana didn't have the courage to tell them she'd visited him at his place and that the situation was even worse.

'But what did you fight about?' Helen asked. This put Ana on the spot. She couldn't find a way to avoid the whole embarrassing incident that morning. She had to find a way to deflect it. She hesitated, playing with her food.

'Spit it out. It can't be that bad. He might be young and reckless but he's a good man,' Pavel encouraged her.

Ana took a deep breath and told them about the argument she'd had with Jan during which he'd called her mother a coward. There was silence in the room when she'd finished talking. Helen had paled, and Pavel was seething, trying to control himself.

'Do you think I'm a coward?' Helen asked.

Ana didn't know how to answer. She did love her mother, but at the same time she hadn't thought highly of her lately.

Ana's silence was enough for Helen. She stood up and left the room.

Pavel watched Helen leave. When he was finally able to control his emotions, he signalled Ana to move with him to the living room so they would be as far as possible from Helen.

'That's it. I've had enough,' he spat. 'You and Jan have no clue what real courage is. Come with me.'

Pavel pulled Ana up and marched her to the door.

***

Pavel was walking so fast Ana had to practically run after him.

They got to the bus station just as one pulled into the stop. Pavel pushed Ana on, and they found a seat.

'Where are we going?'

'You'll see.'

It took nearly an hour before the bus reached its final stop.

Ana found herself staring at a fortress with a gate that had a sign saying: 'Arbeit Macht Frei'. Her German was rusty, but she could just about work out that it meant 'Work Will Free You'.

'Where are we?' she asked.

'This is Terezín. It used to be a holiday resort reserved for Czech nobility. The Nazis turned it into a concentration camp. This is where your mum spent her teenage years.

For the next hour and a half, they hardly spoke. There was no need; the sights told Ana everything: the barracks where people slept; the photos of the hard labour they had to do every day; the starvation, and most of all the length the Nazis went to deceive the world about the horrors that were taking place there.

Ana wept looking at photos of children having to carry heavy loads of dirt. She was moved to tears even more when seeing how the prisoners were forced to use their talents of music and art to entertain their own jailors. In one of the photos, she recognised young Helen playing the piano to a group of German officers.

'You get it now?' Pavel asked her on the way back home. 'Your mother had to go through all that, then be sent to Auschwitz, and still managed to maintain her sanity and humanity. There is more courage in that than any rally speaking events you could go to.'

'How did mum survive?'

'I don't know all the details. But she used the fact that she was a great piano player to entertain them, and for a while it kept her alive. After that, she had to learn when to keep her head down and when to speak up. And then, when they had enough, they sent her to that hellhole Auschwitz. To survive that place, she had to find a purpose for her life. Those that didn't perished. You have no clue what that place was like.'

Ana watched her father describing her mother's life. As he was talking, his eyes filled with tears. 'When I entered the camp,' he continued, 'I couldn't believe anyone could survive in that place. Here were men, women and children who'd lived through hell for nearly three years. Have you any idea how strong they had to be? There is much more bravery in enduring a life when you know there is no way you can succeed if you fight. Her way of fighting the Nazis was making sure she would stay alive and take care of those around her. That's courage.'

Ana had nothing to say, but she realised she might have to look at her mother in a new light.

When they returned, Ana went into her room to study.

There was a knock on her door and Helen walked in. Ana put down her books. She had no idea what to say to her. She felt bad for what had taken place earlier but didn't know how to apologise for it.

'What do you want? I have an exam tomorrow and I need to prepare.' It came out sharper than she'd intended, but at least it was a start.

'I never got to hear why you were concerned for Jan?'

This took Ana by surprise. Of all the questions she had thought her mother would ask, this was not one of them.

'First it was his physical condition. But the thing that scared me most was that there was a fever in his tone when he spoke. I have never seen him like that before.'

'But he's always been passionate about the changes.'

'Since when are you defending him?' Ana questioned, not understanding why her mother was suddenly showing concern for Jan.

'It's not about him. I'm trying to understand you. How come you became so angry with him? Why are you suffering so much from a fight? It's just a disagreement, everyone has them.'

Ana had no clue how to answer that. *What am I really afraid of?* She invited her mother to sit on her bed.

'I didn't think about it at the time. I guess I was disappointed in him. I was afraid it would kill our friendship.'

Helen took Ana's hand and patted it gently. 'But there is more to it, isn't there? That's not all you feel towards Jan?'

For a minute, Ana was afraid Helen had somehow guessed what had taken place at Jan's. It wasn't something she would ever want her parents to know. But after that wave of panic passed, she realised her mother meant something totally different.

Am I? Is she right? How would I know? I've never felt like this before. All those thoughts came down like a cascade and she was left breathless from them. A*nd how does she know it before I do?*

'He always protected you when you were kids,' Helen said. 'It's natural you'd have those feelings towards him.'

'But I thought we were just friends,' Ana said.

'The best relationships start that way. Look at your dad and me. It started when he took care of me after the war. He became my friend and it developed into the greatest love I could ever imagine.'

Ana didn't know how to respond, but she knew now that she wanted much more than just a friendship with Jan. She had to know if he loved her, the way she loves him.

'The strength of a relationship depends on how you go through the tough times, not that you both agree on everything,' Helen continued. 'Again, look at your dad and me. We disagree on most things, however, our love for each other leads our relationship and not the ideas we have about the world around us.'

'But Jan and I share the same ideas.'

Why am I fighting with her? She's giving me hope.

Ana saw Helen's mouth move, but she was more tuned into the voice in her head.

I'm different from her. She doesn't know who I am. She doesn't know I also want him physically. I can't believe I'm thinking about it. I want to have sex with him.

'So, what am I going to do now?' Ana asked; a question that could mask the fact that she hadn't registered what Helen had just said.

'Why don't you invite him over for dinner this Friday? He could obviously use some good food,' she said, with a little sarcasm. As Helen stood up and started to leave the room, Ana realised something.

'But you don't trust or like him, why are you inviting him for dinner?'

'I still think he's a threat to you, but you're my daughter and you love him. I'm not going to lose you over him. You're much more important to me.'

Ana was still trying to process this when Helen turned back towards her before closing the door.

'Besides, I've learned two important lessons in life. First - to choose my battles wisely, and second - to keep my friends close and my enemies even closer.'

After that, Ana was unable to concentrate on her studies. Not only had her mother admitted that she sees Jan as dangerous for her, but she'd also said her love for Ana is stronger than any other threat. That didn't sound like something a coward would say.

This whole day had been one revelation after another. Ana wasn't sure anymore what she thought about her parents, or how she felt towards Jan. Something was changing in her.

I miss the old days when I knew who I was and what I wanted in life, was the last thought she had before falling asleep.

Chapter Eighteen

It's a perfect day, Ana thought to herself as she went to meet Jan down by the river at their special place. She'd managed to hand in all her assignments on time and only had one more exam to do. She felt like she was back on track.

I hope he remembers this time.

She'd packed a nice lunch and had even brought a blanket to sit on. She'd even tried, for the first time, to put on some makeup. Ana had needed to ask Tereza how to do it.

Tereza had turned out to be a source of information for Ana lately. She'd shown her how to put on the makeup; suggesting what colours would suit her best, and had even given her everything she needed.

'You don't have to pay me. I can get more from Tomas. You can keep them. Just go and have fun for heaven's sake. It would do you both good to be less serious,' she'd said when Ana had started to explain that she couldn't pay her for all that.

'I don't know what to say. You're so nice to me. Why? I didn't even think you liked me.' Tereza burst out laughing, which made Ana even more uncomfortable. She regretted saying it.

'I don't know why you think I don't like you. But one thing is true: we're different. I find you fascinating. You're such a mix of contradictions. On the one hand you're this passionate, dedicated woman fighting to change the world. On the other hand, you're so conventional and stuck in an old mode of thinking. I don't know how you manage it.'

'You think I'm fake?'

'No. I just think that it's like there are two Anas. I find it interesting to see which one will have the upper hand at any moment.'

Ana was thinking of Tereza's words when she reached the river. Jan was still not there, but she was early. She found their spot, which was hidden from the people that passed along the promenade.

Well, I guess I'll have to find out which Ana will show up today.

She couldn't wait to spread out the blanket and soak up the sun on this beautiful day. The sky was a breath-taking shade of blue and the clouds looked like fluffy cotton candy. She lay back and let herself get lost in the serene beauty of the sky above.

The smell of freshly-cut grass and the sweet aroma of the Magnolia trees filled her senses, making her feel truly alive. The gentle breeze carried the delicate petals of cherry blossoms, creating a blanket of soft pink flowers around her. It was a moment of pure joy; one she hadn't felt in a long time. She closed her eyes and let herself fully embrace the happiness of the moment.

Today was shaping up to be a truly great day.

'You look like a fairy resting on a flower,' said a figure appearing before her. The sun was in her eyes, so she could only see Jan's silhouette standing above her. She immediately sat up.

'Don't. It was a lovely picture,' Jan said as he sat down next to her. Immediately Ana felt tense. She didn't know what to do now.

They both sat in silence for a few minutes.

'Mum made us some lunch. Would you like to have some?'

'Helen knows we're meeting? She actually gave her approval? I thought I was branded as an evil influence on you forever.'

'You're still considered "bad" for me, but she worries about you. She still remembers you protected me when we were kids. That stands in your favour.'

'Well, I guess I did something good. But honestly, Ana, I would never do anything to harm you. You're too precious to me.' Ana felt her cheeks becoming red.

Silly, that's what you wanted to hear from him. She tried hiding her embarrassment by taking out the lunch Helen had made for them and organising it on the blanket. Jan took one of the sandwiches and gobbled it up.

'God, Helen's food is always so good. You're so lucky to have such parents. Even though I disagree with everything Helen stands for, she's a fantastic mum.'

Ana wasn't sure how to respond. The last thing she wanted was to talk about her parents. Actually, the last thing she wanted was to talk.

I wish I could be a bit more like Tereza, doing what I want. What would she do now?

'You really see me as precious to you?' she asked. 'What am I to you, really?' She couldn't believe she'd asked it; the question that had been on her mind for so long. She could feel how the mere fact of saying the words allowed her to breathe easier. She never realised how much it took from her to hold it in.

Jan was still chewing on his second helping of food. He allowed himself to finish before he said anything.

'You're my oldest friend. You're the woman I admire and you're the one I love.'

That was it. Ana didn't need anything else.

'I thought we were only friends. I love you too.'

'I know. Everyone knows. And I'm happy you realised it. That's why I would never do anything to hurt you. You're the one I can talk to about anything. I never had anyone else like you in my life.'

Ana reached out to Jan. He took her hand and kissed it.

She wanted more.

She got closer to him and, without any thought, kissed him on his lips. It felt strange. She could taste her mum's melted cheese in that kiss. Now, Jan continued that kiss with a long, tender one.

Within seconds, Ana found herself falling into a world of one kiss after another. She didn't know where one ended and the other started. It was like falling into a pool of senses.

She closed her eyes and surrendered to it.

Finally, she had to raise her head to breathe again. The world stopped spinning.

She took a deep breath and stared at Jan. He looked just as excited as she was. She wanted more, but her rational side was holding her back.

'So, where does this leave us?' she asked him.

'What do you mean?'

'You can't deny that we are attracted to each other. We're good friends. We see the world, most of the time, in the same way. So, what does it make us?'

'I'm not sure what you mean,' he said, 'but for me you're the person I want to be with. You excite me, you challenge me, you're unstoppable. How can any man not want to be with you?'

Ana was taken aback by the number of compliments she'd just got from Jan in one sentence. She had never thought that he saw her in that way. Tereza had told her something along those lines, but she hadn't believed her. She'd thought Tereza was making fun of her.

'I'm flattered you see me that way. You are the first person who ever really saw me. But more than that, you're the one that challenged me to be more than what I thought I was. You're the one that opened the door for me to see that there is so much more to this world than what I had thought… You're…'

She wanted to say more. She wanted to say that he was her knight in shining armour, that he was the most attractive man she'd ever seen. That the first time she saw him, when he returned to Prague, her heart had skipped a beat. But she didn't have the courage to say all that.

'I'm what?'

'You're the one I love. When I think of love, I see you.'

That was as much as she could muster.

There was nothing more to say after that. They sat watching the cherry flowers dropping from the trees, watching people taking their Sunday strolls along the river.

It's a perfect day, she thought. *Probably the best day of my life!*

Chapter Nineteen

Ana couldn't believe that her last exam of the year had arrived. Despite a few struggles throughout the semester, she felt a sense of excitement and optimism as she walked into the classroom.

To her surprise, the test was easier than she had anticipated. As she confidently turned in her completed exam, she felt a renewed sense of hope that she could still come out on top of her class. Though the stakes were high, Ana was determined to give it her all, knowing that her hard work and dedication would pay off in the end.

When she left the examination hall, Ana bumped into Tereza. It was unusual to see her in the halls during examination times.

'How was your exam?' Tereza asked.

'Better than I expected. Did you have an exam too?'

Unlikely. She never knew what to say to Tereza. She always felt inexperienced. Tereza always had a witty reply to anything anyone said, and was always quick in saying it.

'How did your date with Jan go?' Ana instantly turned red. 'Oh, that good? Well done. Did you like it? Come on, I'm dying to hear!' Tereza encouraged her.

Ana had never thought that these things should be shared. Ludmila used to talk endlessly about what she used to do on her dates, but Ana never really listened.

'Is he a good kisser?' Tereza continued. 'With those lips, he sure should be.'

That was way too much for Ana. She didn't want to insult

Tereza, but she felt like she was sticking her nose into something that wasn't her business.

'I wouldn't know if he is good. But it was good for me.' It was as much as she was willing to say, and she hoped it would end the conversation. But Tereza had no limits.

'Good for you. That's what is important. You should always tell the guy what makes you feel good. Don't let them do only what's good for them.'

Ana wasn't following what Tereza was saying but didn't ask her to clarify. *This conversation is so embarrassing,* she thought.

'Let's celebrate you becoming a woman,' Tereza said. 'Let's go to Tomas's place. It's always fun there.'

It suddenly hit Ana what Tereza had meant.

Sex.

She had no intention of correcting her. *That would be too humiliating.*

Once they got to Tomas's, Ana again had the feeling like she was falling down the rabbit hole into Wonderland.

Tomas's place was dark no matter what time of day you walked into it. The fairy lights were everywhere, casting an air of magic. The heavy smell of the marijuana was part of the place just like the walls and the cushions that were scattered around it.

When Tereza and Ana walked in, Tomas came over, giving a long and passionate kiss to Tereza.

'My favourite woman in the world. Hi there, Ana, you're my second favourite one after this goddess.'

'We're celebrating,' Tereza said excitedly, 'Ana and Jan had finally "done it"!'

Ana thought she would die. If she could turn around and flee the place she would, but somehow her legs were glued to the spot.

'Congratulations. What do you know? Next, Ana will be asking for pot! In any case, welcome to "Free Love". Now you are officially part of the freedom movement.' Tomas and Tereza laughed.

Ana wasn't sure if they were laughing at her or being genuinely happy for her. There was no way in hell that she would tell them that all she and Jan had done was kiss. That would make her look so childish. Yet, she knew that if there was one person who could tell her how to take it further with Jan beyond kissing, it was Tereza.

How the hell can I ask her?

Ana dropped down to sit on one of the huge cushions that was used as a chair, while Tereza and Tomas sat opposite her on one of the mattresses. Sitting was an exaggeration - they were practically lying on top of each other. But somehow, it didn't bother Ana.

A bottle of beer was shoved into her hand. Ana gulped it. It immediately had an effect on her. She felt dizzy, and she noticed how her body was relaxing.

'What's "Free Love"?' she asked Tomas.

'It means that the state has no right to determine who we should have sex with, Tereza answered instantly. 'That marriage, sex and love are separate issues. That you have the right to enjoy your body in whatever form you wish.'

'So, how is it that you see me as part of the "Free Love" movement now?'

'Because you ditched the idea of having sex only with the one that you marry. You are willing to enjoy sex and not see it as an obligation that comes with marriage.'

Ana had never thought about those issues before. Again, she realised Tereza's view on freedom had far more implications than what she and Jan had been talking about.

Ana was still processing what Tereza was telling her, when Tomas came and sat next to her. He started fondling her legs, sending shivers along her back.

'Take your hands off me. I didn't give you permission to do this.' She slapped his hand away.

'My apologies. I wanted to see how you would respond. You see, this is another aspect of "Free Love". You choose who can touch you and who can't. Like I said, you're my second favourite woman. Love your energy.'

With that, he went back to sit next to Tereza and kissed her behind her ear, which made her giggle.

'You don't mind that he did that?' Ana asked Tereza.

'He's free to do what he wants, same as I am free to do what I want. I don't own him, and he doesn't own me.'

'Well, I guess that's stretching the word "freedom" way too much for me. I'm not so sure I would not be jealous or hurt if Jan made out with another woman in front of me.'

'Well, you should test it. Or better, test what he would do if *you* made out with someone else,' Tomas suggested with a cynical tone.

'But I don't want to make out with someone else. I like doing it with Jan. He's the one for me.'

'If you feel that way,' Tereza smirked, 'But remember, he's your first. Maybe there is someone out there that can give you more pleasure than him. I've seen how Pjoter looks at you. I'm sure he would love to get the opportunity to pleasure you. He's been in love with you for over a year.'

Ana wasn't sure what she was more shocked about: the fact that she was having this kind of conversation with Tomas and Tereza, or discovering that Pjoter was in love with her. By now, she trusted Tereza's social intuition enough that if she thought Pjoter was in love with her, there would likely be some truth in it.

'Well, I guess I'm not yet ready for all this "Free Love" stuff,' Ana said nervously. 'I guess I'm still a bit conventional.'

With that, Ana stood up and walked out. She'd had enough new learning for one day.

Chapter Twenty

Even though Ana couldn't feel comfortable with what Tomas and Tereza called 'Free Love', it intrigued her.

She decided to do what she does best: read about it. She found out that the idea was not a new idea at all. It had its roots in the 19th century. Not just that, but at the start of the Communist Revolution it was looked upon in favour. It was only when Stalin took over the Communist Party that his traditional views about family became the party's line.

Ana wanted to talk with Jan about it, but never had the courage to bring it up. After the day they'd spent together, he was absent-minded again.

But at least his place has improved, she told herself.

They were meeting there more frequently, spending more time touching each other and kissing than talking about politics. But each time she thought, *this time it will happen,* Jan would stop and start talking about his ideas for further changes. It frustrated her, but she didn't know what else to do.

This afternoon, they'd agreed to meet not far from Tomas's place. There was a rally planned to demand further changes.

When Ana arrived, she noticed the usual crowd. She could see from a distance Tereza's head and Pjoter's, too. Jan wasn't far from them. Everyone carried signs calling for freedom and change.

She joined Jan and they started marching down the street, calling their usual slogans for freedom and support for Dubček.

Unlike other times, some of the students carried with them guitars and started singing songs supporting the new wave and calling it the 'new hope'. The atmosphere was heightened. People were jubilant, and Ana was caught up in that spirit.

When they reached the National Museum, she grabbed the megaphone from one of the students.

'Pjoter, pick me up on your shoulders,' she called out. Pjoter immediately raised her up on his tall shoulders and she could see the whole crowd.

It wasn't like her to speak in front of people without having a speech prepared. But somehow, this time it was different. The music, the songs, and maybe the whole notion that freedom is much bigger than politics, had finally dawned on her. She wanted to experience what it would be like to speak freely, without any preparation or censorship.

Totally instinctively.

All she knew was that she wanted to tell the crowd that they were not alone. That what they are asking for were basic human rights.

Their right to choose.

'Students in Paris are protesting regulations, students in Poland are demonstrating and demanding to let go of censorship. We are part of a movement. It's time for us, for the young generation. We cannot continue to let the old generation decide how we should live our lives!'

Ana was so engaged with what she had to say that she didn't notice the police had started breaking down the rally. It was only when Pjoter took her down and Jan grabbed the megaphone from her that she registered the chaos taking place.

Two policemen grabbed Ana, put handcuffs on her and pushed her towards a van where other students were already detained.

Only when she was in the van did it dawn on Ana the gravity of the situation.

Everything Helen had warned her about had just transpired.

***

Ana, Pjoter, Jan and Tereza spent the night in cells in the central prison. It was a night she would never forget.

The prison was a grim maze of cells linked by a zig-zagging corridor, which was lit by bleak lights and enlivened by a low, weirdly pink ceiling and fat, pink water pipes. She could easily see how people could disappear in this prison without anyone ever knowing about it. She prayed that she would not be one of those statistics.

She'd been separated from the others as they'd entered the prison. Ana was now all alone in a tiny cell where she couldn't take more than three steps. For the first time in her life, she was grateful for her height. She could stand in that cell without hitting her head.

Tereza would not be that lucky.

At first, she had been busy trying to calm herself down. She had conversations with Helen in her head, trying to explain how it had all happened. But as the hours passed, the solitude and the silence caved in on her. She wasn't sure she'd ever get out of there, and she became more and more agitated. She even tried calling out to her friends, only to hear her own voice echoing back.

Sometime during that long night Ana managed to fall asleep. The next morning, she could hear the sound of keys jangling on a chain; a policeman was walking down the corridor.

'Ana Sveboda?' she heard him call.

'Here. That's me.'

'You're free to go,' he said as he unlocked the door to her cell.

'What about my friends?' she asked.

'None of your business. Go now, before I change my mind.'

The light outside nearly blinded her. Ana saw her dad standing in the square, waiting for her. He looked as if he hadn't slept the whole night.

On their way back home, they said nothing, but she could feel the anger emanating from Pavel.

'Thank God, you're alive,' were Helen's first words to her.

Ana thought that might be a good sign. Her parents' relief that she was well would be a better result than anger.

'What got into you?' Helen continued. 'What were you thinking? Not only did you join that rally, but you also encouraged them and spoke against the government. Are you out of your mind? Have you no consideration what it would do to me? I would die if something happened to you. Don't you get it?'

And there it is. It's always about her. Never about me.

'I'm tired. I don't want to go into this debate anymore. Remember, I'm twenty. I'm not your kid anymore and I will do what I think is right.'

'Don't you dare speak like that to your mum,' Pavel's voice roared. 'I had to pull a lot of favours today to get you out of there. There are consequences to your actions. So, you better think about them.'

This was unexpected. Having Helen angry at her was one thing, but her dad? That was painful.

'I'm sorry. I get that you worry for me. I get that I'm all that mum has. I get that you need to protect mum. But I'm tired of trying to please you both. I'm tired of being the "good girl" and doing what you expect me to do. I don't intend to hurt either of you. I love you both very much. But I'm a grown woman now and I must live my life the way I think fit. And now, if you don't mind, I'm going to take a shower and go to sleep.'

***

Ana wanted to know what had happened to her friends, but neither Helen nor Pavel left her side for the next few days. Everywhere she went, either Helen or Pavel had an excuse to go with her. She knew she wouldn't be able to look for them while her parents were around.

Therefore, she was surprised to find Jan on her doorstep when she was about to leave the house. Without thinking, she gave him a hug, not caring who might be watching her.

'Just came to let you know we're all fine,' he said.

'How did you get released? My dad had to pull a lot of strings for me.'

'Well, thanks to Tereza, or shall we say Tomas and his "connections", we were all released a few hours after you.'

Ana wished to continue the conversation with Jan, but Helen suddenly appeared at the door.

'You!' she spat. 'I don't want to see you here anymore. You've been filling Ana's head with all those dangerous ideas. Get out!'

'Mum, you can't say that. He's my friend and I choose who I will see and who not to.'

'Not under my roof. I don't want to see him here again,' Helen repeated.

'It's OK, Ana. I can understand her concern. I'll leave now. I'm just happy to see that you are well.'

'Not thanks to you,' Helen said, and went back into the house.

'I'll walk with you,' Ana suggested.

'No. Stay with her. Give her a few more days and she'll calm down. We can always meet in our usual place. See you.'

Ana wondered what he meant.

Chapter Twenty-One

'What on earth is that?'

Ana rushed to the window as a horrendous noise boomed through the apartment. The clear blue skies over Prague were filled with the dark shapes of planes, like birds of prey over carrion. The building shook as tanks rolled through the streets and past Ana's home, with dead-eyed soldiers marching straight ahead. Unease roiled in Ana's belly at the spectacle.

'And so it begins,' Pavel sighed, putting his arm around Helen.

Ana could see how it was affecting her mother: she was white and trembling, wringing her hands and picking at the faded tattoo on her arm. Ana knew she should feel sorry for her mother, but for some reason exasperation surfaced instead.

'Why are they here?' Ana demanded.

'I told you,' Helen spoke in clipped sentences; she was trying to keep hold of her terror. 'This is what happens when people don't keep their heads down!'

'Don't start, mama.' Ana finally moved away from the window, grabbing her bag. 'I have to find Jan. I've got to make sure he's okay.'

'No, Ana – it's not safe!' Helen's words fell on Ana's back as she rushed from the room.

Ana made her way out of her apartment building, only to be swept along the street by a surge of other tenants wanting to know what was going on. She became a part of a sea of people streaming down towards Wenceslas Square. She stopped pushing and resisting, allowing herself to be carried towards the source of the fracas.

Tanks were lined up there; an ominous sight blocking all main thoroughfares. Crowds of young people swarmed around them. Their arms were full of flowers and billboards. A rainbow of hand-painted signs reading slogans, from mild: 'Nepovolanym Vstup Prisne Zakazan' ('entry to unauthorised persons is strictly prohibited'), to the more extreme: 'betze domu bastardi' ('go home, bastards').

'What's happening?' Ana cried out in the throng, to no one in particular.

'The Russians are coming!'

'Watch out!' someone called back to her. Ana instinctively ducked as a piece of rubble whistled through the air where her head had been moments earlier. There was no time to digest the near miss. It was a cacophony of noise; she could hear people shrieking and yelling, both in anger and fear.

There was a stirring feeling of unease in the air.

'They're going to take the radio station!'

'The what?'

'The radio station! Get down there now!'

Ana started running towards the radio station, observing the flattened metal of upended trams that created a barricade, which Soviet tanks were crushing with ease as they rolled over them. Even before she saw them, Ana could smell the rancid smell of tanks on fire.

Beyond the barricade, Ana spotted Jan and Tereza organising

students to stand in line to protect the free radio station. The whole street was shaking as if an earthquake was taking place. Ana crossed over the barricade and joined hands with Tereza on one side and Jan on the other.

'What are we doing here?' she asked Jan.

'We have to stop them from entering the radio station,' Tereza responded before Jan had a chance to.

'The radio station is Dubček's symbol of freedom of speech. Allowing them to enter would mean the end of the little freedom we have,' Jan continued, while organising the rest of the students to create more barricades.

'How the hell are we supposed to stop them? They have guns!' she yelled to Jan above the roaring noise of people, tanks and shotguns.

'We have creativity and faith on our side. Nothing can stop you when you believe in what you're doing. Do you believe in it, Ana?' Jan cried back to her, before rushing to organise another line of students to block the entrance to the radio station.

Ana felt she had to prove to Jan that she believed.

She had an idea.

She rushed to the other side of the street where some bicycles were locked to the side of the rails. 'Whose bicycles are those?' she shouted.

'Mine,' several students responded.

'Come with me,' she commanded them.

Six students joined her. They unlocked their bikes and created one long metal chain from their locks. Once done, they ran to the entrance of the radio station and wrapped the chains on the doors, locking the people inside.

At the same time, the reporters in the radio station put out speakers so that people on the streets could hear the broadcast taking place.

'At 1:55 a.m. this morning five Warsaw Pact countries invaded our country. It's estimated that quarter of a million soldiers from national ally states flooded into Czechoslovakia. Thousands of enemy tanks, some of which arrived on Soviet army planes at Prague airport, are now rolling through our country.

'Unarmed civilians have been gathering outside our station from the early hours to try to prevent enemy troops from taking control. We are the last point of freedom. The demonstrators are trying to protect us from being shut down.

'By the time the Soviet soldiers got here, a large crowd had already amassed. People are building barricades out of trams and buses, but when the tanks arrived, they just rolled over them. Demonstrators surround the tanks. They even set one of them on fire here at the crossroads, and that caused an ammunition vehicle to explode, destroying one of the buildings.

'All the pretence of Moscow allowing us to run our country in freedom was shot down today.'

Not for the first time, Ana realised the risk those reporters were taking. 'The reporters should come out,' Ana said to Tereza. Tereza was agog.

'Are you serious? They are making a stand for freedom!'

'But they could get sent to the gulag! they could get executed!'

'Then all the more reason to support them, no?'

At this moment, Ana realised her life would never be the same. She was part of the Student Union which was leading the support for change.

I can kiss goodbye to becoming a doctor.

Looking around, she noticed another tank rolling into the street. It was stopped by a courageous group of students who stood in front of the tank blocking its way. The hood of the tank was raised, and four soldiers emerged from it. The people around the tank started banging on it, singing Czech folklore songs, when one of them - who seemed to be the commander - raised his rifle and fired a few shots in the air.

Seconds later, an explosion rocked the area from an adjacent truck carrying ammunition, the noise echoing like the loudest crack of thunder. Everybody crouched down for cover as debris flew upwards and then rained down like metal hailstones.

A nearby building collapsed, and in the dust and smoke a cacophony of coughing could be heard. People cautiously stood up, but seconds later the sound of shooting, shouts and screams came from the direction of the radio station. Everyone fell to the ground.

Within seconds the students around Jan, Ana and Tereza stood up and moved back towards the radio station, creating a human shield around the entrance.

Meanwhile, another tank rolled into the street from the other side and, on his way, knocked down a parked bus. Following the tank, a whole unit of soldiers marched into the street. Ana could hear their commander giving orders but couldn't hear what was said. The next sound was another round of gunfire and hand grenades that were thrown at the protestors on the other side of the street.

By now, Ana couldn't see through the smoke. All she sensed were the hands of her fellow students. They moved backwards until they were pressed into the front of the radio station building. Ana could feel the chains she'd put on the doors pressing against her back, but her focus was on the group of soldiers marching towards them.

The line of soldiers was now facing them with rifles in their hands and helmets on their heads. It was so strange for Ana, who'd never seen a rifle in her life, let alone in such proximity. The line of the soldiers halted, pointing their rifles at the students. It seemed as if they had no idea what to do and were simply waiting for orders.

Ana stared at one of the soldiers standing in front of her. The more she looked at him, the less monstrous he looked. She noticed how, from a faceless enemy, he was turning into a human being. When she focused on him even more, she detected that, though he was holding a rifle to her face, he was as scared and confused as she was.

Once the firing ended, an eerie silence descended, but it was more like the lull before the storm. The two lines; soldiers and students, were facing each other, and nothing was happening.

Suddenly, gunshots cracked across the sky, people began screaming, and the line of soldiers pushed forward towards Ana and her friends who were protecting the radio station.

In the chaos that was taking place, the soldiers in front of Ana were still waiting for instructions. They were pushed and squashed on both sides by protesters. It didn't take a genius to understand that sooner or later, someone was going to pay the price.

The next thing Ana heard was a loud noise next to her which made her ears ring and buzz. She instinctively dropped down to the ground when another round of shots was taken. Looking to her side, she spotted a fellow student falling to the ground with blood streaming from his head. Panic took over her and all she could think to do was to crawl between the legs of the soldiers to get out of there, but she was barricaded.

She was suffocating.

Ana's medical experience hadn't prepared her for such a situation. She tried taking control of her breathing, but it wasn't working. All she could do was keep on the ground and try to seek space. It was as if her body was separated from her mind, doing what it needed to do while her mind was trying to catch up with it.

Dragging herself out of the mess of people, Ana touched a rifle on the ground. She grabbed it, stood up, and fired a shot in a bid to find a pathway out of there.

She never expected the rifle to be that heavy, or the blast to be so strong.

The next thing she saw was a young soldier dropping at her feet, the life going out of his eyes.

'NOOOOO,' she screamed, dropping the rifle.

'Run!' Tereza yelled.

Chapter Twenty-Two

Ana managed to find her way to the other side of the street and crouched behind the turned-over bus, peeking to see if anyone except Tereza had seen what happened. But in all the chaos around the place, it seemed no one was looking for her.

Ana looked around and saw soldiers storming the radio station while her friends were being beaten down with clubs. She knew she couldn't do anything for them; her thoughts were on how to get the hell out of there without anyone connecting her to what had taken place.

Having been born in Prague and having lived there her whole life, Ana knew every single pathway, street and alley in this part of the city. She mapped a route in her head, making sure to avoid any major streets that would be taken by the army. She remembered a shortcut she'd used whenever she needed to get quickly from the university to the hospital. If only she could get to that alley without anyone noticing her, she knew she would be safe.

Ana took a deep breath, stood up and ran as if chased by demons from hell.

The deserted alley was like a separate world from the madness that was taking place in the next street.

Thank god for Prague's ancient, hidden streets.

Ana walked as fast as she could, moving from one alley to another. Suddenly, she found herself at a dead-end. She looked around and located a back garden fence. She climbed over it, but as she jumped down she slashed her hand on the barbed wire. She stopped for a minute and took off her undershirt, tearing it and wrapping it around her wrist to stop the bleeding. Looking around to make sure no one could see her, she noticed some men's clothes hanging out to dry. It hit her that the main problem she would have was how to get into her home without the *three witches* noticing her. She grabbed the men's clothes and found another deserted alley where she could exchange her outfit.

Ana was in luck. In one of the pockets there was a cap big enough to hide half of her face. She rolled her long hair up in a knot and pushed it under the cap, which made it sit firmly on her head. The outfit was two sizes bigger, which meant she could wear it over her own clothes and create a distorted figure. No one would recognize her if she rushed into her building.

When she reached her parents' courtyard, Ana crossed it and entered using a different entrance than her parents'. If anyone was looking, they could only say they saw a man entering the courtyard and going in a different direction than her parents' place.

Once she was inside the building, Ana scanned the outside to see if she could see any faces in the surrounding windows, but they were all shut and the curtains drawn. She ran up the stairs, jumping two at a time, and had to stop on the top floor to catch her breath. She looked around... *Now what?*

Noticing a trap door in the ceiling, which she anticipated would lead her to the roof, Ana speculated that she could cross the roof to the other side of the building where her parents' apartment was. She thanked her lucky stars it had no locks on it. She climbed the rickety ladder and pushed the trap door open.

It fell, banging on the roof.

Ana held her breath in horror, fearing someone would come out to check what had caused the commotion. As fast as she could, she squeezed herself through it and shut down the trap door.

Ana was on the roof looking down into the courtyard. It felt strange being up there, able to see everywhere, yet somehow invisible. She could see all the way down to the river. Her muscles were shaking from all the running and her short breath. She knew from her studies that her adrenalin was high, pushing her into safety, which meant getting home. She crossed the roof until she reached another trap door, which she prayed would get her into her parents' building. She pulled the handle with as much force as she could and, though it squeaked and protested, she was able to open it.

Descending the ladder, Ana discovered to her horror that it wasn't firmly nailed to the wall.

For an agonising few seconds, she pleaded to an unseen greater power that she would reach the floor before it fell. It seemed as if this whole day she had been protected by angels, and she could only pray that her luck hadn't run out. Finally, Ana felt the safety of the floor beneath her feet, and she wasted no time in sprinting to her parents' apartment.

Before she knew it, Ana was inside her home being hugged by a tearful Helen and Pavel, who looked like a weight had been lifted from his shoulders.

Pure relief for them all.

Chapter Twenty-Three

Ana fell into Helen's arms. She could finally allow herself to let go. She felt like a rag doll and the world around her went blank. She could hear her parents asking her questions, but she was unable to answer or even understand what they were saying.

All she could see in front of her was the face of that dead soldier she killed.

I killed someone, she kept repeating in her head. She didn't want to repeat it; it just kept coming back. *I'm a murderer. I took a life. I wanted to save lives and now I killed someone. I can never forgive myself.*

I can never be a doctor.

Ana wasn't aware of what she was doing, but somehow, she found herself on the sofa being hugged by her mother, with her father kneeling in front of her holding her hands and staring at her. Ana was mumbling incoherent words, and the only thing she could do was stare into her father's eyes without truly seeing him.

Pavel was familiar with this look. He'd seen enough young men going into this state after their first battle or kill. He knew there was nothing to do right now for her. The only thing they could do was make sure that whatever had happened to her would not be traced back to them. He glanced at Helen, who was sitting by Ana's side.

All at once, Helen took charge of the situation. 'Undress. I want you out of these clothes. Pavel, go make her something strong and sweet to drink.'

Ana was not responding. Helen raised Ana's hands so she could help her take off her shirt. She unbuttoned Ana's trousers and took them off along with the cap, then bundled them all together into a tight package. Helen would have to find a way to get rid of them without anyone seeing.

Pavel returned with the hot drink. Ana's hands were shaking too much to hold it, so Helen helped her, knowing the effect a hot, sweet liquid has when experiencing trauma. She never imagined it would affect her own daughter. As expected, once Ana was able to swallow the drink, her shaking stopped.

'Listen carefully,' Helen said firmly. 'Did anyone see you come back here?'

Ana shook her head 'no'.

'Are you sure?' Ana nodded. 'Good. Then listen carefully. You never left the apartment today. Is that clear?' Ana nodded again. 'You were sick and didn't feel good. Pavel, go to Mrs. Fischer and ask her for some aspirin. Tell her Ana was feeling sick the whole day, but we were afraid of going out to the pharmacy due to the invasion.'

'Why Mrs. Fischer, that's two floors below? I can go to Mrs. Novak next door.'

'Yes. But she will not tell anyone. The 'witch', on the other hand, will. I want her to spread that news.'

Once Pavel left, Helen turned to Ana. 'You must sleep. The next few days are going to be tough. But you have to pretend as if you're sick. Do you understand what I'm saying? Just nod if you do. No need to speak.'

Ana nodded. She stood up to walk to her room, but apparently too quickly: she was swaying and needed Helen's help to prevent her from falling. Helen helped Ana get into bed and before Pavel returned, Ana was fast asleep.

Once Pavel was back, Helen felt safer. As always, he was her rock. 'Something terrible happened to her,' she said to him.

'Something hideous happened to this whole country,' he replied. 'We need to prepare for dark times. It's not just Ana who is in danger now. All of us are, and we better stick together.'

'I knew it. For months I kept telling you and her that Moscow would retaliate. But no, why would you listen to me? Why would she listen to her feeble mother? She wanted to be a hero, like you. And that Jan. He filled up her head with all those crazy dreams. I don't want to see that boy in this house ever again.'

Pavel sighed a soft sigh. It wasn't that he didn't agree with what Helen said, but he knew Jan was not the one to blame. Deep inside, he knew that if he had been a few years younger, he would have done exactly what Ana had.

Being young means believing nothing is impossible. It's about reaching for the stars, especially when basic rights of freedom were at a hand's reach. Who could blame those young people for fighting for it? It was a fight worth fighting for.

But now, his daughter was in danger. He had no clue what it was all about. The only thing he knew was that he had to help her. He looked at Helen. She was exhausted from the stress of the last few hours. He admired how she was still holding on.

'Go to bed,' he encouraged her, 'I'll stay awake to make sure everything is OK with her. No point in both of us having a sleepless night.'

Helen agreed and walked to their bedroom, giving him a small kiss on his cheek as she passed him.

Pavel remembered a doctor friend who'd once told him that trauma is never truly gone; it's always one step behind you. The only way not to let it take over you, is by becoming a bigger person. This way, the event of the trauma begins to look smaller, and you're able to handle it better. At first, Pavel didn't understand what his friend was saying. He'd asked him to explain more.

'Remember when we were small,' he'd continued, 'and at the back of your parents' garden there was this huge wall? We thought we could never climb it. Remember?' Pavel had smiled. Of course he remembered that wall. It had been their daily game to attempt to climb over it, to see who could do it fastest. 'Well,' his friend continued, 'imagine that wall is Helen's trauma. It's her experience of the concentration camps. It's when she encountered such a huge force of brutality - it made her feel small, insignificant and helpless.'

'OK,' Pavel had said. 'But I'm still not clear.'

'Today, if you and I would go to your parents' garden, would that wall look as huge as it was when we were kids?'

Now, Pavel got it. After the war, he'd visited his parents and noticed how that wall only reached his waist. He could go over it simply by lifting his leg over it. He'd smiled and nodded.

'The only way to get over a trauma is to become a bigger person; to acknowledge it took place when we were young and small and couldn't do much about it. Even if the event took place when the person was a mature age, the trauma will have made them feel small. But it doesn't have to determine who they are for the rest of their lives. They need to become bigger than that event. They should notice how strong that event made them and focus on that. That way, they overcome it.'

Pavel now thought about Helen. If she could overcome her trauma, Ana would definitely be able to, too.

Chapter Twenty-Four

'Police. Open up!'

Pavel and Helen woke with a fright the next morning as police pounded on the door.

Helen checked on Ana, who was sitting up in bed, signalling to her to stay in bed and pretend she was asleep. 'Remember, not a word. You were here the whole day.'

Helen left Ana's room and gestured to Pavel to open the door while she sat down, busying herself with some mending of clothes from a basket by the sofa.

Three policemen stormed into the house, followed by four soldiers.

'Who lives here besides you two?'

'Only our daughter. She's sick in bed,' Pavel answered.

One of the soldiers went down the corridor and opened Ana's bedroom door.

'She's here,' he called back to his commander.

'She's too sick,' Helen pleaded, 'she's been like that for a few days and she's too weak to get out of bed.'

'We need to take her for interrogation. She's on the list as one of the leaders of the Student Union.'

'She's been at home these past few days,' Pavel said. 'Ask anyone in the building. They would have seen if she'd left the place.'

'Besides. Taking her into interrogation now wouldn't help you,' Helen added. 'She can't speak. She lost her voice.'

'Why don't you give her a few days to recover and then come back, if you insist,' Pavel suggested.

'Fine. We'll check with the neighbours and return if we don't get satisfying answers.'

With that, the whole party left and moved to knock on the next door on their list.

***

The next few days Ana spent in bed. Her parents didn't have to convince her of it. She felt drained, like the world had shut down on her. She didn't want to read any papers or listen to the radio. Anything that had to do with the outside world scared her.

Ana kept seeing the dead soldier's face in her dreams and each time she closed her eyes. She started fearing falling asleep. She would sit up late, reading her books, playing the piano and even attempting to learn to knit.

Both Pavel and Helen were constantly around her. They wouldn't leave her alone. Ana was grateful they never pushed her to reveal what had actually taken place that dreadful day. She knew they deserved to know, but she didn't have the courage to tell them.

One night, Ana woke up from yet another nightmare. She sat up in bed, sobbing, unaware that she had screamed out until her dad came running. Pavel sat on the bed holding her hands. He allowed her to cry as much as she needed. When at last she couldn't cry anymore and had managed to control her breathing, Pavel wrapped his arms around her in a bear hug. For Ana, it had always felt the safest place to be.

'Dad, when you were in the war, did you kill someone?'

Pavel looked alarmed by the question, but quickly regained his calm facial expression. 'It was a different time; why do you ask?'

'I killed someone that day.'

And just like that, she finally told her story: how she and the students had tried to block the tanks and soldiers from entering the radio station; how they'd pushed and shoved them. About the riot, the gunshots, the hand grenades, the smoke, and how she'd picked up a rifle in an attempt to make way for herself between the sea of people but had ended up killing a soldier.

'Now, his face and dead eyes are haunting me each time I close my eyes.' Ana looked at her father, hoping to get some reassurance that it would all disappear.

Pavel took Ana's hands in his. 'Give it time. Time is the best and most powerful healer. Remember, you never meant it to happen. You were trying to fight for your own life. It's not an excuse; it doesn't justify it, but it's a fact. No one will accuse you; at least not those who understand the circumstances. The only one that judges you now, is you. You will need to forgive yourself, and that will take time.'

'Is that what you did? How long did it take you?'

'It took a long time for me, but remember, my case was different. I was ordered to kill them. My actions were calculated, planned and executed with the intention of killing people. People I didn't know; people who I'd never seen before in my life. I didn't think of them as human beings, or as someone's son or father. They were the enemy for me. I kept them faceless on purpose. I had to learn to love and respect myself first in order to forgive myself. That's not what happened to you.'

'But I still killed someone. I wanted to save lives by being a doctor. How can I make the vow of "do no harm" when I've killed someone?'

'How about we cross that bridge when it comes?' Pavel said softly. 'Would you like some warm milk and honey? That always helped your mother when her nightmares took over her.'

'I'd like that very much.' It felt good to be taken care of by her father. Ana sensed he understood what she was going through and wasn't going to sugar-coat it for her. He would be there for her as she went through this nightmare.

Pavel walked out of Ana's room to prepare the familiar, comforting drink that he'd made so many times before for Helen. He never dreamt that history would be repeated, and he would find himself making that same drink for his own daughter.

By the time he returned to Ana's room, she was asleep.

Best medicine for her, he thought. He left the cup of warm milk next to her bed and tiptoed out of the room, leaving the door open in case she would wake up and need him.

Chapter Twenty-Five

The next few weeks passed in a haze for Ana.

She stayed at home listening to the radio, dreading hearing any mention of a dead soldier. Pavel and Helen scanned the newspapers, but nothing was mentioned. However, they all knew the news was now monitored by the Soviets. Nothing could be trusted. The propaganda machine was back working full time, making sure people would follow the hard line dictated by Moscow. Some news was true.

Today, they were listening to the radio, which was once more under Soviet control. Dubček was addressing the nation, his speech punctuated with long periods of silence. They understood why he was struggling to control his emotions. He appealed for calm, saying there mustn't be provocation. After a week of being on what Ana called her own 'house arrest', she couldn't take it anymore. She waited for her mother to go shopping and, once she saw Helen disappearing down the street, she grabbed her stuff and got out of the house.

It was a warm summer's day. On any other day she would have enjoyed wandering down the streets of her beloved city, strolling towards the river to enjoy the sights. But now, the city was under a spell.

It was late morning, and the streets were deserted. She noticed shop windows were broken and shreds of glass were everywhere. The smell of gun smoke was still lingering over the city. The scent made her tremble. She was certain that if she couldn't take control, she'd lose it right there in the middle of the street. By now, she was able to identify the signs within her body when something triggered the memories of the day she and her friends had defended the radio station.

'Get a hold of yourself,' she uttered in an attempt to stop the trembling. Though it didn't stop it, she felt like she was back in control of her body. It was the first step towards accomplishing what she'd set out to do when she left her house.

She had not heard anything from Jan or any of her friends. She *had* to know what was going on. She had no clue where to find them. The only place she could think of was the university. She quickly crossed over Charles Bridge and took the shortest route she knew towards its main building, but even before reaching the entrance she was stopped by a group of soldiers.

'No entry to this area unless you have a special permit,' one of them told her while the others blocked her way.

'But I'm a student and I need to get to the library.' This seemed to make them even more suspicious of her.

'The university is now on lock down and no students are allowed to enter.'

'When will it be opened again? I must get my papers that I left there.' The soldiers only shrugged their shoulders.

'No idea. We only follow orders.'

Ana saw there was no point arguing with them. She turned around and walked away.

Now what? Where will I find the others?

Ana stood on the pavement, not knowing what to do. She looked around and caught her reflection in one of the shops that still had a window.

Follow the breadcrumbs, she thought, and suddenly what she had to do was clear.

Ana quickened her steps and walked down several streets until she reached her destination: their favourite bar and cafe. The place was of course locked, but she knew Franz, the owner, had a small flat above it. The place looked deserted. She knocked on the door in hope of waking Franz, but after a few minutes of knocking she lost her confidence.

Just as she was turning to leave the place, she heard a whisper coming from below the pavement. She looked and noticed steps leading down under the building to a basement. She could see Franz's head. He was indicating to her to go into an alley between the buildings. Ana did so and found herself at a dead end. She wondered if she had misunderstood Franz's gestures. Suddenly a door, which she had not seen before, opened and Franz grabbed her hand and pulled her in, closing the door as quick as he had opened it.

'Are you mad? What are you doing here? Don't you know how dangerous it is now to come here? I'm hiding and putting on a show that I'm not here. They've already searched the place twice and ransacked everything. You're lucky I saw you from my hiding place.'

'I'm sorry. I didn't think this through. It's just that I've also been sort of hiding for the past ten days. I wanted to know what happened to the others. I was separated from them during the riots around the radio station and never saw them again. I'm worried.'

'You should be. Anyone that is even suspected of being there was arrested. God knows what they will do to them.'

'You sound like my mother,' Ana said. 'Do you know if Jan or Tereza are among those who were arrested?'

In response, Franz led Ana into what used to be his bar and cafe. Now, it looked more like a place that had gone through an earthquake. Tables and chairs barred the street entrance and on the floor were mattresses. On what used to be the bar was a printing machine.

God knows where they got it from.

Jan appeared out of nowhere and rushed to give her a hug.

'Great. You're here.'

Ana was expecting Jan to be concerned and ask her how she was doing. She'd hoped she could confide in him and tell him about her nightmares. Instead, he shook her shoulders.

'We don't have the luxury to dwell on what happened,' he said in a cold and distant tone. 'We must continue the fight.'

'What fight? The Communists shut down the radio station, and they arrested hundreds of people. God knows what will happen to them. Dubček was taken to Moscow like a small child that misbehaved. They are probably going to put him on trial and torture him until he signs a fake confession like they did in the fifties.'

'That's just the reason we need to keep up the fight. We need to remind people what we were fighting for. We need to resist what they call "normalisation"'.

Ana wasn't sure what Jan was trying to say. 'What do you mean by "normalisation?"' she asked, hoping to stop him from his fervent talk.

'That's what the Soviets are trying to convince us of. They are trying to tell us that what we had before was "normal". That what Dubček was trying to do was *not* normal. How can that be *not normal* when all we want is freedom, which *is* the normal way for people?'

'How on earth do you suggest we do this?' Ana cried. 'I mean, for crying out loud, we were invaded. What more can we do? The radio, the papers and the TV are all censored again by Moscow. What more do you expect from people? To die? Do you get it that more than a hundred people died already, and that's before they put those they arrested on trial?'

Ana was shaking from anger, *or maybe it's frustration*, she thought. She knew she was expressing Helen's ideas, and she wasn't happy with it, but she wasn't sure anymore what she believed in.

'You see, that's what most people believe, but we need to remind them we cannot give up on freedom so quickly. It's a cause worth fighting for till the end. What kind of people would we be if we agreed to such violence and aggression?'

'Alive ones?' she said. But that didn't appear to alter Jan's opinion.

When she looked closely, Ana noticed there was a fire in Jan's eyes, as though he was talking to her but seeing something else in his mind. He looked as if he was standing in front of a huge stadium of people, attempting to get them all marching for his cause. Ana resented him for not asking her how she was after the traumatic event she'd endured. She recognised that he was in his prophetic mood, which scared her.

'So, how do you go about doing this?' she asked, in an attempt to make him more grounded. This seemed to do the trick. When he stared at her again, he was his old self. In response, he took her hand and led her to the bar where the printing machine was. Behind the bar were piles of pamphlets and posters advocating for and encouraging people to continue in their support of Dubček. 'Socialism with a human face cannot die,' some of them said. Others said: 'No to normalisation.'

'Besides plastering these posters all over the town at night, there are still some pirate radio stations that are broadcasting. What we do is trick the Soviet soldiers by moving the street signs so they can never find those stations. After all, they have no clue what Prague looks like. Do you want to come with us tonight?'

Ana hesitated. She knew her mother would never agree to it. But what else could she do? Being locked in her own home wasn't such an enticing idea. Her future as a doctor was not any clearer. The only thing she could do was fight for what she thought she believed in. She could still remember the rush and excitement of how powerful she'd felt when she was giving her speeches. She recalled Jan's admiration for her.

She wanted that experience again.

Most of all, she wanted his adoring eyes on her.

She had to admit to herself that she still wanted to impress him. 'I'm sure my mum wouldn't allow me, but I'll come with you tonight. I'll meet you outside our building. Wait for me in the alley next to it. I don't want anyone seeing you or me leaving the building.'

'Good thinking. You can't trust anyone these days. I'll meet you there around nine tonight.'

All at once, Ana became aware of the time. Her mum would probably be back home soon and would be out of her mind with worry if she discovered Ana wasn't at home.

'I have to go back home. Mum will probably put me under lock and key if I'm not home before she returns. See you tonight.'

Ana rushed out to the street. She was praying she'd be able to get home before Helen, especially now that she was planning on sneaking out tonight.

Her prayers were answered. She managed to arrive only a few minutes before Helen entered the house.

Helen looked at what Ana was wearing, and from the look she gave, Ana knew she hadn't fooled her mother. Ana was preparing an explanation, but to her surprise, Helen didn't even address it.

Chapter Twenty-Six

That night after dinner Ana excused herself from the table and told her parents she was going to have an early night. She didn't see the looks Pavel and Helen exchanged between them. If she had, she would know they didn't buy her story.

Ana waited in her room until she heard her mother putting on one of her favourite classical music records. When the house was filled with the sound of the beautiful and hypnotic music, it was her time to move. Her bedroom had a window to the fire escape, so her plan was to get out through the fire escape to the alley next to her building where Jan would be waiting for her. However, when she was halfway through the window, her mother entered the room.

'Where do you think you're going?' Helen said in a tone that meant 'no arguments'. After ten days at home with her mother, and after seeing Jan that morning, Ana was determined not to listen to her mother anymore. She was twenty years old. What kind of twenty-year-old still follows her mother's instructions? Ana felt rebellious again.

'I'm going out to meet Jan,' she said with as much confidence as she could muster. She really didn't want to have an argument about it with her mother.

'Are you mad? There's a curfew in an hour. Anyone who is found on the street after ten o'clock is arrested and accused of espionage or disobedience.'

Ana returned to her room and marched into the living room.

Her father was sitting reading his book. He was aware of the exchange she'd had with Helen. It seemed he wasn't going to take part in this argument, *which is good.*

'If you care for me,' Helen continued, following her, 'you won't go out tonight. I can't lose you. I can't lose another family member.' It was a sign to Ana that her mother would not stand in her way if she insisted.

'Mum, you won't lose me. Dad, please tell her?' Ana attempted to bring her father in to help on this issue.

'The Soviets believe it's over now Helen, they captured the radio station. They won't be looking for her.'

That was enough for Ana. She stepped out of the door only to hear her mother call after her, 'Choose wisely what you're doing!'

Jan was waiting for her in the alley.

'How did you manage to escape Helen?'

'I didn't, she caught me climbing out of the window. But I insisted on going out and promised her to act wisely.'

'Good one. Seems like you're starting to stand up to her.'

Ana wasn't sure whether this was a compliment or not. It sounded like one, but somehow she felt as if it was a condescending one.

Ana and Jan moved quickly between dark alleys, taking down street signs and putting others in their place.

They arrived at a building and knocked on the door. Someone opened it and handed them a note. Jan read it.

'The next address is twenty minutes' walk from here.'

They surveyed the street before moving from their hideaway.

As they prepared to move, they heard the sound of soldiers marching on the cobbled street making a ruckus. The leader had a map of Prague and was trying to navigate his way according to it through the narrow streets. Ana and Jan crouched down behind a parked car, holding their breaths. Ana found herself praying for the second time that day.

Please don't let them find us.

'It shouldn't be too far,' said the commander. 'According to the map, the pirate station is broadcasting from down this street, then to the left and to the right until the end.'

Ana and Jan crouched down further while the soldiers passed their hiding spot. Once the soldiers disappeared around the corner, Ana released a sigh of relief.

'They're gonna look for a long time for that station. They're walking in the opposite direction!'

Jan and Ana shared a moment of quiet laughter, and Ana wished this moment would continue, but Jan was already on his way to the next place to misdirect the Soviet troops and make them even more confused in the city.

At that moment, with a sinking feeling, Ana realised Jan had no clue how she felt towards him.

Chapter Twenty-Seven

BOSTON - 1989

'He's a jerk.' Yael said, cutting off Ana's story. 'I have no clue why you liked him so much. He seems like he was only focused on himself and his ideas. Besides, you keep saying grandma Helen was stopping you. But in the end you did what you wanted… just like me.'

Out of the mouths of babes.

'You're right about Helen, and it took me a long time to realise that. But you're totally wrong about Jan. We had a history together. We started as childhood friends. He was my first real friend.'

'I still don't get it. It sounds to me like he never really listened to you or cared what you thought.'

'OK. Let me tell you how I first met Jan.'

***

PRAGUE - 1958

'Jid.'

'Jidan.'

'Dirty Jid.'

'You don't belong here, Jid.'

Ana could still hear those shouts as she raced back home from school. The whole day she had managed to hold back the tears. Now, rushing back home as fast as her feet could carry her, the tears came rolling down her cheeks. She tried her hardest to block those words and the roars of laughter that kept playing over in her mind like a broken record. For the first time, she was grateful for the cold, February wind that blew in her face. It gave her an excuse for the tears. She had no clue why they'd called her those names. Worse, she had no idea what those words meant. It was an insult, for sure, and no one stood up for her, not even her friend Ludmila.

Maybe she's not my friend? This made it even more painful.

It had all started when they'd got their test results back. As usual, she'd got the highest mark in class. For some reason, the teacher had to mention it in front of everyone.

In principle, Ana strived to keep her results secret. She believed that if the other kids didn't know how easy it was for her, she might have more friends in this new school. Ana loved going to school. She enjoyed reading and learning. The fact she excelled was like a bonus reward. She sensed it made her parents proud, and she relished making her mum smile. She never could understand the reason why, but she always assumed it was her job to make Helen happy and proud of her. Being a 'good girl' and doing well in school was the key to it.

Ana's old school was just around the corner from her home. However, she hadn't liked that school because she had been bored in class. She would finish the work the teacher gave in half the time, and no one cared about it. Most of the time she would read further in her textbook than the teacher had instructed. When it became too much for her, she told her parents she was bored at school. Her parents went to speak with her teachers. She hoped they would give her more work to challenge her. To her surprise, the decision was made to move her to a new school. Both her parents and the teachers agreed that the new school would be better suited for her. Ana had no idea what 'better suited' meant, but it seemed like it was a compliment. Looking at her mum, who had been shining with pride, it appeared as if it was an important event that she was admitted to this new school.

Ana had soon discovered that there was nothing special about this new school. The only difference was that it was further from her home. While her first school had only been five minutes' walk away, she now had to walk more than thirty minutes to school. She had to wake up earlier than before. It wasn't bad when the weather was good, but when winter came, she regretted moving to that school because she had to leave the house in the dark and come back in the dark as well. It was as if school stole all the daylight from her.

Another reason she hated her new school was that she had no friends. In her old school, she knew all the kids; they all lived in her building. Here, she knew no one, and no one even tried to get to know her. The only exception was Ludmila, who until today she'd thought was her friend, but now she wasn't so sure.

Lately, each time any teacher praised her on her grades she could hear the other kids talking behind her back. She knew they were talking about her, but she never understood what they were saying. They would call her names she didn't understand.

Today had been the worst. During lunch break, a gang of boys circled her and started making rude jokes about how she looked, calling her 'Jid' and 'Jidan'.

I have to check in the dictionary what it means. But in her heart, she knew those words would not appear in a proper dictionary.

I'll have to ask dad. She didn't have the nerve to repeat those words to her mum. In her opinion, Helen was fragile and would not be able to express what those words were and why they seemed so insulting.

Usually, Ana enjoyed being alone; reading, playing on the piano or even working in the small garden in their courtyard where the older women were planting flowers and vegetables. There was something refreshing about digging in the soil. The attack on her today felt different than usual. The boys had managed to penetrate her glass wall and hurt her more than ever.

I really need to ask dad what that word means, she thought, while wiping a tear that escaped her eye. *But he won't be back until later. I'm not sure I can wait that long.*

As usual, when Ana entered her home the smell of food being prepared welcomed her. Her mum had that sixth sense to know exactly when she would arrive back from school and have food ready for her.

'Why the long face?'

All of a sudden, telling mum didn't seem like such a terrible thing. *She might have the answer right away.*

'Mum, what does 'Jid' or 'Jidan' mean?' The look on her mum's face confirmed that it wasn't a word she would have found in the dictionary.

'Where did you hear this word?' Helen asked.

'The kids in school called me that today. I don't know what it means, but it felt bad.'

'I'll talk to your teachers. Those kids should be punished for calling you that.' Ana could see her mother was furious.

'But what does it mean?'

'It means Jewish, but in a negative way.'

'What is Jewish? Are we Jewish?'

'You are.'

'Are you?'

'Yes, I am,' Helen replied with heaviness in her tone.

'And dad?'

'No, dad isn't. But today there is no religion, so no one is Jewish or Christian. The state does not allow religious practices.'

'Why not?' A whole new dimension had opened for Ana which she had no clue about. She was determined to get to the bottom of it.

'Enough for today, I'm going to talk to your teachers. Those kids should pay for their behaviour.'

Ana knew her mother was hiding something from her, but Helen's tone was so rigid that Ana knew better not to continue the conversation just yet.

Maybe when dad is back, I can ask him about it, she told herself.

In any case, she wrote down in her little notebook: 'Learn more what Jewish means.'

Chapter Twenty-Eight

Spring is in the air, Ana thought as she walked back from school.

Equidistant between the Baltic and the Mediterranean, Prague was Central Europe personified; harsh winters and scorching summers, but spring was perfect. Everything seemed possible at that time of year.

The days were longer. At last, there was daylight when Ana got back from school. It allowed her some time to work in the small garden.

I should plant some bulbs today. But it wasn't only the change of weather which made the difference. Ever since the day she'd returned home crying to discover she and her mother were Jewish, things had changed at home, which she appreciated.

Friday meals were different, for example. Helen would light the candles and bless them, which changed the whole atmosphere in the house. It was as if the rhythm of time slowed down. Her parents weren't always stressed, but somehow, once the candles were lit and they'd finished their dinner, tranquillity set in. Instead of listening to the radio, they would either listen to Helen playing the piano or to records. They would even play games, which had been a rare thing before, but had occurred more frequently lately.

Ana hadn't, however, learned more about her mother. Helen was still unwilling to talk about what had happened to her during the war. There were still nights when Ana would wake up to hear her mum screaming and her dad calming her.

The days after such incidents were always gloomy. Helen would be moving through the small apartment like a ghost, not talking to anyone. However, after a few days of such a heavy atmosphere, she would be back to her normal, steely persona.

Thinking of her mum, Ana recalled how she used to think that the blue number on Helen's wrist was because she was a Communist, and that she was sent to a concentration camp by the Nazis for being one. She never imagined it was because she was Jewish. No one talked about the war around Ana. Not in school. Not in the building's courtyard (which was like the town's council). It was as if the war had never happened.

**

Ana was walking through the narrow alley leading to her building when she noticed the same group of boys who'd bullied her blocking the exit. There was no way out except walking by them. Ana took a deep breath, raised her head, and started walking towards them. It was soon clear that they had been waiting for her.

Every muscle in Ana's body tensed. She started perspiring and could smell her own sweat. She knew she would have to confront them but was clueless how to do it. All of a sudden, her hand was held by someone else's.

'Don't worry, they wouldn't dare to do anything now,' said a male voice.

Ana raised her head and saw Jan, the new kid in class, holding her hand. 'How do you know they won't do anything to me?'

'Because they are cowards. They only trouble you when no one is watching, like all bullies and cowards.' He smiled at her.

'I've been watching them for a while now. They only bully those they think are weaker than them, and only when they are all together.'

Ana stared at him as if he was someone who'd stepped out of one of the books she loved reading. She couldn't believe someone in school even noticed her, let alone gave her any attention. Here was this cute boy that all the other girls were talking about, defending her. Ana never thought he would give her the time of the day. Now, here he was saving her from her bullies.

'Why are you doing this?' she asked. Once the words were out of her mouth, she couldn't believe she'd said them, but it didn't seem to affect him at all.

'Because it's the right thing to do. Let's go. Lead the way. I love discovering new places in this wonderful city.'

He held her hand and they walked to the end of the alley. Nikola, the ringleader, was looking at Jan with a fierce look. Ana could see he wanted to throw something at Jan but was hesitating. Instead, he whispered something to the other kids once they passed them.

'Jid lover,' they shouted at Jan. Then, 'Jan loves the dirty Jid, Ana.'

This stopped Jan in his tracks. He turned around and started walking back towards Nikola. Ana was terrified.

'Forget it, it's not important, leave them,' she begged, pulling Jan's hand back.

'If you don't stand up to bullies, they will always come back at you. The only way to stop them is to show them you're not afraid of them.'

Ana thought about it, and had to admit that it made sense,

but she knew she was still scared of them. Jan left her standing a few metres away and walked up to Nikola and his group. He stood only a few centimetres from Nikola and looked him straight in the eye.

'What's your problem with Ana? Is it that she's too smart for you?'

Ana couldn't believe what she heard. She blushed. She knew she was smart, but to think that *he* thinks it too was the best compliment she could ever dream of. By now, her fear of Nikola and his gang was disappearing.

'She's just like all those filthy Jews. She thinks she's better than us. Father Luka says that her people killed Christ. Pity Hitler didn't finish them all off in the war.'

Ana wasn't sure what shocked her more: hearing that Jews killed Christ, or Nikola mentioning the name no one was allowed to say.

Jan was as horrified as she was. He turned around to see how she was taking this exchange. Though she was shocked, she seemed to have more strength now that she had Jan.

'Father Luka is a drunk who doesn't know what he's talking about,' Jan said, focussing his attention back on Nikola. 'If you would have listened to your teachers more than you listened to him, you would have learned that the person you mentioned was the Devil.'

Jan started walking away from them back to Ana when he suddenly turned around. 'And just for the record, Christ was born and died as a Jew, so was he also a dirty Jid?'

Once he got back to Ana, Jan took her hand and proceeded to escort her home, not allowing her to look back at the alley.

***

'I met someone new today,' Ana told her parents when they'd finished dinner that evening. She could see that her parents were pleased for her.

'Tell us. How did you meet each other?' her father said, smiling at her and encouraging her to tell them more.

'He stopped Nikola and his gang from insulting me.'

'I thought the school had taken care of those thugs?' Helen said with a concerned tone.

'Jan, that's his name. He says that they probably were punished. And that's why they are now trying to bully me outside of school. He called them cowards. You should have seen how he made Nikola look. It was priceless.'

'I like the guy. And he's right. Nikola and his gang are bullies, and like all bullies they are basically cowards,' her father confirmed. Ana was happy to hear that her father seemed to like Jan. She wanted to see him more, and the fact that her parents liked him was crucial.

'What else did he say?' her mum asked.

'He told Nikola that I'm smarter than him and that's why he hates me.' Ana couldn't take the grin of her face when she told her parents that.

'He must be a smart boy himself,' her mum concluded. Helen stood up to clear the table when Ana remembered something.

'Mum, did the Jews really kill Christ?' Helen had to sit down from that unexpected question.

'Where did you hear this nonsense?' her father interjected before Helen could respond.

'Nikola said that this is what Father Luka says.' Ana couldn't ignore the look that passed between her mum and dad.

'Father Luka is a drunk,' her mother quickly replied.

'That's what Jan told Nikola.'

'Like I said, I like the boy,' her father said.

'But is it true?... Oh, Jan also said that Christ was born and died as a Jew, is that true too?'

The room was silenced suddenly. Ana kept looking at the faces of her parents, waiting for them to answer.

Why is it so difficult to get an answer to this simple question? Ana thought impatiently.

'God is dead and there is no religion anymore. That should be enough for you.' Helen stood up and left the room.

'But I want to know more about this Jewish thing,' Ana called after her. 'Why can't I get a straight answer from you?'

Ana turned towards her father, expecting to get some answers from him, but none came. Ana's good mood had been spoiled by the gloomy feeling Helen had left when she'd exited the room.

Typical of her to spoil the one day I was truly happy.

Ana was about to clear the table from the remains of their dinner, when her dad touched her hand.

'Leave it. Please, sit down.'

Ana sat down immediately. Knowing her father, he'd try to give her some sort of explanation that would shed some light about her mother. It might not make sense, but at least it was something.

'It's hard for your mum to talk about Judaism. For her, God died in Auschwitz with the rest of her family. She refuses to accept that any kind of God could have allowed such atrocities to take place. For her, the fact that it happened is proof there is no God and no religion.'

'But she still lights candles on Friday and blesses the Challah. I want to understand what all this means. I'm sure it means more than just having light and eating bread. No?'

'I can't answer. I have no clue about it,' he admitted. 'She will not talk about it. Why don't you go to the Old Jewish Quarter in the Old City? See if you can find one of the older people that might be willing to tell you more.'

'Oh… that's a great idea! I can ask Jan to come with me. I'm sure he'd love this adventure.'

'Great. That would also relax your mum, knowing you're not wandering around all by yourself. Why don't you invite him over, so she gets to know him better?'

Ana felt good again. Not only had she gained a friend, her parents liked him even before they'd met him. Now, she could learn more about her roots.

Chapter Twenty-Nine

The next weekend, Ana and Jan marched into the Old Town. They called it their 'private quest'. Ana had discovered that, while she was enchanted by science and physics, Jan loved anything that had to do with history and literature. For him, this adventure was as if it was taken out of one of his favourite stories about lost treasure and secrets buried for centuries.

They had no idea where to go. Ana's initial idea was to go to the synagogue. When she asked where it was, very few people could direct her to it. Or maybe they were afraid of being known as Jews.

After wandering for a long time between the winding alleys and streets, they found themselves in a small square surrounded by old trees.

'How about we take a break? Let's rest for a while before coming up with another plan,' Jan suggested.

'Good idea. Mum packed us something to eat.'

'Bless her heart. She always thinks about the small things.'

Ana didn't want to argue with Jan. But for her, Helen's efforts were more about smothering her than caring.

If she really cared for me, she would have given me what I wanted. She would have answered my questions and not kept me in the dark.

Ana and Jan were eating their sandwiches when a voice behind them made them startle.

'May I join you?' They hadn't seen anyone in the street before, so this man had taken them by surprise.

'Oh, I'm sorry I startled you. My name is Rabbi Siddon.'

Ana remembered her mum's constant warnings against talking to anyone who is not familiar. Rather than being irritated or threatened by the man, she felt angry at herself. She was acting as her mother expected her to, even though Jan was with her.

'Oh, it's OK,' she said. 'You just took us by surprise. We didn't expect anyone. I'm Ana, by the way, and this is Jan.'

'Nice to meet you, Ana by the way.'

Ana and Jan laughed. They noticed how their laughter released their initial anxiety.

'I learned a long time ago that laughter always helps to calm people. God knows we need some tension release these days.'

Ana found that after her initial scare, she became quite at ease with this strange man. She had no idea what a Rabbi was, but she assumed it was some type of title.

'What is a Rabbi?' she dared to ask him.

'It's like a priest combined with a teacher.'

He didn't look like a Rabbi; not that she would even know what one looked like. But this man looked more like a *hippy* than a Rabbi. For a start, he was way younger than what she would expect a religious teacher to be. He was also wearing colourful clothes and not the traditional black clothes she'd heard Jewish people would wear. The only sign that gave him away was the small cap on his head. Ana was intrigued.

'Aren't you afraid of introducing yourself as a Rabbi? My mum says that it's not allowed to be religious anymore. She says religious people are thrown in jail,' Jan asked, staring at him just as Ana had.

Rabbi Siddon laughed out loud. He had an infectious laugh that made them want to join him. 'Are you an informer?' he asked when he regained his breath.

'No. But what if we were?' Jan replied, which made Rabbi Siddon become serious again.

'You're right, these are challenging times, and one should be careful.'

'Now *you* sound like my mother,' Ana responded.

'Sounds like your mother is a smart woman,' Rabbi Siddon continued with a kind smile. Ana felt like he'd heard her disapproving attitude towards her own mother in her mind. It made Ana feel ashamed.

'Well, she would say that about anything, but it's understandable when you come to know her history.'

'I'm happy to hear that you can understand your mother's reasons for wanting you to be safe. Though I can imagine it can sometimes be irritating for a young person like you. This proves you're a wise person, too.'

It took Ana by surprise to hear someone who doesn't know her giving her a compliment. For some reason, she felt like she trusted this strange and intriguing man.

'The truth is,' she said. 'I don't *really* know her history. That's why I'm here with my friend.'

'Why here? What are you looking for?'

'I want to know more about my mum's religion. She says we're Jewish, but I have no clue what it means. She won't talk about it, so my dad suggested I come to the Old Town and find someone who can tell me more.'

The man looked intensely at Ana and Jan. It seemed as if he

was contemplating something. 'And are you Jewish, too?' he asked Jan.

'No. I'm just her friend. I'm trying to help her find what she's looking for.'

'That's a good friend you have there,' Rabbi Siddon said to Ana. 'Why do you think you're Jewish?' he asked her.

'My mum told me after some kids called me "Jid". I didn't know what it meant. Also, she has this blue number on her arm and my dad says she was in Auschwitz and that's where she got it.'

Rabbi Siddon sighed a heavy sigh. 'I guess you can thank the Communists for your ignorance, not your mum. The Nazis tried to eradicate her physically. However, the Communists are worse. They don't allow us; those that escaped hell, to keep our faith, or to maintain our culture and the way of life that kept us alive for two thousand years. They might destroy us more than the Nazis did.'

'Can you teach me about it?' Ana asked.

'I guess I should. There are no coincidences. We met here today, so I guess I am supposed to be your guide. How about we meet here in this square every Sunday? I'll try and teach you as much as I can.'

Ana couldn't ask for a better solution. From that day onwards, every Sunday, she would meet Rabbi Siddon on that bench and have him answer her questions. She discovered a whole new world. But the more she learned about her roots, the more she was furious at Helen for not sharing it with her. It didn't matter that Rabbi Siddon kept telling her that it wasn't Helen's fault;

that it was the government's fault. For Ana, the government was a faceless entity. She needed someone to blame for her ignorance, and her mother was her only option.

***

For two years, Ana enjoyed her weekly meeting with Rabbi Siddon, but one day he never showed up. Ana tried to look for him, but no one could tell her where he had disappeared to.

She kept returning to their bench for weeks, only to be disappointed time and again. Ana had even roped Jan into helping her find Rabbi Siddon, without any success.

Jan became her best friend, and he was fun to be around. They would spend their days together, and she was excited to see that her parents took a liking to him. At times, Jan would stay and talk with her father for even longer than he would with Ana. Ana thought it was because Jan's own father was never around.

One day, Jan told Ana that his father had never wanted to return to the city; he'd preferred country life. But his mother couldn't take it any longer, especially because she wanted Jan to have a better education than what they'd had in their village.

Chapter Thirty

PRAGUE - 1960

Ana was working in her little garden. She enjoyed it, especially now that summer was here. The air was warm, and the skies were cloudless. The colour of the sky on such days reminded her of Jan's eyes; so blue and so intense it took her breath away.

Ana knew everyone was talking behind her back, saying that he was her boyfriend. She could hear the snide jokes about their friendship when walking down the school's corridors, and even in the courtyard. For some reason this didn't seem to bother Jan, but Ana kept feeling embarrassed for him having to suffer those remarks because of their friendship. For Ana, Jan was a friend like the ones she used to read about in books. She had no thoughts of anything romantic with him. He was her anchor and confidant. He was the one she could talk to about anything. He was more than a friend; he was like her brother. As such, she couldn't think of him in romantic terms, like everyone was suggesting. Even Mrs. Hudek stopped nagging her and insinuating that she should take the first step with Jan.

What is it with all these old women, that they think that the only thing on my mind is catching a boy? As if I'm unable to lead my life without one. It's so unfair.

It was the first week of summer vacation. Nothing could change Ana's good mood, not even the *three witches*, who were sitting in their usual corner of the courtyard. Nothing could ruin this great feeling she had.

Ana heard cackling and sniggering, which meant someone

had entered the courtyard. With her back to the entrance, Ana couldn't see who it was until a hand was on her shoulder. Jan stood above her, silhouetted by the bright sun.

'Can we talk?' he asked in a serious voice, which made Ana feel uneasy. His voice was usually cheerful - as long as he wasn't discussing history with Pavel.

What could be the matter?

'Sure. Let me wash my hands and we can go to the river. No one will be listening to us there.'

Ana found that, when she wanted to talk freely with Jan, it was better to do it somewhere outside of the confined space of their neighbourhood. Besides, it was such a lovely day. A stroll along the river with its fresh smells and the view of the forests around Prague can only make this day even more perfect.

She rushed up the stairs to wash the dirt from her hands.

'Mum, I'm going for a walk along the river with Jan.'

'That's good,' her mum replied to Ana's surprise. 'Tell Jan he's welcome to come and have dinner with us when you return from your walk.'

She's probably having one of her good days, Ana thought as she skipped back down the stairs to meet Jan in the courtyard.

'Let's go,' she said to Jan, 'before she changes her mood. You never know with her. One minute she's all fine and next I'm this fragile thing that needs to be protected all the time.'

'I know what you're talking about. It's the same with my father. It's like that character in the book we were reading. You know, the one that had two people in one body. What was it?'

'Dr. Jekyll and Mr. Hyde?'

'Yes, that one. Though I don't think your mum is as dangerous as my father.'

Ana had never told Jan what the *three witches* had said about his dad; that he's an alcoholic and that when he has an attack, he beats Jan and his mother.

Maybe that's why there are days when Jan doesn't show up at school. He probably has to take care of his mum. Ana shook her head; she didn't want to think these dark thoughts on such a lovely day.

Ana and Jan crossed the city through narrow lanes and alleys until they reached the riverfront. It never ceased to amaze Ana how the city changes so suddenly. From narrow streets where houses crash upon each other, to Charles Bridge where all you see is the Vltava river flowing peacefully.

They found their favourite spot: a bench along the trail looking over the river.

'Ana, I have to tell you something,' Jan said again with a serious look in his eyes.

Ana could see it was hard for him, but she had no idea what to say to make it easier. So, she stayed silent, allowing him to find his own way.

After minutes of silence, he finally mumbled, 'I'm leaving Prague.'

'What?'

'We're leaving Prague at the end of the summer,' he repeated.

'Why?'

'It's my parents. They are getting a divorce. My mum can't afford to stay in the city. We're moving back to my grandparents' place in the village.'

'Can't you stay here?'

'I wish I could, but we both know it's not possible. But I promise I'll write to you every week.'

Ana had no clue how to answer that. How could letters replace what they had between them?

'Are you sad your parents are getting a divorce?' she asked to avoid the pain she was feeling, knowing she would miss him.

'No. I think it's best for my mother. But I wish we could stay in Prague. I asked my mum if there was any way we could stay. She told me that, because she's not in any of the Unions, she has no chance of finding any work here.'

'Can't she join one?'

'It's the chicken and egg story. You can only join the Union when you have a job, but the chances you'll get a job without being a Union member are impossible, so she's stuck.'

Jan gave Ana a peek at a whole new world: the grownup world. She never thought about those things, and she suddenly realised there were so many things she took for granted: work, jobs, money, and who knows what else. But for now, she just felt like she was being punched in her guts. As of next year, she would be all on her own again.

'I thought we're going to have a glorious day today,' she said, more to herself than to Jan.

'We can still have one,' he said. 'We have the whole summer in front of us. Let's make it one that we will never forget.' He took her hand and pulled her up from their bench.

I'll never forget it for sure, she thought. *It's the summer I learned nothing good lasts forever.*

'I'm good,' she said. 'Let's go back home. My mum said you can stay for dinner if you want.'

Chapter Thirty-One

BOSTON - 1989

'So, you see, Jan was my "Knight in Shining Armour." He was there for me when I was bullied because of antisemitism. He helped me to understand more about my own heritage and roots. You don't forget someone like that.'

'I get it now. But then how did you escape Czechoslovakia? How did you end up here?' Yael asked.

Ana was about to answer when the phone rang. Dan picked it up. He was listening to someone on the other side. He then handed the phone to Ana.

'It's Monica. They need you in the centre. I can drive you there.'

Ana took the phone and could hear Monica on the other end of the line. She knew she couldn't refuse her.

'I'll be there in thirty minutes,' she said, putting the phone down. She turned to Yael, who already knew what was coming.

'I know, you have to go,' she said with a sigh. 'Go. But you have to continue this tomorrow.'

Ana nodded.

***

'Samaritan Centre, how can I help you? ... I'm here for you.'

Though the sentences came automatically to her lips, Ana made sure the person on the other side of the line could sense she was invested in them and their problems. These were the calls that made her come back to the centre time and again.

Tiredness and exhaustion had not come into consideration when Monica had called her that evening. That had all become secondary, even after Ana's long day as a surgeon in Beith Israel Hospital. Monica knew she would always come and would never abuse Ana's desire to help.

As she'd entered the centre, Ana had instantly understood Monica's reason for calling her. The whole place was on fire. Phones were ringing off the hook and the night shift staff were totally unprepared for the deluge. Ana's ability to handle calamity in a calm way was what this place needed tonight.

For Ana, the centre was a place where she could drop her armour and dare to show some vulnerability. Here, there was no need to play the strong and powerful doctor. Even with Dan, Ana didn't allow herself to be as exposed as she was here. A different kind of strength was expected of her, which made it so much easier.

Without wasting any time, Ana had sat down in one of the stations where the phone was ringing and had answered it without hesitation. As the caller spoke, she'd lost track of time; the whole world beyond disappeared. There was only her and the caller. She understood that those who took the time to ring needed someone to hear their pain; to acknowledge their existence.

'I can't find any reason to keep on... I've been struggling for so long... What's the point? What's the purpose for this kind of life?' they asked.

If only I had a penny each time I heard this, Ana thought.

Ana had no idea how long the call had been. Once she put down the receiver, she noticed the tiredness in her body and the pain in her lower back. There was a hand on her shoulder. She raised her head and saw Monica standing behind her with her eternally soft smile.

'Take a break.'

'When did you come in? Didn't notice you when I arrived.'

'You were with that person on the line for three hours. No wonder you didn't notice.'

'Was it really three hours? Didn't feel like it.'

'Well, it was more like four hours,' Monica chuckled, before her expression became sympathetic again, 'but when you do your work coming from the heart, time disappears and becomes irrelevant. Let's take a break and have coffee? Dan passed by and brought you some food. He made me feel guilty when he mentioned you hadn't had time for dinner when I called.'

'Good old Dan. Always taking care of me,' Ana joked with Monica as they walked to the small kitchen.

'Yes, he is. He's a keeper.' Monica said.

They stepped into a small kitchen that had seen better days. There was a small corner table with barely enough space for two chairs. Though the place was spotless, there were signs of obvious neglect in the unventilated space: faded paint on the walls, chipped cups, the acrid smell of sweat lingering in the air no matter how cold it was outside.

Monica dumped tea bags into two cups, pouring hot water from the urn. Ana had been volunteering so long at the centre, she didn't even need to tell Monica how she liked hers: black, two sugars. Ana smiled as Monica placed the mug in front of her.

'That's better,' Ana said, taking a tentative sip. It was still very hot.

Monica sat down opposite her. 'You know, you never told me why you were interested in volunteering in this centre?'

Ana's smile froze as she played for time. 'Didn't I? I thought I did. I thought it was one of your questions in my interview?'

Don't look back, Ana heard her mother's voice. *You promised never to look back.*

'It's a long story.' Ana sighed. Ana could sense Monica was even more intrigued, but before her friend could say anything, the door to the kitchen opened and Dan was standing there.

'Ready to go?' he asked.

'Always on time.' Ana grinned. She grabbed her bag from the back of the chair. As she did so, Monica's hand grabbed Ana's.

'Saved by the bell, but you still owe me that story.'

'Yes, I do,' Ana said, 'but not right now. Rain check?'

'I'll hold you to that.'

Chapter Thirty-Two

The next day after dinner, Yael couldn't wait for Ana to continue her story. She didn't care that her mum was exhausted after her night shift at the centre, followed by a morning shift at the hospital. She wanted the full story.

'You promised to continue,' she reminded her. Ana was tired beyond words, but her daughter's request and Monica's words last night had made her realise that telling her story might be the thing she needs to do.

She's right. It's time to be done with it.

'Fine. Let's take the dessert to the living room. I'll continue there.'

***

PRAGUE - 1968

Years later, when Ana tried to recall the month after the invasion, the period was stuck in her mind as a time of confusion, frustration and the feeling of being lost.

She couldn't find her place in the world and had been going about her daily life like a robot. She had been hoping the restrictions on students would be lifted once the new year started, but to her dismay it was announced that Charles University was to be shut down and the Communist Party had dismissed all teachers who were suspected of supporting Dubček.

'I wonder who's left to teach?' Ana remarked when Pavel read it from the newspaper. 'I saw many of my teachers in the meetings we had.'

'Now you will see them cleaning streets, if they are lucky,' her mother said.

'You can't be serious, these are esteemed professors,' Ana cried out in a shocked voice.

Her father sniggered bitterly. 'Since when has being an intellectual person been beneficial to the collective? Don't forget, the Communist regime sees any intellectual as an enemy of the state, unless they preach for socialism and communist propaganda. Anyone else was on thin ice even before Dubček. Now, they have the excuse to get rid of them.'

Suddenly, Ana became aware of why her mother had been concerned when she became involved with the Student Union. The repercussions dawned on her. In a span of only a few days, her mother no longer sounded feeble and irrational. There was sound logic behind what she said, which Ana had never paid any attention to before.

The following week the real blow came. Ana and many of her friends received a letter informing them they were banned from education. On the evening news it was announced that any student who was a registered Student Union member would be denied admission for the following year.

The only ray of light in those dull days were Ana's nightly activities with Jan, attempting to distract the army from finding the pirate radio stations. But even that had its limits. Ana was no longer sure what she believed in or why she was doing what she was doing.

***

One afternoon, Helen came back home on the edge of an attack. Ana recognized it instantly. She went into the kitchen and prepared her father's drink. By now she knew the effect of the warm, sweet drink on the nerves. It had even managed to relax Ana when she'd had her nightmares.

Once Helen's shaking had stopped, Ana could relax. 'What happened?'

'There were soldiers on the street checking for papers. They said they are looking for a female student who killed a soldier. I thought I would faint on the spot. I was able to keep a straight face and just show them my documents. They let me go, but I had to come back here and warn you.'

Ana was just as frightened by this news as Helen, but she couldn't show it. Ana suddenly felt like the walls were closing in on her. As long as she could remember, all she'd ever wanted was to be a doctor; she couldn't see any kind of life for herself but that. Now that she was banned from studying and the authorities were onto her, all she had ahead of her was a bleak future.

Ana started doubting whether her work supporting freedom and Dubček had been worth it. Worse of all, it had resulted in the death of a human being.

Feeling overwhelmed by the recent news, Ana knew she needed to find a way to regain some sense of normalcy. Desperate to keep up with the latest developments in the field of medicine, she decided to seek out a place where she could read medical magazines and journals. She clung to the hope that, with time, the restrictions would be lifted, and she would be able to return to the university library to continue her studies.

Lost in thought and unsure where to turn, Ana wandered the streets in search of purpose and direction. As she walked, she found herself drawn to a local library.

She stepped inside, feeling a sense of curiosity and intrigue. At first, Ana had to make do with reading outdated magazines and journals. But, as she kept returning to the library and spent most of her time there, she grew friendly with the librarian. When Ana asked about more recent and prestigious magazines that would contain the latest research, the librarian regretfully informed her that they were not allowed. They had been banned because they were from the West.

'After the invasion, all Western literature was banned and confiscated,' the librarian informed her. The librarian could sense Ana's eagerness to read updated material and appreciated her thirst for knowledge.

One day, as she handed Ana the books she requested, the librarian whispered under her breath, 'I'm out for a lunch break at twelve thirty, meet me outside.'

Ana was curious. She could hardly concentrate on her reading and was counting the minutes until she could go outside and meet with the librarian.

When at last the time had come, she stood outside and waited for the librarian.

'If you're looking for those banned publications and books,' whispered the librarian behind her, 'there are some bookstores in town that have been printing them illegally. They have them, but with the cover of another book,' she said quickly. 'But make sure no one hears you asking for them.'

Ana wanted to ask whether she could give her the names of such bookstores, but by the time she turned around, the librarian had vanished. Ana felt excited and became determined to find those shops.

The next day, when Ana returned from the library, she found herself facing three men who were clearly members of the notorious StB (State Security Police). What scared Ana most was the fact they were talking to the *three witches*.

'That's her over there,' Mrs. Kadlek pointed in her direction. There was no way for Ana to escape.

'Please, come with us,' said the one in charge.

'Where are you taking me?' Ana protested loudly. 'I haven't done anything wrong.' Ana hoped that her parents would hear her.

'We just want to ask you a few questions about your whereabouts during August 21st.'

'I was at home all day. I was sick. Ask Mrs. Fischer there,' she said, rehashing the story her parents had concocted.

'That's true. Her father came to ask for some medicine. They didn't want to go out of the apartment that day to get it,' Mrs. Fischer told them.

'That's insignificant. We have someone who says they saw her near the radio station. Move.'

The commander pushed Ana out of the courtyard.

Ana was terrified. She had no idea where they were taking her. There were so many stories of people who simply disappeared after being taken by the StB.

'Where are you taking me?'

'If you haven't done anything, you have nothing to fear. Just come peacefully with us,' the commander said.

'Tell my parents I was taken to Kachlíkárna,' Ana called back to the *three witches*.

The whole way, Ana kept repeating the story in her head, hoping she would remember all the details.

Their march ended at Bartolomějská Ulice number 4, known as Kachlíkárna ('The Tile') on account of the specific kind of tile that was used in its architecture. Just the sight of the place would bring fear to anyone.

The three men took her to what used to be the convent of St. Bartholomew's church, which was just across the street. The convent's cells that had been built in the middle of the 19th century were perfect holding spaces for those unfortunates who ended up there.

Ana was thrown into one of those cells.

It was dark and cold. She could spot a simple bed and a bucket next to it. On the bed there was a blanket. Shivering, she took the blanket to warm up.

'Put the blanket back. It is to be used only at night,' she heard someone shout.

Ana looked around to see where it was coming from but couldn't see anyone. *Someone is watching me. Mum was right. The walls have ears, and the doors have eyes.*

'How long are you going to keep me here? I haven't done anything,' she called out into the empty space. There was no reply.

Ana had no idea how long she had been in the cell. Each time she wanted to sit on the bed, the faceless voice called out to stop her. Tired of standing up, Ana collapsed on the cold and dirty floor.

'Stand up. You're not allowed to sit.'

For the first time, Ana was happy she was so small. Any person with normal height would have banged their head on the ceiling. She started walking and jumping to keep herself warm. Finally, after what seemed like days, one of the men opened the door.

'Step out and follow me,' he called. Ana followed as fast as she could. They climbed up a set of stairs to rooms that looked a bit more modernised.

The room they entered was just as small as her cell. The only difference was that this one was lit. After hours in her dark cell, those fluorescent lights nearly blinded her. There was a small table and two chairs.

'Sit.' He pointed to one of the chairs. Ana sat down. The man sat opposite her. He took out a notepad and a pen. 'Where were you on August 21st?'

'I was at home. I was sick for a few days and that day my temperature was running high. My parents already told you that when you came into our home on August 22nd.'

'We have an eyewitness saying you were part of the group of students defending the radio station.'

'Can't be. I was in bed the whole day. He must be lying or mistaken,' Ana insisted.

'Can anybody, except your parents, testify to it?'

'Ask Mrs. Fischer. She brought medicine for me that night.'

'Yes. Only she never saw you. She only gave it to your father,' the man said with a cynical smile on his face.

Ana had no idea how to answer. They hadn't been prepared for that argument.

Who could have told them that I was at the radio station? Maybe one of the students that was arrested broke down under torture and needed to blame someone.

Suddenly, she had an idea. She wasn't going to betray one of her friends, but she knew who would always be smart enough to corroborate her story without even having to be instructed.

'I do have another person that can prove I was at home. My friend's boyfriend came to bring me some homework that I left at her place. He can testify that I was sick and at home that day.'

The man was utterly surprised. He hadn't been expecting to hear that.

'Who is it? And where does he live?'

'His name is Tomas. My friend Tereza lives with him, and they can both vouch for me.' Ana could see that her interrogator was not happy with it.

You thought you had me, ha, son of a bitch. She didn't dare to smile, but inside a wave of satisfaction rose.

'We'll bring him in and see if that's true. Meanwhile, you'll stay here.' The man left the room and Ana could hear the lock turning. At least now she could sit.

Hours went by. Ana was exhausted from tension and fear. She didn't even want to think about what her mum was going through. She finally saw what Helen had meant by the danger of being associated with activity that was in opposition to the Communist Party. She'd come to appreciate that her mother was talking not from weakness, but from experience.

At last, the door opened, and Tomas and two men stepped into the room.

'Is this the man you spoke about?' one of the men asked her.

'Yes. He can tell you that I was sick in bed on August 21st,' she blurted as quickly as she could. 'He brought me my papers from his apartment. His girlfriend Tereza, who is a colleague of mine, lives there with him.'

'Is that true?'

'Yes. Like she said. I came to her place. She could hardly get out of bed. I only gave her the papers my girlfriend gave me. I left as soon as I could. I didn't want to be on the streets too much that day.'

Ana thanked her lucky stars that Tomas was so quick to understand what she needed. She tried hard not to show it on her face.

'So, you see. I couldn't have been near the radio station. You must release me.'

'We have a problem,' said one of the men. 'We have one person who says that not only you were there, but you were the one that shot the soldier that died. Now, we have this man who says you were at home. We need to figure out who is lying. We can't release you yet.'

'She isn't who you're looking for,' Tomas said in a very calm way.

'What do you mean?'

'I know who killed that soldier, and it isn't her.'

'Who was it?' both men said in unison.

'First, release her, and then I'll tell you.'

The two men whispered to each other and, after a short debate, turned to Tomas.

'OK. we will release her. Now tell us who it was.'

'Not before I see you signing her release form. Also, I want a paper that says she had nothing to do with that killing.'

Ana couldn't believe what was going on in front of her eyes, but she knew better than to interfere. One of the men left the room and came back within seconds with papers and signed them.

'See, it's signed. Now, tell us what you know.'

Ana had no clue how Tomas was going to get himself out of this situation.

'The person who shot the soldier was my girlfriend, Tereza,' he began. 'She admitted it to me that night before she left the city. So, if you're looking for someone, look for her. If you find her, I'd be happy to get back from her the Tuzek vouchers she stole from me worth more than ten thousand korunas.'

Ana was speechless. How could he so calmly frame Tereza for something she had not done? But Ana couldn't say anything, or even look upset.

'So, can I go now?' was the only thing she could utter.

'Yes. But we will be watching you. You were still one of the Student Union leaders.'

Ana walked out. She didn't dare to look at Tomas, afraid that her contempt would be shown on her face.

When she was finally out in the fresh air, Ana took a deep breath, making sure that she really was free from that terrifying place.

Ana didn't remember much of her way back home. Thoughts were plaguing her.

Why did Tomas frame Tereza? I know he loved her. Why protect me and not his girlfriend?

Chapter Thirty-Three

The next morning, Ana was determined to find out why Tomas had framed Tereza. Ana was certain Tomas knew it was her who'd killed that soldier. For the life of her, she couldn't understand why he would do it. She had to find out.

Ignoring Helen's pleas of staying at home, Ana stepped into the street. By now, she knew perfectly well that someone would be watching her. Everyone was a suspect: a woman walking with a baby's pram could be hiding a camera that might take a photo of her; a man on the corner reading a newspaper might be following her. She knew now that eyes and ears were everywhere.

Today, she didn't care.

Ana rushed to Jan's place. She peeked through the window and could see that it was reasonably organised.

If he's taking care of his room, then he isn't in his weird space.

The look on Jan's face when he opened the door was priceless. He hugged her and pulled her into his room. He immediately went to the window to check if there was anyone following her.

'No one followed me. I checked. I now know that the StB really is everywhere.'

'How the hell did Helen allow you to leave the apartment after yesterday?'

'She didn't. But wild horses couldn't hold me back. I must get some answers. Why the hell did Tomas lie and betray Tereza?'

'You should have stayed at home. This time Helen was right.

But we were ready for this day. When you did what you did, we made a decision that no one would connect you to what took place there.'

'What do you mean, cover for me? I killed a soldier! How can you cover that?' Ana couldn't even comprehend how to express her shock, outrage and a whole wave of other emotions that took over her when she heard him say it.

'What you did was unbelievable. We all agreed that if we needed to testify, we would say you were not there. Tomas didn't betray Tereza. It was Tereza's idea. She said that we should point the finger at her.'

'But now she's in danger. Why on earth would she agree to it? Why didn't you stop her? She was your friend, too.'

'First, there is no way to stop Tereza when she has an idea. You of all people should know it. Next, she's not here anymore. That night she arranged with one of Tomas's connections to be taken across the border to Austria. Once there, he arranged a flight for her to the United States. I guess, by now, she's living her dream life there. It's something she always wanted. It gave her the perfect cover to request asylum, saying she's in danger for her life if they refuse her.'

Ana couldn't believe what she was hearing. She knew Tereza had wanted to get out of Czechoslovakia and live in the United States, but to think she used this whole madness to do it was inconceivable.

I never did get her.

'At least one person benefited from this nightmare. She really did want to live in the United States. But for me the nightmares go on. I can't forgive myself for killing that soldier.'

Without any warning, Jan hugged Ana; the kind of hug she'd been longing to get from him since the day outside the radio station.

The day that has changed her life.

She recalled the day he'd kissed her for the first time. She could hear Tereza in her mind.

Do it. Be brave. Don't wait for him, take the first step. Show him you want him.

Maybe it was the thought of what Tereza would advise her, or maybe it was because she'd wanted Jan for so long. She didn't know who she was anymore, but she knew this was her opportunity.

She pressed herself towards his body and kissed him. His lips were just as soft as she remembered. He held her even closer, responding by kissing her hard on her lips and parting them. His tongue was inside her mouth, and she could taste him.

Every kiss became more passionate as Ana's heartbeat rose. Without any thought, she took off her shirt, took Jan's hand and led him to the bed for another long and heated hug. Ana could no longer tell where her body ended and where Jan's began.

Jan took his shirt off. Ana could see the muscles on his back and ran her fingers along them, noticing how Jan responded to her hands playing along his body. There was no doubt in her mind that he wanted her just as much as she wanted him. She could see herself through his eyes, and she liked what she saw. It made her bolder in her movements.

She imagined herself as Tereza. In her head, she could hear her guiding her.

Jan seemed to follow Ana's lead. She was showing him what

gave her pleasure, and he was giving it to her. She'd never imagined it would be like that.

The musky smell of his body.

The dried sweat and dust in his clothes.

A hungry, feral wolf.

She knew he wanted her.

'I'll give it to you,' he murmured, and his hand moved lightly. A touch. Another. 'I promise I'll be tender.'

'And what if I don't want it tenderly?' she teased him.

'I can do that also,' he said, with a hint of humour. 'It would only be what and how you wish it.' He stretched her out on the bed.

By now, they were both totally naked. Ana could see how he was admiring her full body. Just his look brought shivers of delight to her. He started kissing her whole body, and without any warning, he came into her strongly enough that she gave a small, high-pitched cry of release.

I wish I could tell Tereza, Ana thought before she fell asleep. *She was right. Everything has changed between me and Jan.*

Chapter Thirty-Four

It was dark when Ana woke up. At first, she had no idea where she was, but then she turned around to see Jan sleeping next to her.

She knew she needed a shower. She got out of bed and walked towards the bathroom. The smell from the tiny area was overwhelming, and the state of the bathroom was not inviting. Even walking barefoot on the floor felt as if she were walking on something sticky and gooey.

Ana looked at her wristwatch and realised she only had one hour before curfew. She knew her mother would be worried if she didn't make it back by then, so she quickly dressed and left a note for Jan, suggesting they meet at their usual spot by the river the next day.

Ana rushed down the streets and managed to get back home just in time.

'I'm sorry I'm so late. I was with Jan the whole day,' Ana called out as she entered the house. She was hoping an apology would pacify Helen. It seemed to have worked.

'Did anyone follow you?' her dad asked.

'Not that I could see. I'm fine. I'm going to take a shower,' she announced, hoping that by the time she was out of the shower they wouldn't want any more explanations.

When she returned, Helen had prepared something for her to eat.

'I figured you didn't have much to eat if you spent the whole day with Jan,' she said with an unexpected smile, as if she knew what had gone on between her and Jan.

I'm not going to fall into her trap, I'm just going to ignore it.

Pavel turned on the radio and raised the sound to a level no one who might be listening to them could hear.

'Did he tell you what happened to Tereza?'

'Tereza is gone. Probably in the United States by now. God knows how she pulled it off. But that's what she always wanted and I'm happy for her. I can't imagine living in a place where I don't speak the language or know anyone. I hope she finds the happiness she was looking for.'

'I'm happy to hear you're not thinking of doing something foolish like that,' Helen said.

Ana wasn't sure that it was foolish but didn't say anything. She would continue to say only what her mother and anyone listening in would want to hear: that she wasn't planning on leaving the country.

In any case, her words did the trick and put her mum in a good mood. They spent the rest of the night listening to Helen playing the piano, which always put Ana in a quiet space.

When Ana turned off the light in bed that night, she still could feel Jan's hands caressing her body, and she was excited to meet with him the next day.

***

It was a glorious autumn day.

Might be too chilly to go swimming, but still warm enough to enjoy the day.

The ground was covered with falling leaves which created a carpet of red, yellow and brown. Ana was excited. The last time she and Jan had been here, was the first time he'd kissed her. Yesterday's events were still on her mind. She was hoping they could discuss the future of their relationship. She'd made some sandwiches and had brought two bottles of beer to celebrate.

Jan was never one for punctuality, but when the hour stretched and he still hadn't arrived, Ana started worrying.

What if yesterday meant nothing to him? She didn't know how she could face him if it had just been casual sex. *He's not like that, it had to mean something,* she kept telling herself.

Finally, he arrived. It was clear he'd remembered the meeting at the last moment because he was still wearing yesterday's clothes. His hair was ruffled and there was a look on his face that indicated his mind was somewhere else.

'I'm sorry. I found your note only ten minutes ago. I was busy the whole night after you left. I was carried by it the whole morning.'

Ana knew that if she asked him what it was about, the conversation would not go in the direction she wanted. She kept silent. To her disappointment, Jan saw that as an invitation to talk about what had kept him up the whole night.

'Do you remember Vaculík's ideas?'

'Sure. Mum said they are the ideas that would lead us to hell. She said they went against everything the Communist Party stood for. That Moscow will not be pleased if they spread. She kept reminding us of what Stalin did to all the intellectuals and those who had different ideas than the party's line. Seems like she was right. She always ended by saying, "The Gulags are filled with the bodies of those people who thought differently".'

'But we can't live our life in fear.'

'To that she would tell you, "better live in fear and be safe than disappear and die."'

Ana wasn't so sure anymore who was right and who wasn't. 'But what does this have to do with what you were doing yesterday?' she asked Jan.

'Everything. It got me thinking. What we need today are people who are willing to die for their beliefs. We cannot accept this "normalisation" nonsense.'

'So, what are you going to do?' Ana asked again after her initial feeling of shock had subsided.

'I don't know yet. I'm thinking of writing an article about Middle-Age martyrs; those who died for their beliefs, and compare it to what we should do these days.'

Ana couldn't believe what she was hearing. *Has he gone mad? Who would follow such a thing?*

'Did you know,' he continued, 'that Jews in the Middle Ages would rather die than submit to becoming Christians? It was called "Kiddush HaShem". They were hailed as the highest believers. I find it fascinating. It's so brave to be willing to die for what you believe in. We lost that spirit in this country.'

He stopped for a second, then continued as if talking to himself more than to Ana. 'There was even a group of Jewish rebels during the Roman Empire that fortified themselves in a fortress in the desert called Masada. It took the Romans nearly ten months and over fifteen thousand soldiers before they could conquer that fortress. The rebels, when they realised they could not run or win, chose to die by their own hands rather than become slaves. This is the kind of devotion and strong belief which is missing today. Most people would rather become slaves to Moscow than keep on fighting for our way of life and freedom.'

Ana was listening to Jan's words and realised she had no chance of making him see that she was interested in talking about something much more mundane. She was looking for their physical connection. She was waiting to hear him speak about their future, not preach his ideas. She had no idea how to change his fervent talk about ideals into a more personal one. Her only way to continue was to follow his lead.

'Would you have that courage? I mean to die for a belief?' Ana feared his answer, but it was on her mind.

'I think that in my head and heart my answer is yes, but I'm not sure I would be able to go through with it,' he replied with total honesty.

'If you feel so strongly about it, what is holding you back?' She was now curious to hear his answer.

Jan seemed to be waking up from a haze of thoughts. He came to sit next to her on the bench. He was taking his time before answering, which made Ana hope it would be one that would give her some hope for her relationship with him.

'I guess, the main reason that would stop me would be the people I'd leave behind. I'd never want them to think it was their fault, or want them to feel guilty about my actions. I guess what I'm trying to say is... I would probably be able to do it, but only when I see there is no hope, and no one is left that believes in the same cause as I do.'

There was so much sadness in his words that Ana felt her heart was breaking. She wanted to reassure him she would always stand by him; that she would always fight with him, but she couldn't. These days, there was nothing she was absolutely convinced about. For the first time in her life, she had more doubts than certainty.

She couldn't make him a promise she wasn't sure she could keep.

'I hope it won't get to the point where that's the only option.' It appeared as if her comment was the right one. The minute her words were out in the air, his whole attitude changed. He was back to his usual charming and cheerful self.

'You're absolutely right. Enough of this melancholic mood, we still have much to do, and there are more actions we can take.'

It wasn't what she wanted to hear, but it was better seeing him back to his optimistic spirit.

'I have to go,' she said. 'I promised mum I wouldn't be too late today, and it's getting late. How about we meet on Saturday here. It's the last day of autumn. We should enjoy this wonderful weather before winter falls upon us.'

'Perfect. By then I might have the first draft of my article. Would be great to get your input. See you Saturday.'

Jan left in a rush, leaving Ana to her thoughts. She was concerned about him. He was back to his manic behaviour, which scared her. She had no idea what she could do to get the old Jan back.

Her Jan.

Chapter Thirty-Five

The next morning, Ana was going through some of her stuff in her room. Helen had asked her to clear out anything that might incriminate her even more.

Not that it could get any worse. She had no energy to argue with her mum. She *had* had a point in everything she'd warned her about so far.

Ana's room wasn't very big. It had enough space for a bed and a small table where she used to do all her studies. While other students would cover their walls with their favourite idol's posters, Ana had shelves and shelves of books, mostly medical ones. A small cabinet was sufficient for all her clothes. There was no more room beyond it.

To keep her space tidy, she used to keep old stuff in boxes, labelled, under her bed. She started dragging those boxes out. One of the last ones, to her surprise, was not labelled. She opened it out of curiosity and was stunned to discover it contained the notebooks she'd kept when she was young. She opened one of them to discover it contained the Hebrew alphabet. All of a sudden, a wave of memories came rushing in.

It was the year she and Jan had become friends. The year she'd become interested in Judaism. She and Jan had looked for someone in the Jewish Quarter to help her discover more about her roots.

What was his name? He was a rabbi. For the life of me I can't recall his name, but I remember how he looked.

Ana closed the notebook and got up. She knew what she had to do. In his feverish talk yesterday, Jan had mentioned something about Jewish martyrs. If she could find that rabbi, maybe he could give her more information. If he could teach her more about that subject, then maybe she could stop Jan in his downward spiral. She had to find a way to show Jan that martyrdom was not the way to make a difference.

Helen was mending some clothes when Ana stepped out of her room.

'I'm off to the old Jewish Quarter,' Ana said. 'I want to see if I can find that rabbi that taught me years ago.'

'Why are you interested in that stuff again all of a sudden?'

'Something that Jan said yesterday, which troubles me. I want to check if he was right.'

'Fine. Just be back on time before curfew.'

Ana was surprised that her mother didn't argue with her more. *Let's thank small miracles*, she thought as she quickly descended the stairs and headed out into the courtyard.

As Ana made her way towards the Old Town and the Jewish Quarter, Ana tried to recall the details of what Jan had told her. She sensed the key to getting *her* Jan back was to stop him from going down the path of believing that people need to sacrifice themselves; to learn more about what he was talking about and find a counter argument.

When she got to the Jewish Quarter Ana stopped. It suddenly dawned on her that she had no clue where to find the rabbi. She walked towards one of the buildings she knew was used as a synagogue, but it was locked. She walked towards the Spanish synagogue, but that was also locked. For nearly an hour Ana walked around the area, even visiting the old Jewish cemetery. She thought that if there was a funeral taking place, she could ask someone, but there was no one there. She didn't dare knock on doors, but she was close to doing it.

Ana didn't feel like going back home, so she kept walking only to find herself by the river. She sat down on the bench and stared at the river for a long time.

'May I sit here?' a man asked her, which made Ana nearly jump out of her skin, so engrossed in her thoughts that she hadn't seen him arrive. 'Oh, I'm sorry, I didn't mean to startle you. My name is…'

'Rabbi Siddon,' Ana cried out when she recognised the very man she'd been looking for all day.

'Do I know you?' he asked, looking closely at Ana, trying to remember if he'd met her before.

'Yes. But that was years ago. You used to call me Ana, by the way.'

'That sounds like me. I learned a long time ago that laughter…

'Always helps to release tension,' Ana completed his sentence. 'I can't believe I'm seeing you here. I was looking for you the whole day. Just when I gave up, I found you here of all places.'

'How did you recognise me? It's been so long since the last time we met?'

'It's your Kippah. It's so different from the traditional ones. It looks more like a cap than a Kippah.'

Rabbi Siddon smiled. 'Serves me right for trying to be modern. But now I think I remember you. You were interested in learning more about Judaism. You used to have a friend that came with you. He wasn't Jewish as I recall but was just as interested in it as you were.'

'Yes. That was Jan. A lot has changed since then,' Ana said with sadness in her voice.

'Why so sad? I know we're not living in "happy times", but you're young. As much as I remember, you were very smart. You had your whole future in front of you.'

It took Ana by surprise to hear him say that. It regained her confidence in him.

'Well, it doesn't help me much that I'm smart now that I can't do any of the things I had my heart set upon. I can't study what I love. I can't even find a job. It's as if no one will dare to hire me, just because I was in the Student Union, which makes me unemployable.' She had bitterly added the last part, more for herself than for him.

Rabbi Siddon was silent for a while. They both stared at the river.

'What were you studying that you had your heart set on so passionately?' he asked after a few minutes.

It was refreshing for Ana to have someone who would listen to her for a change, without judging, or arguing with, her. Ana experienced him as someone who truly listened without an agenda or a need to educate or challenge others.

'I studied medicine. I really wanted to be a doctor. I thought studying would help me understand the trauma my mother went through and help others like her. She was in Auschwitz. For years I would wake up at night from her screams and nightmares. I was hoping I could ease that pain for others. Funny how life is - now it's me who wakes up from nightmares.'

Ana didn't dare to look at Rabbi Siddon. She felt embarrassed.

'Then why were you looking for me today after all these years?'

This reminded Ana of her goal.

'Remember Jan? He told me Jews in the Middle Ages would die in the name of something called "Kiddush HaShem". He also said there was a group of rebels who fought the Romans and preferred killing themselves rather than surrendering and becoming slaves. Is it true?'

From the surprised look on Rabbi Siddon's face, Ana guessed he hadn't expected such a question. He was flabbergasted.

'For someone who isn't Jewish, he knows a lot more than most Jewish people. But, yes, all that is true. However, I would argue it wasn't our finest hour.'

That was exactly what Ana wanted to hear. She really wanted to get more of Rabbi Siddon's perspective on this topic.

'He also says they were heroes. He thinks we should strive to be like them by fighting against "normalisation" and for our freedom.'

Rabbi Siddon took his time answering Ana. Several times he started saying something, but stopped.

'What do you think?' he said, finally. 'Was it heroism or was it zealotry?'

'What's the difference?' Ana asked.

'Think about it. What about those they left behind? What about those who felt inspired to fight back? It's not a black and white issue. Those that died on "Kiddush Hashem" and the rebels in Masada were zealots. Nothing good comes from being a fanatic.

If you're looking for role models for heroism, look at the

actions of the Spanish Jews during the Inquisition period. They chose to convert, but only on the surface. They managed to keep their Jewish heritage hidden and keep it alive, but in secret. They managed to find a way to stay alive *and* keep their tradition and culture alive. I'd call that heroism.'

Rabbi Siddon stood up ready to leave. 'If you can't find any work,' he said, 'you can always stop by the old Jewish synagogue, I might have some work for you.'

It was precisely what Ana needed to hear. She wanted to run to Jan's place; tell him about those so-called 'heroes'. But she was already late.

It will have to wait for tomorrow.

Chapter Thirty-Six

The next few days, Ana desperately tried to get hold of Jan but without any success. She called him a few times, but there was no reply. On her last attempt, the ringtone indicated the line was dead.

After a week of trying, Ana finally decided to visit him. She knocked on his door but there was no response. She peeked through the window, only to find the place was deserted. It looked as if Jan hadn't been there for days. She could spot a pile of mail on the floor. The clothes he had been wearing the last time she saw him were thrown on the floor. The sink was overflowing with dirty dishes, and, on the table, she could see apples that had seen better days.

It was enough for Ana to know that Jan was again on his downward spiral. She was concerned for his safety, but he was out of reach, and it was clear that he had no desire to see her again. She had to do something. She decided, against every instinct in her body, to leave him a note.

She knew it might be dangerous. *Who knows who might read it and what they might make of it?* But it was her only way of letting Jan know she cared for him and wanted the best for his well-being. She took a piece of paper out of her bag. It took her a long time to decide what to write. She had to find a way to write it so that it would not be interpreted as political. In the end, all she could come up with was, 'Please call me or come and visit. I love you.' She had so many other things to tell him, but anything more might be interpreted in a way that could harm them both. She had to leave it at that. She folded the piece of paper and slid it under the door.

Only after she'd left did another thought come into her head which scared her: *What if he doesn't love me? I've made such a fool of myself.*

***

Ana had no idea whether Jan had read her note or not. Ten days later, she found herself facing him when she was on her daily search for a job. She knew there was no hope for it, but she had to do something. Staying at home with Helen was no option for her.

Ana was just about to turn the corner near the Old Town square, when she nearly bumped into him. He was a mess. His hair was unwashed and ruffled, and he looked as if he'd slept in his clothes for days. He'd developed a five o'clock shadow on his face. This more than anything indicated lack of sleep.

'Hi, Jan,' she said, surprised. 'I hardly recognised you.'

'Oh. Ana. It's you. Sorry. Was busy,' was all that he said. That was too much for her.

'Where have you been all this time? Ever since that day we spent together in your apartment, you disappeared from the face of the earth and totally ignored me. Am I so meaningless to you? Did it mean nothing to you?'

The truth was that she didn't really want to hear what he had to say. She was too afraid to hear that, for him, their sex had meant nothing. She knew it would break her heart to hear it. However, her concern for him took over and she'd blurted it out without any control.

'I have no clue what you're talking about. I have much more important things to deal with. The world doesn't revolve around you, Ana. Have you any clue how much danger we are in? Don't you get it? The most dangerous thing for our cause is inactivity. The one thing that will kill our movement is apathy, and this is what is going on today. I must wake people up. I have to make them see that this "normalisation" is not normal. Don't you get it?'

Ana was fed up with his political speeches. That wasn't what she was talking about. She wanted to know where they were at.

'You're not answering my question. Don't avoid me. I want to know how you feel towards me. Answer me.' She didn't care anymore that they were in the middle of the street, or that people were staring at them. However, Jan seemed to care. He pulled her into an alley where there was no one around before answering her.

'You're acting like a child. What are two people's lives compared to a nation's? There are much more important things at stake these days.'

'If you don't care about me then say it. Don't hide behind this political nonsense. I want to hear the truth from you!' Ana cried out of frustration and anger.

'If you don't know how I feel towards you after all these years, then you're not the person I thought you were. Stop being so immature and act like the powerful person I know you can be!' Jan replied just as heatedly as Ana had.

'Well, I guess I'm not that person, if you're unable to explain yourself,' Ana snarled, and walked away from him.

Chapter Thirty-Seven

Ana couldn't sleep well that night. She kept turning and tossing, thinking of all the things she could have said to Jan, things she should have said and, most importantly, things she would have loved to tell him. When she finally fell asleep, she had terrible dreams. They were a combination of her usual nightmare of the soldier she had killed, but this time, for some reason, when she looked at the soldier, his face was Jan's.

The next morning, as she remembered the dream, she thought it may be a metaphor for her relationship with Jan.

It's as dead as that soldier.

She knew she had to get out of the apartment; to find a quiet place that would feel safe and allow her to deny her fears. A place where she could be occupied enough to focus on something other than those fears and her nightmares.

The only place that came to mind was the local library. She'd finished reading all the medical books and magazines a long time ago, so today she decided she would search for other topics that might capture her heart.

Ana wandered down a section of the library when she came across a book about the Jews of Prague. She noticed that many shelves in this section were half empty. *Interesting. I wonder why?* She asked the librarian, who had a smile on her face.

'It used to be the religious studies section. Many of the books were banned and confiscated after the invasion. But I tricked them,' she whispered with a mischievous twinkle in her eye. 'I managed to hide some of the rare and old books before the StB came to confiscate them. If you ever want to read some interesting philosophical and religious issues, let me know.'

Ana didn't think she had any interest in religion, and certainly not philosophy. 'But why did they leave this book about the Jews, while other religious books were confiscated?' she asked.

'Another spark of genius on my side. I wasn't willing to let those hooligans and ignorant people rob me from my precious books. So, I catalogued many of them under Art and History and even Science. So, when they came in to confiscate the books, they only searched the names of authors or the politics and religion sections. Those were the books they took away. That's how I managed to hide more than six hundred banned books under their noses. Serves them right! Who do they think they are to censor what people can read and learn?' she concluded with cold fury.

Ana liked this woman and her passion for her books. *I wish I could find this kind of passion again.* She recalled the librarian telling her about bookstores that printed banned literature. *Maybe I'll go on a treasure hunt for them - that will give me something to do.* The thought of wandering in the streets of her beloved city hunting for secret bookstores excited her.

The next few weeks, Ana used her vast knowledge of the city to look for those bookstores. She was astonished to find how many new alleys and streets she discovered. Not only that, but she found many stores she had no idea existed. But each time she mentioned names of magazines or books she knew were banned, she was shown the door. She had to find a way to express what she wanted without becoming suspicious.

After weeks of this search, she concluded that, in order to find those shops, she needed someone who would give her an introduction. The only person she knew was the librarian, but she wasn't willing to risk it.

One cold morning, Ana was on her usual search when she bumped into Jan. She had not heard from him in weeks. He looked even more like a homeless person now compared to the Jan she'd known. His clothes had clearly not been washed for weeks. He was never a big guy, but now it seemed as if he was shrinking, and when she looked at his face his eyes were shining with feverish ambition.

'Ana! I'm so happy to bump into you,' he cried out. Ana didn't know how to respond to that. On the one hand she wanted to scream at him for forgetting all about her. On the other hand, her heart fluttered.

Maybe there is still hope.

'I'm organising an important meeting tomorrow at Fritz's Cafe,' he continued. 'It would mean a lot to me if you could join us.'

So no, nothing has changed. There is no hope.

'What is it about?' she asked, trying to sense what she might be getting herself into.

'When you get there, you'll hear, just like everyone else,' he replied, which made Ana uncomfortable.

'What's all this secrecy? I mean, you can trust me,' she remarked in an attempt to get more information.

'Just be there at five. Come from the entrance below, the door will be unlocked.' He then raced down the street before she could ask him anything else.

The next day was one of those cold and windy winter days in Prague, where each step you take the wind pushes you two steps backwards. Ana put her head down and forced herself through the streets, fighting the wind until she reached Fritz's Cafe.

She paused to check there was no one on the street and dashed down the stairs to the basement entrance. The door, as Jan promised, was unlocked and she entered. It took her a few seconds to adjust to the darkness, but also to get her blood circulation back after escaping the freezing cold outside.

She climbed up the stairs and entered the cafe itself. In a dark corner, Ana noticed Jan sitting with a few other students, debating and writing notes. *He still has that leadership quality,* she noted as she approached the group.

'What are you all writing?' she asked to get their attention, as none of them had even noticed her coming in.

'We're going to take a stand against "normalisation". People forgot what we were fighting for,' Jan said, turning towards her and giving her an unexpected hug.

'I don't think people forgot. How can anyone forget such a thing? People are just afraid,' Ana replied.

Jozef, one of the ex-students that was there, made a disagreeing noise. 'Nothing is being done. Dubček came back from Moscow where he signed those damn Moscow Protocols that took away everything we fought for.'

Ana could hear echoes of Jan's statements in the young man's words. She realised Jan now had a group of admirers who were repeating everything he said, just like she had only a few months before. She couldn't help but wish they would think for themselves instead of simply repeating what Jan believed.

'It's only on the surface. Look what happened after we won the game against the Soviets,' she noted, trying to show them another way of looking at what was taking place. But Jozef was not taking it the way she intended. He used it to counter her own argument.

'Exactly. Dubček called for a state of emergency and a police crackdown.'

Ana looked around the table and saw the rest of the group nodding their heads in agreement with his statement.

The moment had come for Jan to reveal what the whole meeting was about.

'It's worse,' he said. People believe there is no other way, that we cannot fight the Soviets. We need to take actions that will shock people.'

Ana became nervous. She hadn't noticed it before, but every time she listened to Jan, she experienced fear and anxiety.

'What do you mean to shock people?'

Jan's reply made it clear he was ready to go all the way, no matter what the price was. 'We must take actions that will set the country on fire.'

That scared Ana. She looked around the table and saw that no one was going to argue with Jan. Even if they had thought he was suggesting something too dangerous, no one would contradict him. Ana was the only one that might stand up to him.

'I agree. But we can't fight a whole army. Staying alive is crucial,' she said.

Jan sniffed with disdain. 'You sound like Helen. Pavel would say it's a man's duty to fight evil with every ounce of his strength.'

Ana was furious. Jan had no right to bring her parents into this discussion. It was OK to say such things between just the two of them, but in public she felt a need to stand by her parents.

'Leave my parents out of this. Listen to what I'm saying. I agree with you, but life is sacred,' she stressed.

'We need to remind people of the spirit of freedom,' he said firmly. 'You're either with us or not. Will you join us?'

Ana looked around and watched the reactions on the faces of the other students. They all looked at her, waiting for her answer. Ana had no intention of making promises before she knew what she was committing herself to. *I've done that before, and it did me no good.*

'First, tell me what you're planning.'

'No, it doesn't work like that.' Jan said. 'First you commit, and then we'll let you know. You need to want freedom so badly you'd be willing to do whatever it takes.' That made Ana feel even more cautious about the whole thing.

'I want freedom, but I have others who I need to think of. They might pay the price for my actions. I can't have it.'

It seemed this time that Jan listened to her, but he wasn't willing to give up. He knew what was disturbing her. 'Don't let Helen's fears determine your decisions.'

Ana thought about it. She wasn't sure anymore whether it was her mother's fears that were holding her back, or her own doubts on the merits of fighting a lost cause; even when it was justified.

'I need to think about it,' she said. She could see Jan's disappointment.

It wasn't meaningful enough for him to withdraw or change his plans. 'You have until the day after tomorrow. If this is your decision, you cannot stay here anymore. We're discussing who's going to be the first one.' This sounded even more ominous.

'The first one for what?'

Jan was determined. She'd never seen him as fierce as he was now. 'When you commit, you'll know.'

Ana stood up, staring at Jan while putting on her coat and scarf. Her gut was telling her that nothing good was going to come out of his plan. She knew she had to say something.

'Don't do something you'll regret. I don't want to lose you,' she mumbled as he helped her with her coat.

He leaned towards her and gave her a long hug. 'Only acts of heroism will make a difference,' he whispered. 'Otherwise, people live a life of quiet desperation. We can't let it happen.' Ana hugged Jan tightly.

Before she left, she turned one more time towards the group, and at that moment an unexpected ray of light broke through the window and shone over Jan's head. It made it look as if he had a halo. Ana saw it as a sign, but whether it was an omen for good or bad, she had no clue. All she knew was that Jan only saw her as a friend.

He'd never loved her the way she'd loved him.

***

On the way home, Ana felt as if a chapter of her life had just closed. She was hurt and even humiliated.

I was nothing to him but a toy to play with. She couldn't forgive herself for allowing him back into her life and derailing her from the track she had been on.

Tears were running down her cheeks by the time she got home. She was so trapped in her thoughts that, when she entered the apartment, she didn't even bother to hide the fact she was crying.

'What's going on? What happened?' Helen asked her when she passed through the living room without saying anything. It was the cue Ana needed. She told her mum all about her meeting with Jan and what had happened.

'You were right all this time, mum. Jan was bad for me. If it wasn't for him, I would have never joined the Student Union and I would still be studying today. Now everything is ruined and it's all his fault. I would have never killed that soldier if I hadn't followed him and believed in his cause.'

She was now crying so badly she couldn't speak anymore. All her mother did was hug her. When she finally stopped crying, Ana was afraid to look at her mum. She was afraid Helen would say, 'I told you so.'

'Whatever he did, he was always a good friend and protected you.'

Ana didn't have the courage to tell her mother that not only did she think he never really loved her, but that she'd lost her virginity to him. *Not the kind of thing you speak about with your mother.* But somehow, Helen was more perceptive than Ana credited her.

'No matter what he did,' she whispered to Ana, 'he will always be your first love, and that is important. It was real.'

Chapter Thirty-Eight

Ana had another restless night.

Hearing her mother approving of her love for Jan had confused her. She was sure Helen disliked Jan to the point of hating him, so why would she tell her he had been a good friend? *A friend,* Ana thought sadly. *Not a boyfriend. Tereza was wrong - he never really adored or wanted me.*

Though she was awake for a long time, Ana didn't have the energy to face her parents; especially Helen, after the talk with her the night before.

There's nothing for me to do, anyway. I might as well spend the day in bed. But after an hour she couldn't take it any longer. She was never one to stay late in bed.

She padded through to the kitchen in her slippers. She could hear her parents in the next room, talking in low voices. As she waited for the water to boil while spreading some of her mother's homemade jam on toast, her mother's low hiss caught her attention.

'No, we can't tell her. It will destroy her.'

Pavel sighed. 'She will find out anyway. We can't keep it from her forever.'

Ana moved to the kitchen doorway in a bid to eavesdrop better. She could hear her mother's intake of shaky breath; the tears in her voice.

'But this was Jan. You can't imagine how much she loved him.'

Loved?

'Why the past tense?'

Both Pavel and Helen visibly jumped as Ana materialised in the living area next to them. They proffered hasty smiles, making a forced attempt to pretend all was well. Both their demeanours were brittle, like they might shatter to pieces on the rug. Ana could sense the sorrow in the air.

'What's happened?' she demanded.

'Nothing…' Helen began, but stopped when Pavel shook his head at her.

'No, Helen. She deserves the truth.'

Fear surged through Ana as Pavel gestured to her to sit down. She heard his low, gentle words as he explained, but struggled to make sense of them.

She rushed to the radio, turning it up.

'A human torch on the steps of the National Museum shocks the nation. Jan Palach, a twenty-year-old philosophy student, has set himself on fire as a symbol of protest against the attitude of acceptance of the new normalisation. In a letter, he said that he's the first of nine other students that will follow the same action until the censorship ceases.'

'No, I don't believe it,' Ana said, her voice flat; almost robot-like. 'Jan wouldn't do that.'

Pavel did not try to dissuade her. Ana looked into his eyes and saw the glassy shine of tears, and finally it clicked.

It was true.

Ana jumped to her feet and rushed towards the front door, her parents' voices behind her, calling her back. She ignored them.

She wrenched open the door and was out into the courtyard, running past the *three witches*, who laughed, asking her what the hurry was when she was still dressed for bed.

Ana raced onwards, snow slush leaking through her thin slippers. Within moments her feet and body became numb, but it didn't matter. The harsh, cold air filled her lungs, catching in the back of her throat.

She had to see for herself.

The museum building was shuttered and all but deserted except for a single soldier standing sentry. He barely flinched as Ana ran pell-mell past him in her pyjamas, until she tried to run up the steps – still cordoned off with incident tape.

Ana felt strong hands grab her by the shoulders, holding her back. Without thinking, she fought and screamed like a child in a tantrum.

'I need to see! I need it!'

The soldier seemed to understand this and let go; or perhaps she slipped from his grasp. Ana made it up onto the steps, her eyes glued to the smoky, burnt spot at the top by the museum doors. Her nose wrinkled as she registered the acrid smell of petrol where, just a few hours earlier, Jan had poured accelerant all over his head and body and set himself alight.

Her love and inspiration were gone.

Gasping from his unexpected run, Pavel appeared beside her, holding a blanket. He wrapped it around Ana, who'd been unaware how hard she was shaking until she felt her father's loving embrace.

'Why? How... How could he do this?' Ana murmured.

'Come on,' Pavel said, 'there are no answers here.'

The strength seemed to leave Ana in an instant. She lurched against her father, unable to hold herself upright. Pavel caught her and kissed the top of her head. He picked her up with ease, holding her like he had when she was a child with nightmares; though this nightmare was only too real.

He carried her home.

When Pavel and Ana entered their apartment, Helen rushed towards Ana and held her in her arms until Ana gasped for air.

'I should have guessed. I should have stopped him. Last night when I left him, I felt as if it was the last time I'd see him… but I would have never guessed he would do something horrific like this.' She started sobbing again.

'You couldn't have stopped him. Why did you think he might do something drastic?' her father asked.

'His last words to me were, "Only acts of heroism will make a difference. Otherwise, people live a life of quiet desperation. We can't let it happen."'

There was silence in the room, only Ana's deep breathing could be heard.

'No one knows the strength of the human soul and the lengths one might go to for something they believe in,' Pavel said after a while. 'In my book, he's a hero.'

This pushed a button for Ana and all at once she stopped crying, her sadness turning into a cold rage.

'No, he's not. He's a fool. Freedom is important, but one shouldn't die for a dream. A dream needs to be something we can live up to, not die for. It cannot be that death is the price for a dream. To think he wanted me to join him! I'm so furious! I can't forgive him.'

Neither Helen nor Pavel knew what to say to her. They both knew how much their daughter loved Jan, and hearing her say those words made them sad. They'd both learned, a long time ago, how difficult it was for forgiveness to take place and that, without it, one would live a haunted life. However, it was too soon to say any of that to Ana.

Suddenly something clicked in Ana's head.

'That reporter… he said there were more, right?'

'He said that Jan wrote he was the first of nine other students that would follow him,' Pavel said.

'Oh no… I know who they are. I was there when they all signed the agreement. I couldn't stop Jan, but I'm damn well going to stop the others from making this foolish mistake.'

Ana was determined; she grabbed her coat and was on her way out when Pavel stopped her.

'You stay here. You can't go out in the state you're in. I'll look for them. Where should I start? Give me their names and I promise I'll find them.'

Ana's cold, furious rage dissipated, and exhaustion overcame her. She was more than happy to let her father search for the others. She also knew that he might be able to convince them better than she could.

'Start at Fritz's Cafe. Here, I'll write down their names.'

By the time she finished, Pavel was dressed to go out into the cold again.

Chapter Thirty-Nine

The next day, Ana woke up with no recollection of how she fell asleep. The last thing she remembered was her mum handing her that sweet, warm drink. After that, everything went black until she woke up. It took her a few minutes before she remembered everything that had happened the day before. She remembered her father's promise to find the other nine students.

Was it only three days ago that I had my last hug with Jan? It felt like a lifetime ago.

Ana dragged herself out of bed into the living room. The radio was on with all kinds of interpretations on the effects of Jan's self-immolation. Reporters were calling him a 'hero'. Ana crossed the room and shut off the radio in anger.

'Where's dad?' she asked Helen, who was clearing up the remains of breakfast from the table.

'He had to go to work. Some of us still need to show up at work.'

Ana ignored the hint of criticism in her mum's words. She didn't want to start a fight with her now that she'd started to appreciate her wisdom.

'Did he manage to find the students I spoke about?'

'I don't think so. He came back early this morning after spending the whole night looking for them. It seems they've disappeared from the face of the earth. I think it's for the best.'

Ana wasn't satisfied with this answer. 'I'm going out to

look for them myself. I can't just sit here. I need to know I did everything I could to stop another person doing this insane act.'

'Ana, it's not on you to do this. They made their own decisions. Isn't that what you were fighting for? For freedom?'

'You don't get it. They are following Jan blindly just as I did. I might have lost my future, but they might lose their lives!'

She grabbed her coat and went out of the house.

This time the *three witches* only gave her a nod of recognition. But after she passed them, she could hear them whispering.

'That Jan, the one who burned himself? That was her Jan. Always a hero.'

Ana wanted to turn around and tell them that he was never 'her' Jan, and nor was he a hero, but finding the other students was more important.

Ana started at the last place she'd seen them at Fritz's Cafe. But the place was deserted. Even the back door was blocked with barrels. She went to all the other places she knew were used as hiding places since the invasion. However, they were all locked or, worse, surrounded by soldiers.

Out of desperation, Ana decided to go to Jan's place. *Maybe I'll find a clue as to where they might be.*

She ran up the stairs to his apartment. The door was locked, but she remembered Jan telling her there was a key hidden in the crack in the wall next to the window. She felt around until she found the crack, and her fingers touched the key. As she pulled it, she scratched her fingers on the rough stone. She was bleeding.

Ana opened Jan's door and looked for a piece of cloth to wrap around her hand.

Looking around the room, she noticed how neglected the place was. It was in even worse condition than when she'd seen it through the window last time.

No time for daydreaming. It's over. Remember why you're here.

She started to search between the different notebooks and papers that were all over the place. She had no idea what she was looking for, but she had to find a clue. It was like looking for a needle in a haystack. Some of Jan's writings made sense, but some were broken sentences that made no sense. She noticed how his handwriting had changed. Some papers were written in beautiful handwriting, and some were so incoherent that she wasn't able to read them. Ana was so engrossed trying to decipher one of those incoherent papers that she didn't hear the door open.

'Who are you?'

Ana nearly jumped out of her skin. She turned around to find herself facing Jan's mother.

'What are you doing here?' his mother asked.

Ana's mouth was dry, and she couldn't find her voice. She knew it looked bad.

'I know you,' Jan's mother said, 'You're that girl he always protected. You're…

'Ana. Ana Sveboda.' The women stood staring at one another.

After a few minutes, Ana finally got a hold of herself.

'I loved him. I had to come here and see if I could make any sense of it.' She could feel the tears building up in her eyes and her throat was burning.

'So, you're the one that wrote that note? I found it yesterday. I don't think he ever saw it. I wish you would have said it to him; maybe it would have stopped him from doing this terrible thing.'

Ana didn't know if she was embarrassed that his mother had read her note, or that she had to discuss this with her.

'I did try to stop him. But he wasn't listening to me. I…'

'If you really loved him, you would have found a way to do it. You were with him these last few months. You saw him and did nothing,' she seethed at Ana. 'It's on you and all those who didn't care enough for him, who allowed him to do this crazy act.'

Ana realised she would never be able to convince Jan's mother of anything different. She could recognise the same anger his mother had in her own. She'd lashed out at her own parents, who had only ever wanted to support her. Jan's mum had no one, so she was lashing out at Ana.

'I'm truly sorry,' Ana said as she made to leave the apartment. 'It hurts me, maybe not as much as you, but believe me it is painful. I honestly can't make sense of his actions.'

Walking back home, Ana suddenly recognised that part of her anger wasn't directed at Jan; it was directed at herself, because she hadn't been able to stop him.

Jan's mother's words had struck a chord.

That's why it hurts so much.

Chapter Forty

Ana returned home late that night, feeling exhausted and anxious. Jan's mother's words were still ringing in her ears. She also hadn't been able to find anyone from the group of students she had met in the café with Jan. It was as her father had said, *they had disappeared into thin air.*

Everywhere she went, people were talking about how Jan was brave, using the same words her father had used, 'a hero'. But Ana couldn't help but disagree with them.

He betrayed me. I lost everything because I followed and believed in him, and now he's gone. What kind of love was that?

Her gut feeling told her that the more people talked about Jan as a hero, the more it would encourage the others to follow in his footsteps. Ana couldn't fathom more young people dying in such a horrific way.

She entered her parents' apartment to find them sitting, waiting for her.

'Did you find them?' her father inquired. From the look on her face, he didn't need an answer.

'Come, I'll warm you some soup,' Helen said. 'You need it after a whole day out in this cold.'

Ana took off her coat and got closer to the fireplace. Only now did she notice how cold she was from hours roaming the streets, following 'breadcrumbs' in search of the students.

'Soup would be heaven,' she said, sitting down at the table.

Both her parents sat opposite her, waiting for her to tell them what was going on. Ana appreciated their silence and the fact they didn't insist on getting information from her immediately. She wasn't ready to talk yet.

The radio was playing some classical music when all at once it stopped and a reporter announced that they had managed to secure an interview with the doctor who had treated Jan.

'Shut off that radio!' Ana didn't wait for her parents to do it. In a few quick steps she shut it off so violently it nearly fell.

'The radio isn't your enemy,' Pavel remarked. However, Ana was not going to back off. She felt angry and furious, which was the only way she could cope right now.

'Anger never solved anything,' Helen said in a soft voice. Ana hadn't expected it, but for some reason her mother's tone calmed her down.

'I met Jan's mother today. She practically blamed me for what he did.'

'She what? How dare she?!' Helen was outraged. Suddenly, Ana comprehended how her mother would always protect her against anyone who would dare to threaten her. *Another side of her I never knew.*

'I can understand it wasn't easy to hear that from her. But why are *you* angry?' her father asked.

Good question. Ana took her time to answer, not because she didn't want to, but because she had to arrange her thoughts.

'I guess the bottom line is that I feel betrayed. He didn't trust me. I trusted him utterly and gave up on everything I ever wanted because I believed in him. He, on the other hand, didn't trust me enough to tell me what he was going to do, and now it's too late. I'm so furious at him! He left me all alone with nothing to believe in. I can't forgive him for stealing away my life and my dream.'

Ana noticed both her parent's faces were gloomy. She didn't know what made them so downhearted; whether it was the situation or how she felt.

I can hardly take care of my own feelings, let alone someone else's.

She was angry at Jan, herself, the Communist Party, and the people in the country who'd given up. Even at her own parents. She knew they were always there for her and constantly on her side. But somehow, this great ball of fire of her anger was drawing them into it. All she saw was red.

'I'm going to sleep,' she announced, walking to her room, knowing very well what she meant to say was *I don't want to talk about it anymore.*

The reports on Jan's condition kept on being the top news everywhere, but Ana refused to listen or read anything that had to do with him. Her only escape was the library.

She hid herself away, pretending to search for new books. She also tried to find those books that were disguised as art but were actually banned ones.

That morning, she was in the children's section when she recognized Rabbi Siddon entering the library. *What is he doing here?* She was about to go and speak with him when she noticed the librarian nodding to him. They then disappeared into one of the remote aisles. Ana became even more curious. She followed them in a parallel aisle and could hear them whispering. She was too far to hear what was exchanged. Rabbi Siddon gave the librarian a package. In return, she gave him a stack of books. That was even more mysterious for Ana. She knew something strange was taking place but couldn't figure it out.

She returned to her table and pretended to read while keeping her eyes on the reception table. When she saw the librarian return, she picked up one of the books and pretended to be returning it.

'Who was that man that just left?' she asked, feigning ignorance. 'I think I recognised him.'

'Oh, that was Mr. Siddon,' the librarian said breezily. 'He returned some books that he borrowed for some sick people in his community.'

'I thought he went by the name Rabbi Siddon? I think he was the one that taught me the Hebrew alphabet when I was young.' That caught the librarian's attention.

'So, you know him? Didn't know you were Jewish. He's a good man.'

'So, what did you give him?' Ana asked, comfortable enough to let on that she'd seen their exchange.

'If you know him, then you should ask him. It's not my place to say.'

'Fine. I'll ask him. Thanks for the books.'

If she was quick enough, she might be able to catch him.

Ana left the library in a hurry. At first, she couldn't see Rabbi Siddon. But once she started walking and turned around a corner to enter a bigger street, she spotted him further down the road. She quickened her steps, but just before she was close to him, she slipped on the icy street. In a split second, someone's hand grabbed her arm, stopping her from falling on her face.

'Thanks,' she said, relieved. 'That was close.' She looked up, only to come face to face with Rabbi Siddon.

'You. Ana, by the way! It seems we always meet in the most unexpected ways,' Rabbi Siddon said with his light humour.

'True. But this time I was trying to catch up with you. I saw you in the library. I also saw the exchange you had with the librarian and wondered what it was all about.'

Rabbi Siddon didn't respond right away. She could see he was contemplating how to answer such a direct question.

'Why don't you come by the Jewish Museum tomorrow and we can talk.'

'Sounds good to me,' Ana answered, recognising that even if he wanted to tell her about it, the middle of the street was not the best place.

'Good. Walk with me now. I think we're going in the same direction.' They started walking in silence.

'What happened to your friend?' he asked after a while. 'The one that spoke about Jewish martyrs?'

'He's the one that self-immolated,' she said in a cold, robotic tone. 'That was Jan, my childhood friend.' That stopped Rabbi Siddon on the spot.

'Oh. I'm so sorry to hear that. I should have put two and two together. You're probably devastated. Is there anything I can do to help you in this painful time?'

'I'm just angry. I'm angry the whole time. I'm angry at him. I'm angry at myself. I'm angry at life. All I can think of is how I couldn't stop him from doing this horrific action. The more I think about it, the angrier I become. Can you help with that? No. I don't think you can,' she said bitterly.

Rabbi Siddon stopped walking and found a bench to sit down on. He indicated to Ana to sit next to him.

'You're right. I can't help you. Actually, no one can. The only person that can help you is you. You would have to accept that some things are not in your control. Actually, most things. The only thing that is one hundred percent in your control is how you respond to things.

'Right now, you are reacting, not responding. You are angry. It's human and it's normal and to be expected. But with time, you'll need to accept that it wasn't in your hands to stop him. You'll have to forgive him for choosing that direction. Even more difficult, you'll have to forgive yourself.

'The only advice I can give you is to be kind to yourself. Don't judge yourself so hard.'

Ana could understand what he was saying, but the whole concept was so strange to her that she felt he was talking in a foreign language.

'I wouldn't even know where to start.' she said.

'As I said, why don't you come to the Jewish Museum? I could use some help there. Maybe you'll find something there that will engage you, so you won't think about what happened.'

That sounded like a good thing, so she agreed to visit him the following week.

Chapter Forty-One

The next day was cold and grey, but that didn't stop thousands of people congregating on Wenceslas Square from the early hours. They were waiting for Jan's funeral to begin. They were all dressed in black and some carried Czechoslovakia flags to demonstrate how it was a national funeral, not a private one.

In their apartment, which was overlooking the square, Ana could see the thousands of people gathering on the streets. Even her own parents were going to attend.

'Are you sure you're not coming?' her father asked, standing at the open door looking at her. He was hoping something would convince her to join them in giving respect to Jan, whom he knew Ana had loved with all her heart.

'I can't. I'm still so angry, it would feel as if I'm being dishonest. I definitely can't honour him right now,' she mumbled.

Helen, dressed in her finest black clothes, came to stand next to Ana near the window.

'Remember, he died for something you believed in,' she said in a soft tone.

Instead of making her feel better, this triggered Ana. It felt like someone pouring fuel on the already existing fire inside her. She aggressively turned to face Helen.

'Since when did you support his cause? You always fought him. You thought he was a fool, which he was. You always said he was dangerous, which he was. Unfortunately, to himself rather than to anyone else. Don't be a hypocrite and now start telling me he was brave or a hero.'

'I'm not always right, you know. Maybe I was wrong about Jan,' she replied.

'No. You were right. Nothing is as important as life itself. I can see it now. When you love someone, you do anything to make sure they stay alive. No concept is more important than living a life with the ones you love. He didn't give me this option. I can't forgive him.'

Pavel joined Ana next to the window overlooking the square and beyond. It looked as if the whole city was out.

'Look outside, see what he created with his sacrifice. There are more people in the streets now than when you were resisting the tanks.' He hoped she would be able to see beyond her own personal pain.

'Half a year ago they invaded our country, but they haven't broken our spirit. This is what Jan's legacy is about,' Helen added. But Ana was beyond reason by now.

'I prefer having Jan, not his legacy. I'm done with idealism,' she said in a bitter voice.

'Whether you want it or not, he'll be with you for the rest of your life. At least give yourself a chance to say goodbye to him. Why don't you join us at the funeral?' Pavel urged.

Ana turned her back to her parents so they wouldn't see the tears running down her cheeks.

Pavel and Helen waited at the open door for a while to see if Ana might change her mind. When she didn't turn around, they stepped out of the apartment.

Left alone, Ana turned again to the window and watched thousands of people march in silence, carrying flags in respect of Jan.

All she felt was numb.
Something inside of her died too that day.

Chapter Forty-Two

The day after Jan's funeral Ana, along with the rest of her building, were woken up to the sounds of hammers banging on the street.

A few minutes later a knock on their door came. Pavel went to open it. Standing on the doorstep were two policemen. They handed Pavel a letter addressed to Ana.

A few months before, Ana had written a letter to the university requesting that they reconsider the decision of banning her from studying. She was hoping they had accepted her appeal. She tore the envelope open eagerly, reading it out loud.

'The Council of Higher Education hereby informs you that after serious consideration, you are not permitted to continue your higher education. It has been noted that you have been a registered Student Union member. Not only that, but it has also been mentioned several times that you were one of the leaders of the union, supporting the anti-state demonstration. Thereby, any university in Czechoslovakia is prohibited from allowing you to study.'

Ana dropped the letter. She had to sit down; she wasn't sure she trusted her body to remain upright. She was shaking. It was like hearing her own death sentence.

Up until this moment, Ana had still had hope that, after the dust settled, she would be able to study again to become a doctor. But this letter had closed the door on that chapter of her life. She couldn't conceive of how she could continue.

Helen returned from outside, where she'd gone to see what the police had hung up in the street.

'It's a list of all those they suspect of being subversive to the republic,' she said sombrely. 'Ana is on the list.'

For Ana, it felt like the last nail in her coffin. Being on that list meant no one would even consider giving her a job.

What am I going to do with my life? She had no energy even to cry.

'I know it looks like a bleak future, but you'll find your way,' her father said, as if hearing her thoughts.

'I'm going back to bed,' was her only response. *What else can I do?* She didn't see her parents' sad looks following her to her room.

'There's nothing we can do for her just now,' Pavel said to Helen. 'Time will heal it. Give her time. If I can rise up again after the war, then so can she. She's stronger than me. She will do it.'

***

For the next week, Ana spent most of her time in bed. If it was up to her, she wouldn't have eaten, but Helen would not hear of that. She made sure that Ana had at least one meal a day.

Helen was no stranger to depression, even if she didn't label it as such. She knew the signs. She also trusted that her daughter would be able to get herself out of it. But after a week of showing no signs of wanting to get out of bed, Helen had an idea to encourage Ana.

'Why don't you go to that library you used to go to? I'm sure you'd find something there to get you excited again.'

The thought of being in a library was too painful for Ana. But she appreciated her mother's attempt.

I could use some fresh air.

'I think I'll do it,' she said, and got up and dressed for the first time in a week.

Being outside in the fresh air did wonders for Ana. Though she intended to go to the library, her feet took her in all directions. It seemed as if something inside was guiding her more than her mind.

She first climbed up Petrin Hill and walked around the gardens. She knew Helen would freak out if she knew she was in that area. It was too close to Prague's castle, which was the headquarters of the Communist Party. But at least she had a fantastic view there of her beloved city. If it wasn't so cold, she would have stayed longer.

However, as she walked back to the old city, she noticed the first signs of spring: little white and orange crocus flowers popping up from the frozen ground. *Maybe it's a sign.* This thought cheered her up.

When she finally arrived at the library, Ana was half frozen from her long walk. Her lips were blue, and she could hardly speak.

'Do you have anything interesting you can recommend for me?' she asked the librarian.

'My god, you're freezing. Come, get close to the heater.'

'Oh, that would be fantastic. Thank you.'

The librarian took her to a back room which seemed like her office. There was even a small kitchen. Most importantly, it was much warmer than the library halls. Ana sat down on one of the chairs and rubbed her hands to get her blood circulation back. She then got closer to the small electric heater.

'Oh, I can finally feel my fingers and toes again,' she told the librarian, who handed her a cup of strong, steaming tea.

'I haven't seen you for a long time. What were you thinking wandering around in this cold weather?'

'I had to get some air. I have been in bed these past ten days. It's true it's cold outside, but it's beautiful and there are signs that spring is coming. I wish I could say the same for myself.'

'What do you mean?'

'I feel I'll be forever trapped in winter. There is nothing for me on the horizon and I have no clue what to do with my life.'

Once those words came out of her mouth, Ana had no idea how she could look into the librarian's face. She was so ashamed. *One doesn't express such thoughts to a stranger.*

'Why do you say that? You're young, you're smart, you're alive. Why the long face?'

Ana found herself telling her life story to the librarian: her dream of becoming a doctor, following her heart; ending up being involved with the Student Union due to the fact she fell in love with Jan, which had led to her being banned from higher education for life; and Jan's death. By the time she'd finished, her face was red. Regardless, whether it was the shame or the heater having such an effect on her, Ana finally felt like she could breathe freely; something she hadn't been able to do for weeks. She suddenly felt lighter, as if a heavy load had lifted from her chest.

After a long silence, she dared to raise her eyes and look at the librarian.

'I see now why you think there is no future for you,' she said, looking into Ana's eyes sympathetically. 'I think you have to get out of this country. It's not a place for young people anyway.'

This took Ana by surprise. Of all the things the librarian could have said, that had been the last thing she'd expected. Even if she wanted to do it, she wouldn't know where to start. It seemed as though the librarian heard her thoughts.

'The other day,' she said, 'I saw you speaking to Rabbi Siddon. Go meet with him. He has ways to get people safely to the West.'

Why am I not surprised? Ana thought. 'He did invite me several times to visit him in the Jewish Museum. Maybe I'll take him up on it. Thanks. I'm not sure I'll ever do it, but there's no harm checking it out.'

Chapter Forty-Three

It took several more days for Ana to gather the courage and to go to the Old Quarter. Even when she reached the place, she went around it several times. It was as if once she entered, it would be a declaration; that she was thinking of leaving her family and life behind.

She wasn't sure she was ready for it.

There was a small square just opposite the entrance. Ana sat down on one of the benches to get her thoughts in order.

She had been sitting for a few minutes when, out of the corner of her eye, she noticed two men on a faraway bench. They weren't policemen, but she was sure they were from the StB. They had the look of officials. One of them was staring at her. His look sent chills down her spine.

She wasn't safe anymore.

Ana stood up and started to go back home when the two men blocked her way.

'Ana Sveboda?'

'Yes. That's me.'

'Come with us.'

'Why? Who are you?'

'Who we are is not important. Who you are and what you're doing here in the Jewish Quarter is more important.'

'I'm like you said: Ana Sveboda. Am I under arrest or something?'

'Just come with us quietly. If you have nothing to hide, you'll be released in no time.'

Ana knew there was no point arguing with them. She followed them.

This time, it wasn't to the infamous Bartolomějská Ulice but to a local station, not far from the Jewish Quarter.

Ana was put into a small room with no windows. The door locked behind her. At least it was a warm room and had a table and two chairs. *For interrogation purposes for sure.* Ana couldn't even prepare a story, as she had no clue what it was all about.

It couldn't be about the dead soldier. *Could it?* Even if it was, she could blame Tereza.

After several hours, the door opened, and a heavy-looking woman stepped in. *That's different,* Ana thought. But the look on the woman's face was not reassuring.

'I have no clue why I am here,' Ana said to her. 'I've done nothing illegal.'

'No need to get defensive. It's just a routine check. You've been on the list of members of the Student Union. We need to routinely check on your whereabouts and what you're doing,' the woman said.

'Well, thanks to the "normalisation", I can't study anymore,' Ana replied in a bitter tone.

'You've also been named as the girlfriend of Jan Palach.'

'I wasn't his girlfriend. I knew him when we were young. That's all.'

'So, you're telling me you were not involved with his protest?'

'I hadn't seen Jan for at least two days before the invasion. During the invasion I was sick in bed, and you've already interrogated me on this twice.'

'No need to get upset. I'm just checking what you have been

doing since then. Besides, what were you doing in the Jewish Quarter?'

'I didn't know it was illegal to visit that place.'

What are you doing? Her rational voice scolded her. *Why are you fighting her? Just simply answer, don't get so feisty!*

The woman wasn't provoked and simply stared at Ana, waiting for an answer. It gave Ana an idea.

'I'm volunteering in the Jewish Museum. You can ask Rabbi Siddon,' she blurted out, without even thinking what danger that could put Rabbi Siddon in. She instantly regretted saying it but had no way to take it back.

The woman left the room. Ana could hear her phoning someone but was unable to hear what she was saying. She had no idea what the outcome of her lie would be. She was hoping they would bring Rabbi Siddon in, so that he would see her and maybe collaborate her story.

What if they only ask him if Ana Sveboda volunteers? I'm doomed.

Ana had no idea how much time passed, but it felt like forever.

Then, the door opened.

'You can go,' the woman said. 'Rabbi Siddon says you don't have to come in today, you can continue what you were working on tomorrow.'

Ana couldn't move any faster. Before the woman had even finished her sentence, she was out of the room and heading straight out of the building.

Chapter Forty-Four

Ana knew she had to go and meet Rabbi Siddon, even if just to thank him for covering for her. But Helen was too anxious to let her go after hearing about her 'adventure' with the StB.

'Mum,' Ana pleaded. 'I have to go. Besides, if they are following me, they'll be expecting me to go there today.' It didn't relax Helen, but Ana's point made sense.

It was only when Ana got to the Jewish Quarter that she realised she had no idea where she was supposed to go. *It's not as if I know where the Jewish Museum is.* But it seemed like someone up there had her back. Once she stepped into the small square, she saw Rabbi Siddon.

'Good to see you,' he said. 'We have a lot of work ahead of us.' Ana looked around and spotted the two men that had picked her up the day before. She now understood why Rabbi Siddon had waited for her there.

They stepped into an old building which had a small sign declaring it to be the Jewish Museum. Ana had another 'down the rabbit hole' experience. The whole place was a huge warehouse full of crates and boxes stuffed with artefacts and books. Strange objects, which Ana had never seen before, and scrolls of old manuscripts.

'What is this place?' she asked, in awe.

'This is what is called the Jewish Museum, and what is left from thousands of years of heritage and culture.'

'I still don't get it.'

'God works in mysterious ways. This is what the Nazis confiscated from the Jewish communities they destroyed. They intended to create a museum of the "extinct race" here in Prague. When the Soviets freed Prague, they saw it as an opportunity to prove their superiority over the Nazis by allowing us to keep them. They wanted to demonstrate how "our race" is still standing and rising from the ashes. They intended it to be a thorn in their eyes. Only now, they do not allow me to continue with the work. They are afraid it would be a place for free thinkers and rebels against the Communist doctrine.'

Ana chuckled. 'So, you're in the same predicament I am. Wanting to continue with what you believe is your mission, but a hostage of circumstances. Maybe we could help each other?'

Rabbi Siddon looked at her with interest. 'I'm listening.'

'I'm not allowed to continue with my studies, and you don't have the resources to catalogue all this treasure. I'm looking for something to do with my life. How about we work together? I'll catalogue this beautiful mess while you teach me about it all.'

Before she could finish, Rabbi Siddon had his hand out in front of him.

'You've got yourself a deal, young Ana.'

Ana shook his hand and noted how her heart was filled with the same excitement she used to have when studying for exams or preparing speeches with Jan.

Maybe I've found a new purpose?

***

Discovering a new purpose filled Ana with a wave of energy. She noticed how much she was looking forward to each day's work with Rabbi Siddon. She enjoyed learning more about Judaism. *There's still no censorship on private thoughts. It's not 1984 yet!* she thought when threatening thoughts crossed her mind.

Ana's librarian friend had managed to get her hands on a 'samizdat' copy of the book '1984', and had given it to her to read. Since then, she'd been obsessed with 'thought control' by the government. She loved the book and could identify so much with its protagonist, Winston Smith. She requested more writings of George Orwell, though she understood the danger she was putting the librarian in by searching for it.

'It's my own way of rebellion,' Ana explained. 'It's my way of proving to myself that I'm still not giving up on the idea of freedom and free thought. Though these days, those notions seem so far away.'

'I'll try and get it for you. You'd like it. I read it just after the war when it was first published. I got it from an English friend of mine. Unfortunately, George Orwell's books were banned and confiscated once the Communists took over this country. I couldn't save those books.

'I miss the days when free thinkers were valued, and free speech was encouraged. It feels as if we all have to be moulded into one template. All the colour of being a human is sapped out of us.'

Ana couldn't agree more. It had become clear to her that, though her daily routine consisted of spending hours with Rabbi Siddon, she was actually living a life of rebellion against the so-called 'normalisation'. It dawned on her that she was doing exactly what she was meant to be doing. On the surface, it was as if she'd accepted the invasion and its consequences, but in reality, she kept her hopes and beliefs for freedom while living her life as much as she could according to those ideals.

Ana's work with Rabbi Siddon was exciting. It opened a whole new world for Ana. She was never exposed to this world due to her mother's reluctance to speak about Judaism. Ana discovered she was able to bring the same passion and curiosity she'd had for her medical studies into this world of religion, art and culture.

When she started, she was embarrassed by how ignorant she was, but Rabbi Siddon never saw it as stupidity. On the contrary, he loved her questions and the fact she was eager to learn; he reminded her that it showed how much dedication and strength she had.

In time, Ana became an expert on all the different artefacts and could identify any item simply by looking at it; its region, era and origin. When it came to the scrolls and the written artefacts, she was still struggling, but with Rabbi Siddon's encouragement she'd resumed her Hebrew studies. In time, she was able to read the texts, despite not always understanding them. But even she, with her need for perfection, felt proud of what she had managed to achieve in such a short amount of time.

After nearly nine months of cataloguing all the items in the crates and boxes, Ana found herself writing down the last item in her notebook. For a few minutes she felt elated to have completed what had felt like an impossible mission when she'd started. She felt a sense of completion and success. But then, she experienced a wave of sadness.

Now what?

She couldn't even contemplate ending her work there. When Rabbi Siddon came in that evening to say goodbye, she urged him to find her new projects to help him with.

'This work was an education,' she said. 'Maybe not what I dreamed about, but I can't stop now.'

'How about creating a proper exhibition of these artefacts? Let's see if we can make an enticing showcasing of them in a way that would be a tribute and honour for those souls who died for them.'

Before he could finish, Ana was nodding her head with eagerness. She started measuring the space in her mind, visualising how it would look.

'We can create a timeline starting from the earliest ones to the latest. All we need are bookcases and shelves to put them on, and maybe we can put the more fragile items behind glass. With proper lighting it would look brilliant!'

'We'll need much more, but it's a start,' he said. 'How about you work on a plan of what items to put on display? I'll see where I can get the money for such an exhibition.'

'Sounds like a plan!' Ana said enthusiastically, back to her high-energy mood.

Ana skipped all the way back to her parents' place as if she was a child.

Strange how life is. I never thought I would find a purpose again, and here I am learning about ancient relics. She was so mesmerised in her thoughts that she didn't notice she'd been followed the whole time by the same two men who'd arrested her.

Only when she reached the courtyard did she notice them. They were talking to the *three witches*.

Figures, I always suspected them of being informants. I have nothing to hide.

When she entered her parents' apartment, Ana's cheerful energy was obvious.

'Your librarian friend brought you a package of books,' Helen told her. This was like the icing on the cake to end this cheerful day.

During dinner, Ana told her parents about the new project at the museum, but she was counting the seconds until she could go to her room and look at the package.

Soon after, she excused herself and went to her room.

Ana ripped the newspaper wrapping and searched through the package for the typewritten pages of the 'samizdat' copies of the banned books. The librarian usually hid them between the regular books.

The last thing Ana expected to find was a letter from Tereza. How Tereza had managed to send a letter without StB censorship was beyond Ana's comprehension, as was how it had found its way to the librarian. *Tereza always knew how to get what she wanted in spite of circumstances.*

Reading the letter made Ana happy. Tereza had found happiness in the United States. She was urging Ana to find a way to leave Prague and the old country behind. *Typical of Teresa not to think about limitations.*

Ana had to admit that, more than anyone else, Tereza embodied what freedom was. Ana wasn't sure she could ever be as free as Tereza, but a new hope was starting to rise in her heart.

***

A few weeks later, that hope became stronger.

Rabbi Siddon informed Ana that he'd managed to get a big donation from the Jewish congregation in the United States to create their exhibition, which he'd decided to call 'The Precious Legacy.'

Ana wanted to create a showcase of all the items they had in their possession, but she accepted that it would be impossible. They had over fifteen thousand artefacts, from wedding portraits and infant cradles to Torah scrolls and hand-embroidered synagogue fabrics. There was no way she could give them all credit. She would have to be selective. Her task was made even more difficult when the authorities, once they'd heard about it, said they weren't willing to allow them to display anything that had a direct religious implication.

How on earth can I do that, without killing the purpose of honouring the heritage?

The answer came a few weeks later, when the Communist Party authorities allowed them to present the children's drawings from the concentration camp, Terezín. Ana came up with the idea of presenting the artefacts the drawings were based upon next to them, along with some of the clothing and secret possessions of the camp's residents. Ana felt elated knowing she had outsmarted government restrictions again.

Ana managed to create an exhibition that told the stories of those victims while also educating people about their horrific living conditions, and how Jewish life had been maintained despite this dark period. It was a testament to their heroism, endurance and courage.

For months, Ana worked on that exhibition, even though she knew not many people would ever see it. She comprehended that the Jewish Museum did not have a permit from the authorities to be open to the public. The only thing that put a dampener on her joy was that she was constantly being followed by someone from the StB. Even Helen had started to notice it.

'You need to be more careful,' she'd warned. 'They are constantly keeping an eye on you.'

'Mum, they have nothing on me. I'm not doing anything that is not legal. You have to calm down.' Ana kept reassuring her. But as the weeks turned into months and they didn't cease following Ana, Helen became more and more agitated.

'It has to be because of your work in the museum. You have to stop.'

'No. It's the only thing that keeps me going. You can't take this away from me.' The conversation always ended with Helen having one of her attacks, and Ana feeling either guilty for triggering it or frustrated by it.

Ana realised that, even though she loved working on the exhibition, the work would come to an end sooner or later. *And then what will I do?*

Tereza's letter had shown her that there was the possibility of crossing the border without being shot or killed. She also remembered the librarian telling her that Rabbi Siddon had helped people get to the West.

Maybe it's time for me to leave? She had no idea how to go about it. Approaching Rabbi Siddon directly was too risky.

Chapter Forty-Five

One morning, Ana spotted Rabbi Siddon talking with two older men. There was no doubt those two men were from the West: they were wearing such fine suits you'd never find in any store in Prague; not even the Tuzek ones. Next to them were two other men who were without a doubt the StB. *You can't miss them, it's as if they all came out of the same assembly line.* The two foreigners were not trying to hide the fact they were not from Prague. *Who are they?*

'Here she is,' announced Rabbi Siddon. 'If anyone deserves any compliments on this small exhibition, it's this young lady. May I introduce you? Ana Sveboda, this is Senator Charles Vanik and Mark Talisman, both from the United States.'

Ana didn't want to, but she found herself staring at them as if they were specimens in a zoo. She had never seen anyone from the United States in real life. For her, the United States was as far away as the moon. Rabbi Siddon noticed Ana's bewilderment.

'They are here on a visit as part of a mission of East-West understanding. Charles here is a descendant of a Czech immigrant to the United States. Mark here is a good 'Jewish boy' who heard about our small museum. They wanted to see it. How about you show them your exhibition and maybe take them afterwards for refreshments out the back?' Rabbi Siddon suggested with a wink.

Ana knew exactly what he meant; he wanted her to show them all the other artefacts they had which were not officially allowed to be displayed.

Ana made sure the tour of the small exhibition was long and descriptive. She told stories about each and every item, keeping her eyes on the two secret policemen that accompanied them every step of the way. To her delight, they lost interest after a while and became impatient. When one of them took out a cigarette, she seized the opportunity.

'Please don't smoke here, it's not good for the exhibits. Why not go outside? There is only one entrance to this building.'

The two policemen exchanged some words between them and left.

Ana turned to her guests. 'Now I can show you the *real* treasure.'

She quickly took them to the back of the building where everything was organised with labels. The place was huge. Charles and Mark were astonished to find such precious objects.

'This is only what I was able to organise here in this space,' Ana explained, 'but I have endless crates and boxes full of more religious artefacts. I organised it by periods and geographical areas and took one, two or three specimens from each. The rest is still packed and stored, though I have made an inventory of everything.'

The shock on their faces did not need any explanation. They were clearly impressed.

Once they returned to the main hall, the policemen returned, and Rabbi Siddon joined them.

'Thank you for your hospitality and the nice refreshments,' Charles said. 'This exhibition is so unique; I think it must be displayed in other parts of the world. I wonder if Rabbi Siddon would be willing to consider having it on loan for a while in the United States?'

Ana turned to Rabbi Siddon, who was as surprised as she was.

'It would take a lot of time to organise it. I don't think I'll be able to do it or travel with it,' he began, but Mark intervened.

'What about Ana? She seems to be extremely knowledgeable. She might not be a museum curator, but she is more than capable of organising an impressive exhibition which is both emotional and educational.'

Before either Rabbi Siddon or Ana could say anything, the two Americans started throwing ideas around and making plans for the exhibition. Though Ana's English was good, the speed in which they spoke was too fast for her to catch everything. She could hear the words 'Smithsonian Institute' and 'Jewish Memorial Museum'. She had no clue what the latter was, but the Smithsonian was definitely something she knew of. She couldn't believe her small exhibition would be accepted there.

'We'll take care of the paperwork with the authorities,' Charles said, 'We know it will take time, but start thinking about how to take this exhibition "on the road" as we say in the United States. Oh, and make sure we also get the pleasure of the refreshments we got in the back.' Charles winked at Ana and Rabbi Siddon.

When they'd all left, Ana collapsed into the nearest chair she could find. She'd never imagined in her wildest dreams that her day would end up like this. Not only had she met two people from the United States, but she'd got an official invitation to travel there.

'Is this for real?' she uttered, looking at Rabbi Siddon.

'I thought they would be interested,' he said, just as shocked as she was. 'But I never imagined they would move so fast. It will take at least a year for the paperwork to be finished. We certainly need to think about what to ship, and how to transport them.

'In a way,' he mumbled, more to himself than to Ana, 'it's good we have this time. I'll need your help. No one knows what we have here better than you. I'll make some calls and see what we can come up with. You'll need to head this project. Are you ready to visit the United States?'

That's when Ana realised something she had not thought about before. 'I'm not sure they would allow me to go with the exhibition. I'm under surveillance. I'm certain they would not allow me to leave the country.'

'Do you want to?'

'I'm scared. I'm afraid my parents would pay the price for my actions. I can't do that to them.'

'Do you really think they would prefer that you give up on your hopes and future for their sake?'

Ana had never thought of it that way. 'But the authorities will never let me join this exhibition.'

'I'll find a way,' he said, 'Not for the first time. It's you who has to make the decision.' Rabbi Siddon looked intensely at Ana. 'You have an opportunity here, Ana. I know your heart is still longing to become a doctor. You will never be able to do it here in Czechoslovakia or in any of the Eastern Bloc countries. You're on the blacklist, no matter what you do. Your only hope is getting out of here to the West. Nowhere is better than the United States. When he left, Charles whispered that if, while you're on tour with the exhibition, you want to seek asylum, he'll take care of it. This is your ticket to freedom and fulfilling your dream of becoming a doctor, Ana.'

'I can't leave my parents. My mum would die if I left without ever coming back. I'm all she's got.'

'Your mother will not die. She will miss you very much, but she will not die. From what I gather she's a tough cookie. If the Nazis didn't kill her, then this won't either. If you wish, I could speak with her and show her why this is the best opportunity for you. She will want what's best for you, mark my words.'

Ana wasn't sure Rabbi Siddon was right, but it became clear to her that she needed to get out of Czechoslovakia. *It was nice doing this work, but I still feel like my life's mission is to become a doctor. I will never achieve it here. Maybe all this was a blessing in disguise; preparation for me to leave?*

'I think you're right,' she admitted. 'You work on how to smuggle me out of here, and I'll work on packing this exhibition.'

'That's easy. We'll create a special crate just for you with a double bottom. On the top will be some of the artefacts wrapped up well, but underneath will be another layer with air holes that you can hide in it until we reach Vienna. Lucky for us, your small size will be perfect for these crates.'

'Sounds like you've done this before. Did they all arrive in one piece?'

'I told you; I have my ways. Now, let's get to work.'

Chapter Forty-Six

Convincing Helen hadn't been easy.

Since Jan's death, Ana had valued her mother more than before. She'd adopted her way of looking at life. Helen had been right all along: life trumps idealism. That was Ana's new view of life.

It was because of this exact reason that she couldn't understand why her mother would not give her blessings to this plan. In her mind, this plan allowed her the chance to live the life she was meant to have. She was certain, more than ever, that she was destined to be a doctor. But no matter what she did, this could never happen if she stayed in Prague.

Ana kept arguing with Helen at any given opportunity, trying to convince her that the risk was not that high. Even Rabbi Siddon came over and shared with Helen how he'd managed to smuggle more than thirty Jewish people across the border to Vienna. However, when Helen heard that Ana would be cramped in a crate for more than twenty-four hours, her objections were raised again.

'What if she doesn't have enough air in there? What if they inspect the crates more thoroughly? I can't take the risk of losing her.'

Pavel tried to get Helen to agree. Ana was glad for the support, although he did point out that, in the end, they would be the ones to pay the price for her defection.

'Even if they fire me, we could always move out of Prague,' he reasoned.

'Where would we go?' Helen asked.

'I have a small house in the mountains. You remember Romain? My friend from the war? He always told me I could use it whenever I needed it. It's not much, but it's a place away from probing eyes and investigations.'

Helen still wasn't convinced that danger wasn't around the corner, no matter what Pavel or Ana told her. Nothing helped: Helen was not backing down.

Ana thought her mother was as stubborn as a mule. *I guess that's where I get my determination from*, she thought.

However, that did not stop Ana from continuing to plan her escape. She and Rabbi Siddon even had a plan B in place. Ana spoke with Tomas, Tereza's old boyfriend. Though officially he was working in the Tuzek shop, in reality he was smuggling illegal goods into Czechoslovakia. He had all the connections needed to cross the border without leaving a trace.

Ana wasn't aware how many months had passed since Charles Vanik and his aide had visited. At times, she thought it had only been a dream. Months passed and nothing was announced, but she kept on packing exhibits and 'refreshments'. She kept a tight inventory and, each time she sealed a box, she made a small prayer that the official approval would come soon.

***

In the blink of an eye, the sixties were over. A new decade.

Jan's memory had faded in the public's view, but not for Ana. She still couldn't read or listen to any news about politics. It reminded her of him, and she wasn't willing to forgive him for his betrayal and for ruining her life. Even now, when she had the chance to get out of Czechoslovakia, it would be at the price of losing her family, and *that's on him,* she kept telling herself.

One spring day she entered the museum at her usual time to find Rabbi Siddon waiting for her with a huge smile on his face.

'It's done. We got the approval. We're leaving in three days. As expected, they didn't give you permission to join me as an assistant. However, the document states that I can bring one assistant with me. One of the other volunteers will join me until Vienna. I will meet you in Vienna and you will board the plane with their papers.'

The next few days passed so fast Ana could hardly breathe. So much needed to be done.

Ana soon found herself spending her last night at her parents' place trying to pack for the journey.

'Mum, would you be willing to help me pack? You're so much better than me at packing,' Ana asked her mother in an attempt to get her on board. But Helen refused, locking herself in her bedroom and pretending as if none of it was happening.

Ana knew she had to pack so it would look as if the assistant was returning. The plan was that the assistant would take Ana's suitcase with her, while Ana was smuggled across the border to Vienna in Tomas's car. She couldn't take everything she wanted. She had only one suitcase, although it was an ancient one and therefore slightly bigger than the modern ones she'd seen in shops. It still didn't have the space for all that was dear to her. Each item she picked, she had to think twice whether to put it into the suitcase or not.

She looked around her room and picked up a few photos of

her and her parents. Behind one of those photos, she found a photo of her and Jan.

She hesitated.

In the end, she picked it up, wrapped it with a scarf and gently packed it into her suitcase. When she raised her head, she saw her father standing in the doorway watching her.

'Are you ready?' he asked, looking around at the mess in her room.

'How do you pack a lifetime into a small suitcase?' Ana asked with tears in her eyes. The realisation that this might be the last time she would ever see her parents had finally hit her, and the sheer sadness of it was hard for her to take.

'Don't think too much. Think like you're packing for a long vacation,' her father replied.

Ana appreciated her dad's attempt to sound practical, but it wasn't so easy to do when you were aware that the destination was one-way.

'I'll miss you so much, ' she said, hugging him. 'Promise you'll take care of mum. I know it's hard for her, but I really must do this.'

Her father smiled. 'I know you do. As for your mother, I've always taken care of her and always will. Don't worry, she knows she needs to let you go, but it'll just take her time to adjust.'

Both of them were astounded to hear the door of Helen's bedroom open. Helen stepped out, holding something that looked like a gift.

'Your father is right. I knew the whole time that it's the right thing for you to do, but I couldn't bear saying goodbye. But I'd never forgive myself if I don't.'

Ana, who already had tears, couldn't control them anymore and rushed to hug her mother, who stopped her.

'I have something for you.' She unwrapped the package. To Ana's surprise it was the Sabbath candlesticks. 'They belonged to my grandmother. I was hoping to give them to you on your wedding day, but I guess today is as good a time as any. Who knows if I will ever get to see you married.'

Ana wrapped the candlesticks and packed them inside her suitcase. She did it with such care and honour, as though they might break at any moment. She wanted to give them the respect they deserved, and most of all to let her mother know how much she appreciated the gesture. Once she was sure it was packed safely, she turned to hug her mother.

'You both gave me the foundation to know where I came from, and the wings to fly wherever I wish. If I ever have kids, I'll remember this as the greatest gift I could give them. I promise I'll honour you by doing it.'

The next morning Ana, Rabbi Siddon and the assistant were on the platform waiting for the train that would take them to Vienna. They said their goodbyes and, once the train left, Ana walked home, where Tomas was waiting for her in his Skoda car.

'We need to move now if we want to get to the border before night falls,' Tomas whispered to Ana as he hugged her tightly.

'Let me just say one last goodbye to my parents. I need to make it look like we're going on a short drive to the country.'

'Fine. But do it fast.'

To Ana's horror, the *three witches* were in the courtyard watching her hug with Tomas.

'So, you now have a new boyfriend. He looks much better than the previous one,' Mrs. Hudek croaked as Ana passed them.

'Why don't you mind your own business?' Ana couldn't resist the retort. *How much harm could she do to me now?*

Ana went up to her parents' apartment.

She had no clue what to say to them. To her relief, neither of them expected any more words. They simply held each other.

When Ana gave her mum a final hug, Helen whispered one last piece of advice.

'Don't be Lot's wife. Once you get there, never turn back. Go and live your life and make the best out of it.'

She then grabbed Pavel's hand and, with the other, pushed Ana out of the door and locked it behind her.

Ana had to dry her eyes before stepping into the courtyard where she knew the *three witches* would be watching her like a hawk. She put on a big smile as she rushed across the courtyard to Tomas.

'Can't wait to meet him?' the *three witches* laughed. 'Wrong strategy. Let him wait for you! Young women, they don't know how to get a man interested in them these days!'

Chapter Forty-Seven

Ana didn't know if she was expected to talk with Tomas or not. Regardless, she was too nervous to say anything.

'It's a two and half hours' drive to Mikulov,' he told her. 'It's the closest town to the border. You will have to hide under the luggage compartment. This model has a wider space, though with your size you could fit in any model,' Tomas laughed.

'I guess it's better than being trapped in the crate for three days. Thanks so much for this,' was all she could say back to him.

'Don't mention it. Just promise me that when you get to the United States, you'll try and find Tereza and send her my love.'

'I promise.' The rest of the way they remained silent, each trapped in their own thoughts.

Once they got to the outskirts of Mikulov, Tomas took a side road and stopped at an abandoned field. Ana got out of the passenger seat and climbed into a chamber that was under the luggage compartment.

'Most important now is that, when you hear the car stop, you can't move or make any noise. Be totally silent. It won't be for a long time. Just an hour or an hour and a half, depending on how long they stop me at the border. Once we cross to Austria you can get out,' Tomas reassured her before shutting the false floor on her. She could hear him putting something into the luggage compartment to make it look like he was on a business trip.

Ana had no idea how long they had been driving until she felt the car slowing to a halt. She heard Tomas get out and exchange a few words with someone but couldn't hear what they were saying. Suddenly, she heard them approaching the back of the car and began to understand parts of the conversation.

'I was looking forward to meeting Andre here today, what happened to him?' Tomas was saying.

'It was his shift, but his wife called him just an hour ago. She's in labour and he had to go back home to take her to the hospital.'

'Oh, I remember he told me that his wife was pregnant. Well, I guess it's a happy occasion. Anyway, you checked my papers, can I continue? I really want to get to Vienna before dark. I hate driving at night.'

'Open the luggage compartment and you can be on your way. We got a special alert this afternoon to thoroughly check all cars crossing the border.'

'More than usual? Why?'

'Don't know. Something about possible defectors that might cross the border. Someone that was part of Dubček's supporters. As if any of them would try anything these days. Damn them, they make my work more complicated.'

Ana nearly stopped breathing hearing that exchange. She felt sweat starting to trickle down her face, but she didn't dare move to wipe it.

She heard the soldier opening the trunk and froze. The soldier moved the different boxes Tomas had put there.

'Take them out,' the man ordered Tomas. 'I need to check the floor of the trunk.' Ana thought she was going to faint.

'You've checked the trunk twice now,' Tomas complained.

'What do you think you're going to find there? Do I look like someone who would risk my job aiding someone to escape? I just want to finish this run and get back home.'

'I know. But I have my orders. You see, there in the booth, that's my superior, I need to make a good impression on him.'

'Got you. I'll tell you what. I'll give you a hand in taking the boxes out.'

Ana could feel her heart beating so loudly she was sure it could be heard outside the car. She didn't know what to do. She heard Tomas and the soldier pulling one of the boxes out. Next, she heard Tomas whispering something to him which she couldn't hear. Then. the box was returned into the trunk, and the trunk was closed.

Ana could finally release her breath.

'All good. You can go. I'll send your regards and congratulations to Andre,' she heard the soldier say to Tomas.

Within seconds the engine started, and they were on their way again.

Not long after, Tomas stopped the car and helped Ana climb out of the trunk and back into the passenger seat.

She was free.

Ana relaxed into the notion that she was safe and out of Czechoslovakia. 'How did you convince him not to examine the car?'

'Good old-fashioned bribery. He knew I used to give Andre Tuzek vouchers to purchase illegal goods, so I offered them to him in a way that his supervisor wouldn't see.'

***

NEW YORK

Nothing could have prepared Ana for her first encounter with New York when she and Rabbi Siddon landed. Years later, watching 'The Wizard of Oz' with Yael, the words of Dorothy were the best expression of how she felt when she'd landed in La Guardia airport.

I've a feeling we're not in Kansas anymore.

Even at busy times, Prague seemed peaceful compared to the hustle and bustle of New York. Both Ana and Rabbi Siddon were awestruck by the noise and how fast everything was moving. For Ana, the thing that kept astonishing her was how big everything was and the abundance and variety of things.

She could still remember how small she felt when walking into a supermarket for the first time. She'd stand for hours looking at the different varieties of morning cereals. Never in her life could she imagine such abundance.

Walking on the streets and doing what she later learned was called 'window shopping' was her favourite way to spend her spare time.

The Jewish community kept Ana and Rabbi Siddon busy all the time. It felt as if everyone wanted to meet with them.

For the first time in her life, she participated in a fully religious Friday night meal, went to a synagogue, and even celebrated landmark dates like a Bar-Mitzvah and a wedding. At each of those events, even though she didn't know anyone, Ana was treated as if she was the guest of honour, and people even insisted on remaining friends with her afterwards. Within a few weeks she had more people who called her their friend than she'd had her whole life in Prague.

Another aspect of American life that took her by complete surprise was how everyone was so open and direct. Back at home, people would speak in hushed tones in case anyone was listening. Here, there was nothing to worry about. People were loud: they would call each other from one side of the street to the other, and exchange gossip from one balcony to another. No one was afraid of saying whatever they wanted. That was mind-blowing for Ana.

At last, she understood what freedom felt like.

Ana remembered how Tereza described it in one of her letters. *It's as if my whole life I was breathing through a tube, and now I can breathe fully, filling my lungs.* Ana literally tried it one day when she was walking through Central Park. She stopped and breathed in deeply, just to feel her lungs expanding to their fullest. She nearly fainted when her head became dizzy with so much oxygen coming so fast into her body, which was not accustomed to breathing in such a way.

The only thing that kept reminding her that all this might be temporary was the fact that she still had to find a way of getting her papers sorted so that she could become legal.

Charles Vanik had managed to get the documents to get the exhibition out of Czechoslovakia, but the process in The United States was not yet finalised. Ana welcomed this situation, as it ensured they could stay longer without raising suspicion from the Czech authorities.

But how long will it last?

Chapter Forty-Eight

NEW YORK

Dan Lavinsky was dreading his weekly Friday meal with his parents. He was trying to make the journey from his place in Manhattan to their place in Brooklyn as long as it could be.

Why am I doing this? he asked himself for the millionth time. He knew exactly what was going to happen once he entered his parents' apartment. His mother would be smiling as if she had a secret gift for him. She'd hug him and whisper, *'wait and see who we invited for dinner tonight,'* and would then scold him for not wearing proper attire for a Friday meal. His father would chide him for not wearing a Yamaka and would offer him one while asking, *'How's business?'* so as not to make a big fuss out of something Dan knew was important to his father. Then, they would all walk into the dining room and present him with a young Jewish girl that his parents approved of and wished him to marry.

At the age of twenty-nine, Dan was perfect husband material in the Jewish community of Brooklyn. He was good-looking, had a successful advertisement agency, and was marked as one of the uprising political figures for the Democratic Party. He wasn't sure if he wanted to run, but he knew people expected him to. However, he hadn't yet made up his mind about it.

'I'd rather run my own company, helping others with my marketing skills, than run for politics,' he used to say when people asked him why he wasn't running. The truth was that, in order to run, he had to be certain he could win. Dan never went into anything unless he knew, in advance, that his chances were high. For that reason, he accepted that having a wife by his side was crucial.

Yet, it was something he was not ready for.

Though his parents had been married for nearly thirty-five years, Dan would never want a relationship like they had. He wanted a woman by his side that would be strong enough to lead her own life; one that didn't need him to create one for her. He definitely didn't want a clingy, needy one whose whole world would revolve around him the way his mother's had revolved around his father.

Unfortunately, Dan hadn't met a girl like that. Most of the girls he'd dated, although having been university graduates, seemed to still be trapped in a world where 'catching' a husband would be their greatest achievement. If there was a girl that seemed a bit different, she'd end up being a 'shiksa' (not Jewish). This would certainly be a big NO for his parents now that his father had become the head of the Jewish Federation. He couldn't do that to his family.

So, Dan kept his weekly visits to them, knowing very well that each Friday dinner would bring a new candidate for his hand in marriage. He would be nice and charming and take her out on dates for a few weeks. Then, when she raised the famous question, *'Where is this relationship going?'* he would disappoint her, her parents and his parents yet again. He wasn't proud of it. But Dan knew he couldn't live with himself if his private life was based on a lie. Ticking all the right boxes felt like too much of a lie to live with. He wanted someone who would be a partner for his life's adventures, a friend and, if possible, attractive. Therefore, nothing had prepared him for his first meeting with Ana.

When he entered his parents' dining room, the table was already set for dinner, and everyone was sitting around the table. The Sabbath candlesticks were lit. There were many more people than he'd anticipated. His younger sister smiled and waved to him across the table.

'We are graced by your presence, dear brother,' she said in a sarcastic tone. For some reason, he blushed. Next to his sister, as usual, sat the 'intended bride'. However, this time there was something different about her. First, she wasn't accompanied by anyone that looked like her parents. What most captured his attention was the fact she wasn't as bubbly and talkative as all the others before her. This one was serious and quiet. She appeared to be captivated by all the sights in the room, as if seeing them for the first time. Only when introductions were made did he understand the reason.

'This is Rabbi Siddon,' his father pointed to the man who sat next to him. *Strange looking Rabbi* was Dan's first thought.

Before he could put his finger on what it was, his mother proudly announced, 'This is Ana Sveboda. She and Rabbi Siddon are part of the Czech delegation preparing the upcoming exhibition of the 'Precious Legacy Exhibition'. Isn't that exciting?'

All Dan could do was nod, but he couldn't take his eyes off Ana. Her behaviour and looks were so different to what he was used to. First, she wasn't interested in him; she was much more focused on how his father conducted the traditional Friday meal with the different prayers and blessings. Next, she didn't talk much and, when she did, it tended to be questions about things she didn't know.

What a relief meeting someone who doesn't talk about herself all the time and knows how to listen, Dan thought. But if he was honest with himself, he knew perfectly well that what attracted him to Ana was how she looked. If he'd have seen her on the street, he would never have thought she was Jewish. She was what his sister once described as 'petite'. She had sharp features. Her long nose and wide mouth were at times in contrast, but it was what made her face so attractive. She wasn't what you would call a traditional beauty, but she certainly made people's heads turn with her long blonde hair, which was currently wrapped around her head in a loose knot. Then there were her eyes; big, green eyes that at times seemed bluer depending on the light in the room. Dan had never expected to be impressed by any woman at a Friday dinner, yet here in front of him was someone that, without even exchanging any words with, he was totally interested in.

I just hope she won't spoil it by saying something stupid. But nothing like that happened. Dan wanted to know more about what she was doing in New York.

'We're preparing our exhibition of Judaica, which is a small part of what we had in Prague,' she explained.

'How did you manage to get out beyond the Iron Curtain? Isn't Czechoslovakia under Moscow's control?' he asked, trying to impress her with what he knew had taken place in Prague only a few years before. Noticing a flash of pain behind her eyes when he mentioned it, he regretted raising the issue. He hadn't intended to bring up painful memories for her, only to make a conversation, but she recovered quickly.

'Oh, we were fortunate to have Senator Vanik do all the pulling of diplomatic strings for us. We're here as a demonstration of good relationships between East and West.'

From the pattern of her speech, Dan recognised it was rehearsed. He had no idea why she had to rehearse it, but he was hoping he could talk more with her alone.

'Where is your exhibition going to be?'

'It was promised to be in the Smithsonian in Washington, DC, but now, because they were not ready for us, we are thinking of doing it here in New York. Once they have space for us, we can move on to the Smithsonian.'

'How many items do you have in the exhibition?'

'Three hundred.'

The number made Dan gasp. 'That many?'

His reaction made both Ana and Rabbi Siddon laugh.

'Back in Prague we had over one hundred and fifty thousand items,' she explained. 'It took me and four other assistants nearly two years just to document them. I had to choose the minimum number of items I could to create an exhibition that would provide a small glimpse into the cultural world the Nazis destroyed.'

Her answers proved to Dan that this woman was indeed different from any he had met before. He was determined to meet her again.

'How about I go with you next week to scout for some locations for the exhibition?'

'That would be lovely,' Ana replied immediately before anyone else could say anything.

***

The next few weeks passed so fast, Dan couldn't believe it.

The more he met with Ana, the more he was infatuated by her. She never stopped surprising him with the wealth of knowledge she had.

He had been raised as a Jew his whole life. He'd been to a Jewish school, studied the religious books, and yet she still knew more about their heritage and customs; things he had never paid any attention to or even cared for.

For him, being Jewish was like having brown hair or being tall. You don't think about it; it's just part of you. Most of the time you don't pay any attention to it, the same as you don't pay attention to your right hand. When he first told Ana this, she immediately understood what he was talking about.

'Until your hand is amputated, or you turn blind,' she said. 'That's when you start thinking about it. You start realising how much you miss it, or how you took it for granted.'

At first, Dan assumed it was some kind of dark humour. But when she explained that, until three years ago, she had had no clue what being Jewish meant, he understood the reason for her constant excitement about anything that had to do with Judaism.

***

Two weeks later, Dan and Ana were still looking for the perfect place for the exhibition in New York. Dan's father used his connections to find places, yet still nothing was found to be suitable for the needs of such a special exhibition.

What became clear to Dan was that Ana was growing on him, and he could no longer bear the thought of not spending time with her. The more he got to know her, the more intriguing she became.

Dan wasn't sure what Ana's feelings towards him were and was hesitant to ask. *Coward,* he said to himself each time he planned to, but ended up asking a trivial question instead.

One day, while they were walking in Central Park, Ana opened up to him, telling him her story. She didn't leave any details out. She'd never even told Rabbi Siddon that she'd killed a soldier during the invasion. Now here she was telling it all to someone who she'd only known for a few weeks.

'My whole life,' she said, 'I knew it was my destiny to become a doctor. Now, because I trusted someone and followed his ideas against my better judgement, I'm not allowed to continue my studies back at home. Not only that, I'm also not allowed to work in any medical institute.

'On the one hand it pushed me into discovering my roots and finding this work with Rabbi Siddon, which has been wonderful, but that's not what I want to do for the rest of my life.

'Now that I've escaped, I can never go back. I need to find a way to become legal here.'

Ana stopped for a second to take a deep breath, all the while aware of Dan's reactions. He hadn't even flinched when she told him she'd accidentally killed someone. He had, however, looked a bit disappointed when she'd mentioned Jan and how betrayed she'd felt by him.

'Senator Vanik promised me that when we got here, he would help me so I could complete my studies and become a doctor. But I'm unable to reach him. I need someone to help me get my papers legal. Could you help me with this?'

Even before this moment, Dan had thought Ana was a remarkable woman. Now, he was certain of it. He had never met anyone as brave or as smart as her. *How on earth can anyone survive that ordeal and continue living? I'm not sure I could.*

'I'm not sure exactly how to do it, but I'm going to find a way to make sure you stay here,' he reassured Ana. 'God knows how I'm going to do it, but hey, God works in mysterious ways, doesn't he?'

He was trying to lighten the mood, and it worked. Ana smiled, which made Dan very happy.

Chapter Forty-Nine

Ana was nervous about how Dan would help her, but for the time being her hands were full with the work that needed to be done to prepare the exhibition.

After weeks searching for a place in New York without success, they'd finally got a message updating them that the Smithsonian could now give them a proper space for the exhibition. Within two days, Ana and Rabbi Siddon had to be ready to go to Washington with their precious cargo. Ana managed to send a message to Dan.

When they arrived in Washington, Ana and Rabbi Siddon were welcomed by a host of specialists and professionals; some historians, and some curators of famous exhibitions who had much more experience and knowledge than Ana could ever dream of.

To her delight, they all complimented her on the choice of items she had brought and the careful and detailed information she had prepared for each item. Ana was relieved to hear that they would take it from there - all they needed from her were her notes.

At first Ana felt redundant, but as the days wore on the curators called on her more and more to give her opinion on how to structure the exhibition. She felt respected that such knowledgeable people would consider her ideas and was grateful for it.

Without noticing, three weeks passed, and opening night was upon them.

Ana was excited and worried at the same time. She and Rabbi Siddon were the guests of honour. Ana had never been to such a grand event.

Debra, the curator, had taken her shopping for an appropriate dress for such a gala. Again, Ana had been struck by the wealth and abundance American shops displayed. She chose a simple blue gown that, to her, seemed like it had been taken from a fairy tale. It was the most lavish gown she had ever seen.

Ana was talking with some of the guests when she saw Dan across the room. For a second, her heart missed a beat. *He is truly good looking,* she swooned, but quickly took control of her priorities: she needed to know that she could stay in the United States legally.

'You look stunning,' Dan said, making her blush.

'You're not half bad yourself.' Once she'd said it, she had no clue what to do with herself. She'd never imagined she would say such a thing to anyone.

To her relief, Dan smiled and accepted the compliment as easily as if she had spoken about the weather.

'Did you find a solution for me?' she asked brazenly. 'I don't have much time. Our papers state that from opening night we only have three weeks' permit to stay. From then on, I'm illegal here.'

'OK. I'll make it short,' Dan said matter-of-factly. 'There is a process, but it takes months. But there is another way you could become legal immediately. It could be done as soon as tomorrow.'

'I'll take it,' Ana said without a second's thought. 'What is it?'

'You can marry me,' he said with a smile.

Chapter Fifty

BOSTON - DECEMBER 1989

Ana loved the last days of the year. She used them to complete things, evaluate what she had done that year; how far she had got and what she would like to achieve the following year. Some people called it goal-making, but Ana preferred the term 'dreams'.

'People think dreams don't come true, but I'm proof that dreams do come true. You just have to put in the effort to turn them into reality,' she'd told Dan.

Once she'd married Dan, Ana had turned her focus onto getting her degree and taking care of her family.

When Dan had proposed to her that day at the Smithsonian, she hadn't hesitated for a second. There was something in Dan that reminded her of her father, Pavel, and she knew she would be safe with him and could achieve her life's dream of becoming a doctor.

What she hadn't expected was to fall in love with him so soon.

Her work as a surgeon defined her. Whenever she had a wobble due to the stress of work, housekeeping or child-rearing, Dan had been there to tell her how proud he was of her and to encourage her never to stop. That was another aspect of him which reminded her of Pavel.

These last few weeks Ana had been thinking about her parents more than ever. 'The Velvet Revolution' as they called it, had made her aware that she might be able to reunite with her father.

Now lounging on the sofa with Dan, watching Vaclav Havel getting sworn in as the first president of free Czechoslovakia, it was proof that change was afoot in her beloved home country.

'I met him once,' Ana told Dan. 'We were all standing together next to the radio station waiting for Dubček to come and deliver his famous speech about 'socialism with a human face'. We were cheering for him, oblivious to the destruction it would bring only a few months later.'

Dan watched Ana carefully. Even after all these years together, he still admired her spirit. She rarely spoke about her time in Prague. Hearing her talk about it now brought some hope that she would finally let go of her guilt.

Guilt for killing a man. Guilt for leaving her parents.

Most of all, he hoped she would be able to let go of her anger towards Jan and towards herself for doing what they did.

Deep down in his heart, Dan knew Jan was Ana's first love. He understood he would never be able to take Jan's place. He wasn't jealous or worried about it. Everyone has a first love, but not everyone's first love was a hero. No matter what Ana told him, he could tell that she was still haunted by those two major events in her life.

Their life together was happy. Dan was confident Ana loved him; maybe not in the same way as he loved her at first, but no two loves are the same. He'd watched with awe over the years how she'd striven to become the best at what she does. Whether as a student or a surgeon, a homemaker or a mother.

He'd accepted that it would take some time for Ana to fall in love with him, but once she did, her love for him had grown over the years. They were now lovers, partners, and best friends.

It was exactly what he had always dreamed when thinking of his 'perfect' relationship.

So, dreams do come true.

They were still watching the inauguration when Dan said, 'You know, you can now finally visit your father without any risk. Would you like to?'

Ana wanted to but had reservations. After years of attempting to forget her life in Prague, the way her mother had advised her, it was hard to overcome. The fact it was now possible did not mean that in her mind it was.

Dan was waiting patiently for her to answer. Normally, she'd have given a prompt and direct one, but just as she was about to, she remembered a story her father once told her.

'Did you know that, in the old days, when they had animals in the circus, the way they would train an elephant not to run away was to tie his legs to a pole when he was small. No matter how hard he pulled, he wasn't able to move further than what the rope allowed.

'As he grew up, they made the pole smaller and smaller, and by the time the elephant was big and strong, the pole was nothing more than a stick. By this time, the elephant had come to believe he could never get away.

'What tied him down wasn't the rope or the pole, it was his own mind. I guess I'm like that elephant. I still can't believe I can go back there. I'll need a bit more time.'

Chapter Fifty-One

BOSTON - SAMARITAN CENTER, 1989

Ana glanced at the room one last time to make sure it all looked perfect before opening the doors and welcoming her weekly support group for people who had lost someone to suicide.

Years ago, when she'd started it, she'd never expected it would become a healing place for her. She'd started it only because she loved the idea of supporting people who had lost loved ones like she had. She knew what they were going through and wanted to give them hope that life would go on.

Ana knew all too well the stages of grief they went through. Whether it was numbness, denial or anger. The endless *what if?* questions and the feelings of guilt, and above all the deep sorrow and pain that leads to depression. She kept telling people that *time will heal*, and in the end, they would reach acceptance.

Deep inside, she'd prayed that she could reach it too.

Ana still blamed Jan for having to flee Prague.

In the last few years, she'd also had another reason to blame him. She hadn't been able to return for her own mother's funeral for fear of being detained. It had broken her heart. She'd wondered what it would take for her to be able to reach acceptance.

Tonight was special.

It was the end of the year, which always seemed to attract more attendees. They too realised another year had passed, and it was a place they could check in and see if anything had changed.

Some sought energy and reassurance to keep on going for another year. Unfortunately, the end of the year was also a time when more suicides took place, and for some who came in it was a memorial to the person they had lost.

Ana had trained herself to be fully present for anyone who needed listening to without judgement or agenda. Tonight, the focus had been on reaching a place of acceptance and completion with their loved ones who'd died.

One participant really struck a chord with Ana.

She was a mother whose son had killed himself. She'd been coming to these meetings for nearly four years, during which time she'd struggled to forgive herself for not seeing the signs.

Tonight, she looked different. Instead of her usual weeping, she was smiling when she spoke, her face beaming.

'I was going through his things,' she was telling the group. 'I do it every year around this time, just to clean around his room and keep his memory alive. When I was straightening one of his books a note fell out addressed to me.

'I couldn't believe it. For years I kept asking myself why he hadn't left a note, and there it was. He wrote that he couldn't take it anymore. That he knows I love him very much and that I try to help him in all ways possible. But he felt like he was stopping me from living my own life. He couldn't take it anymore.

'He begged me to respect his choice. He wrote, "If you really love me, mum, please be proud of me. Realise I'm not a coward. I'm making the hardest choice there is, and I'm making it because I love you and I know nothing can help me. I'm making this hard choice, but it's the only one I can see."'

When she'd finished sharing, there were tears flowing down her cheeks, but this time it was tears of joy.

'I'm at peace now,' she said, 'I know I couldn't help him more than I did. I accept that sometimes, as a mother, I have to let my child choose their way, even if it is against everything I believe in.

'I'm going to continue on with my life honouring his choice, and in my memory he will always be the bravest boy that ever lived.'

There wasn't a dry eye in the room.

When the meeting was over, the woman had been surrounded by many of the participants telling her how much they appreciated her sharing, and what it had meant to them.

After everyone was gone and Ana and her assistant had finished clearing the space, Ana kept thinking about what the mother had said. She was waiting for Dan to come and pick her up.

Ana realised, with sudden clarity, that she had Jan to thank for the life she had today. If he had not convinced her to become involved in politics, she would have continued her studies in Prague and would never have met Dan, who was the love of her life.

If Jan hadn't died after setting fire to himself, she wouldn't have been able to run the helpline and start the groups that had given her life a much deeper purpose.

In a strange way, she had only been able to fulfil her purpose in life because of Jan's presence in it.

Now, she could pinpoint Dan's role in her life. It was similar to Jan's, only in a much healthier way. While Jan had always been her protector, he'd done it in a way that took away her own power. Dan, on the other hand, had been there to support and help her while empowering her to live the life she'd dreamt about.

By the time Dan arrived to pick her up, Ana was experiencing peace and joy. It was as if someone had pulled the curtain away, and she could see clearly.

Her heart was singing.

'Dan,' she said breathlessly as she got into the car. 'Let's go to Prague in spring.'

Epilogue

PRAGUE - APRIL 1990

Ana had forgotten how beautiful Prague was in Spring. The trees around the city were bright green. The river was flowing, and the sunlight bounced off of all the towers of churches, bridges and the citadel to reflect the beauty of the city.

Only once she'd returned did she realise how much she had missed the special music: Prague's church bells. Each one had a different sound and timing, and you knew by each distinct tune which church was ringing.

The meeting with Ana's father had been emotional for everyone. He still lived in their old apartment, and it looked as if nothing had changed since the day she left. Except, instead of a radio, her father now had a TV in the living room.

After spending days roaming the streets, showing Dan and Yael the places where she grew up, she knew she had to face the real reason she'd returned.

***

On a warm, spring day, Ana walked to Wenceslas square, which she'd been avoiding up until this moment. She stood in the centre and looked all around.

So many memories came rushing in: pictures, sounds, pieces of conversations. Everything swept over and around her as if she was watching her old life playing out before her. For a moment, she believed she would faint, but then the memories fell into order and only one piece of the puzzle was left.

At a flower shop on the corner of the square, Ana purchased a bouquet of flowers and slowly advanced towards the fountain in front of the National Museum.

There was a modest memorial.

Modest, the way you were, she thought. Two low, round mounds stuck out of the pavement, connected together with a cross, which looked like a human figure of a torch.

Perfect. She felt the place honoured who Jan was and what he had done in the short period he'd spent on earth.

Ana laid her bouquet of flowers next to his name, kissed her hand and stroked the letters of his name.

'Goodbye old friend, and thank you for being in my life,' she whispered.

When she stood up, she could hear the bells ringing all over the town.

Prague was playing her song.

THE END

Crime Cleaners
by Vered Neta
Publication Date – 2024

After an abused woman kills her husband, her mother, and her friends, a group of women in their late 60s help her to hide the body but are forced to start a cleaning service of murder scenes for the mob.

****

The Yoga Club's weekly gatherings were a joyful escape for Jessie, Megan, Lily, and Vi. Stretching, giggles, and a delightful lunch were their cherished routines. But one sunny afternoon spun their lives into an adventure they never saw coming.

After a laughter-filled lunch, Jessie and Megan decided to pop by Jessie's daughter Becca's place. What they found was beyond belief—Becca, stunned, revealed she accidentally ended Rob's life, her abusive and controlling husband. Determined to shield Becca from more pain, Jessie hatched a bold plan: make Rob disappear and let Becca breathe again.

With Megan, a surrogate mom to Becca, joining in, they began their audacious scheme to vanish Rob's body and secrets. Soon, Lily and Vi, their yoga buddies, became unexpected allies. Each brought their unique talents, crafting a tale that painted Rob as a runaway in love.

Little did they know, their adventure was just beginning.

A knock on Becca's door introduced them to the enigmatic "Crime Boss" Dominic. Rob's secret criminal life was exposed, with stolen goods and danger hanging in the balance.

Fearing for Becca, the group made a deal with Dominic, diving headfirst into his world. But Detective Sam's arrival said it trouble, and the group was now navigating crime, detective work, and friendship like never before.

As tension mounted, Jessie realised they had to escape Dominic's grasp while guarding their loved ones. Twists and turns await them—each choice a step toward redemption or ruin. With their bond tested, secrets on the line, and morality at stake, could they save themselves from a life they never chose?

Things We Do For Love
by Vered Neta
Publication Date – June 2023

When an ageing therapist gets desperate for a child, her overbearing mother develops Alzheimer's. She must decide between her wish for a child or caring for her increasingly helpless mother, whose tyranny drove the family apart.

****

Daisy Bach, a therapist, has always been certain that she did not want to have children. Her childhood experiences with an overbearing and controlling mother, Verity, who tore the family apart, further cemented this decision. However, at the age of forty-five, Daisy finds herself reconsidering this choice.

Unfortunately, her decision to try and conceive is complicated by her mother's diagnosis of Alzheimer's disease. With strained family relationships, Daisy faces the daunting task of caring for her elderly parents while also attempting to conceive. As she navigates this challenging time, Daisy is forced to confront her deep-seated resentment towards Verity.

This journey leads her to re-evaluate her beliefs about motherhood, forgiveness, and the true meaning of a "happy" family. Will Daisy find a way to reconcile with her past and make peace with her present? Only time will tell.

****

PRAISES FOR "THINGS WE DO FOR LOVE"

*"**Things We Do For Love**" by Vered Neta is a superb family drama that highlights damage and redemption, hope and healing, and the power of family ties.*

Mix together a derisive mother with a joie de vivre, a reclusive, highly intelligent father, and three sisters at loggerheads and you have the 'Bach' family.

In **Things We Do For Love**, the happy-family preconception is pulled apart string by string. In the agonizing sadness of watching their parents decline, the three sisters will individually understand something vitally important about themselves and finally allow acceptance in.

Vered Neta's eloquent writing style draws the reader in and holds them fast. Her characters are heartfelt and real, and her portrayal of a not-so-normal family will tug on your heartstrings. Neta has given each of the characters in the story their own vulnerable and genuine role within the family. I really warmed to the fact that Neta divided the story into the five family viewpoints so that we could truly understand events from their unique perspectives. This is a fantastically raw story about love, grief, and family dynamics.

Things We Do For Love by Vered Neta is a wonderful unique, character-driven, moving tale that will sweep you away.

ChickLit Cafe

****

Wow! What a story! Vered's beautifully written story exploring family dynamics, complex emotions, fractured relationships, difficult choices, forgiveness, and making peace with yourself and others… It completely sucked me in, chewed me up, and spat me out the other end with a more positive, hopeful, and reflective mindset with regards to my own demon's, trauma, and fractured relationships.

Vered does a brilliant job of teaching her readers that no one family is ever perfect. That there will always be a difference of opinion, conflicting personality traits, an action, or even words that will cause obstacles along this journey we call life. But what's important is that we listen, ask questions, process, accept.

Vered's characters are immensely realistic and even more relatable… Her portrayal of Alzheimer's is raw, honest, heartbreaking, and heartwarming all at the same time, and she does it with a balance of reality, tact, sympathy, and empathy. Vered is an author who leaves a seamless imprint on your heart and mind."

Rebbeca Scammell – (she_loves_to_read)

****

"This book has my heart and soul!… A thought provoking read and it explores the tough issues and the relationships we have with our family. I'm so excited to read more of this author's books because if this one is anything to go by they will be brilliant."

Leanne Dagan – (leannebookstagram)

****

"This book broke my heart into a million little pieces and then put it back together again…. There was a paragraph that has stuck with me, it's not often I highlight things. But I physically felt this one. So I'll leave you with it.. just know I wholeheartedly recommend that you read this book!

Pattrice Gotting – *(*https://prdgreads.home.blog/*)*

****

Things We Do For Love *with pull on your heartstrings and may make you cry. The story is written beautifully and tackles some hard topics like Alzheimer's and childhood experiences like a controlling mum but Vered Neta tackles them well in the book.*

Emma Fitzgerald – https://tealeavesandbookleaves.blogspot.com/

****

"The writing is enchanting and moving. I truly felt I was experiencing the story along with the characters as a part of the family. All of the characters were relatable and well fleshed out… I thoroughly enjoyed reading this book"

Laura Gorman – https://www.instagram.com/bookish_belfast/

****

*"**Things We Do For Love**" by Vered Neta is a beautiful contemporary novel about a family… exploring complex relationships within a family. I loved it. There are some difficult topics, sensitively portrayed. In the end, we can say that within this family, love wins.*

Julia Wilson – http://www.christianbookaholic.com/

www.ingramcontent.com/pod-product-compliance
Lightning Source LLC
LaVergne TN
LVHW091530060526
838200LV00036B/555